About the Author

Preeti Shenoy, among the top five highest-selling authors in the country, is on the *Forbes India* longlist of the most influential celebrities. Her work has been translated into many languages.

She has bagged the 'Indian of the Year' Brands Academy Award 2017 for her contribution to Literature. She has also received the Academia Award for Business Excellence by the New Delhi Institute of Management. She has given talks in many premier educational institutes such as IITs and IIMs, and corporate organisations like KPMG, ISRO, Infosys, Accenture and many others. She is also an artist, specialising in portraiture and illustrated journalling.

Her short stories and poetry have been published in various magazines such as *Conde Nast* and *Verve*. She has been featured on BBC World, *Cosmopolitan, The Hindu, The Times of India* and all other major media.

She has a very popular blog and also wrote a weekly column in *The Financial Chronicle* for many years. Her other interests are travel, photography and yoga.

: *www.preetishenoy.com*

: *Blog.preetishenoy.com*

: *http://preeti.io/fb*

: *@Preetishenoy*

: *Preeti.Shenoy and Preetishenoyart*

: *Preeti.Shenoy*

Praise for the author and her works

One of India's most popular authors.

– Cosmopolitan

India's top-selling female author.

– BBC World

Feel-good air, crisp and easy-to-grasp writing.

– New Woman

Quick-paced read.

– DNA

Positive and full of life.

– Financial World

Woven intelligently with simple language… leaves a profound impact.

– Exotica

Amazing how deftly she weaves her stories.

– Eve's Times

Keeps the reader hooked from the first page to last.

– Afternoon Voice

Magnetic, engrossing and unputdownable.

– One India One People

Intense fiction that plays with your emotions.

– The New India Express

Preeti Shenoy makes it work.

– The Hindu

Has something for everyone.

– The Hindu

Heart-warming love story.

– Bangalore Mirror

Show-stealer.

– Deccan Chronicle

Keenly observant mind.

– DNA

Wonderful, passionate, common story.

– The Sentinel

Wake Up, Life is Calling

When your mind is your greatest enemy

Always stay positive!
with love
Preeti Shenoy

PREETI SHENOY

Srishti
PUBLISHERS & DISTRIBUTORS

Srishti Publishers & Distributors
Registered Office: N-16, C.R. Park
New Delhi – 110 019
Corporate Office: 212A, Peacock Lane
Shahpur Jat, New Delhi – 110 049
editorial@srishtipublishers.com

First published by
Srishti Publishers & Distributors in 2019

Copyright © Preeti Shenoy, 2019

10 9 8 7 6 5 4 3 2 1

This is a work of fiction. The characters, places, organisations and events described in this book are either a work of the author's imagination or have been used fictitiously. Any resemblance to people, living or dead, places, events, communities or organisations is purely coincidental.

The author asserts the moral right to be identified as the author of this work.

All rights reserved. No part of this publication may be reproduced, stored in a retrieval system, or transmitted, in any form or by any means, electronic, mechanical, photocopying, recording or otherwise, without the prior written permission of the Publishers.

Note: Since the story is set in the early 1990s, Mumbai has been referred to as Bombay , Chennai as Madras, and Kochi as Cochin. The names were officially changed in 1995-96.

Printed and bound in India

For Purvi, Atul and Satish

Prologue

I sit on the windowsill, staring out at the parking lot, so utterly alone as I watch people going about their daily lives. I dread waking up in the morning and having to face another day.

The book I am attempting to read lies next to me. I don't know what I am doing anymore. The hours stretch on endlessly. I've been trying hard to finish an assignment, due when college reopens. But I am unable to focus. I feel inadequate, worthless, inferior. I should have never joined this creative writing course. I have no original ideas, really. Even my professor said so. I am just a sham. A pretender. Someone who couldn't do her MBA and joined this course just to escape. All of this is so pointless and painful. Today is a holiday, but soon I will have to go back to college. And face them. I don't want to. I want to stay where I am. A thought hisses and spits in my head like a snake:

Drop out of this course. This is not for you.

The more I think about it, the surer I am. I am considering how to tell my parents that I want to drop out. *A second time.*

That's when I hear the door to my room open. I know it is my father.

I sit up straight. Not the medication again. I am sure I am unable to think because of the damn medicines. My parents insist I take them. But my head feels heavy when I do. My tongue becomes so thick that I am unable to talk. I am unable to think.

'Please go away, I don't want to take it,' I say even before he speaks.

'Look, I spoke to Dr Neeraj and he says you can take these. They helped you earlier, didn't they? It was all good, remember?' says my father as he stands there with the pills in his hand.

'It was good not because of the medicines, but because I tried hard,' I reply.

'Of course you tried hard. Now be a good girl and take these,' says my father as he extends his hand.

'*No, no, no.*' My fists are clenched into tight balls and I refuse to meet my father's eye. I don't want to look at him. Or at my mother who is right behind him. I can't stand the helpless expression on their faces, the pleading looks, their panic, but mostly it's the depth of their love that I can't bear. They don't deserve this. I have had enough. I cannot face them anymore. I don't want to be a part of any of this. I have given them enough pain in the last one year when I had to be admitted to a mental hospital.

'Please, Ankita,' my father pleads. I detest the whine in his voice.

'*Don't... Don't say anything. Don't enter my room. Get out!*' I yell, my eyes blazing, my voice high-pitched.

It is as though there is another person speaking from within me.

'Listen, Ankita, if you don't take the medication, you will become worse. Don't you remember what happened?' my father says in a calm voice.

I remember. I remember every single thing.

'Please, Ankita. Just this one tablet. Take it, please?' My father refuses to give up.

'*Get the fuck out. Now!*' I scream.

'*Watch your words!*' my mother yells at me. If there is one thing she cannot stand, it is my talking back, and refusing to do as I am told.

'*You…. You shut up!*' I yell back louder. I am shaking in rage now.

I pick up a paperweight and fling it at my father. It catches him by surprise, and hits him on the forehead. He drops the pills he is carrying, his hand going up instinctively to his forehead. I watch impassively as blood gushes out from the skin split open. His face contorts in pain.

'You witch! Look at what you have done!' my mother screams, as she rushes forward to help him.

He has backed off now, wincing in pain, clutching the handle of the door.

My mother rushes to the fridge to get some ice.

I am still standing there, rooted to the spot, staring at him. I cannot believe I did this.

I watch as he leaves my room.

Then I shut the door.

I fling myself on the bed and weep loudly, my wails smothered by the pillow. I don't want them to hear me cry. My body heaves as I shout into the pillow, crying, sobbing. I don't recognise the primeval noises coming from deep within me. I clutch the pillow hard. I hate what I am doing to my parents. I want this to end.

How much more do I have to endure? How much more? Weren't all those months at the hospital enough? This is unfair… unfair… unfair. I recall the months at the hospital, the electric shock treatments, the occupational therapy, my life there and how I struggled to read, to get back to normalcy. I thought I had won. I thought I had succeeded. I thought I had conquered my mind.

I thought all this was behind me. I thought I had overcome all of it. But how wrong I was! The monster I presumed to have defeated has come back with a vengeance.

The pills my father dropped are lying by the door. I hate them. I have had enough of medication, doctors, psychiatrists. I don't want any more of it.

A small voice of reason in my head speaks up. 'Take the tablets. Take them,' it says. I know if I don't take them, I will probably have to be admitted once more. My father is right.

But the medication takes away everything. Makes me numb, drowsy, not myself. Wipes away my thoughts, empties my imagination. It is supposed to help me. But all it does is kill me. Kill me from inside.

I am frightened now. If I could lose control like that and hurt my father, there is no telling what I will do next.

I pick up the pills and walk out of the room. My father is sitting on the sofa with an ice-pack to his head. My mother glares at me.

'I… I am sorry, Dad. I will take the medication,' I choke on my words. 'Are you hurt?'

'It's nothing, Ankita. Just a small cut,' he says.

I start crying again. I know there is no escape now. I have been getting progressively worse.

'Please make an appointment. Take me to the doctor,' I say.

My worst fears have come true. The nightmare has started once again. Trapped in my body, trapped in my head, I am my own prisoner.

There is no escape.

1

Just Like Starting Over

Bombay
October, 1993

When you have survived something that almost destroyed you and have clawed your way back to normalcy, little by little, you think everything will be okay from now on. You are desperate to put the nightmares of your past behind you, looking for the smallest signs of hope. You clutch at even the tiniest positive bits, convincing yourself that they are signs that point towards a brighter future.

I was no different. I was full of hope, eager to start my new life. I had tied up my past neatly, sealed it tight in cardboard cartons with duct tape and kicked them out of sight. No more mental hospitals. No more Occupational Therapy. No more psychiatrists. I was going to a new college, a new course – Creative Writing at that! It had always been my dream, and I couldn't believe I was now living it.

Though a tiny part of me felt guilty for wasting my parents' money on the MBA course (they had paid the entire fees in advance – non-refundable), what took precedence was that I was finally back in the 'normal world', a world where *I belonged*, and

1

would be soon doing a course that I *loved*. I did not care that the college timing was 1.00 p.m. to 7.00 p.m., as Creative Writing was still not viewed as one of the mainstream courses, which were all in the mornings.

I did not care that I had to travel by the electric trains in Bombay. Getting into and out of these trains was an art in itself. Once inside, you had to know in advance which side of the train you had to get out of, as the platform could be on either side. Accordingly, you had to choose your position and park yourself there. The pushing would start precisely ten seconds before the train came to a halt. You could not evade the mass of tightly squashed human bodies, all exerting force in the same direction. You flowed out helplessly with the sea, gasping for breath when you emerged on the platform. The old me would have shuddered at the thought of all this. But this was the new me – freshly minted, raring to go.

My parents were still treating me like a delicate flower, even though it had been two months since I was out of the National Mental Health Institute (NMHI). They were protective and accompanied me everywhere. My every little wish was their command.

When I said I wanted to eat ice cream one night, my father drove all the way to Juhu, to a fancy ice cream parlour that had just opened.

I wasn't used to my parents behaving like this towards me. I think they were afraid I would have another breakdown. Though I protested, I secretly liked it.

'I am fine now! You don't have to listen to everything I say,' I said at the ice cream parlour.

'We know. But this is a chance for us to pamper you. It is only for a little while, so enjoy it,' said my mother.

'Besides, it is also a chance for me to eat ice cream,' my father added, and we all laughed.

They took me shopping to buy new clothes for college. They insisted that I should get a new backpack, new notebooks, and some nice stationery.

'I don't need any of this!' I said, laughing.

'It's a new start, Ankita. We gave away your old college bag and notebooks when we moved here,' my mother said.

While I was in the hospital, my parents had moved homes. The apartment was in a new building in Bandra, a coveted locality – a coastal suburb with a nice neighbourhood, large shady trees, a lot of greenery, pleasant neighbours and all modern amenities like a pool, a gym, shops as well as restaurants within walking distance. My mother loved it. I did too, but for different reasons. It meant that nobody knew me here, nobody knew my past, nobody knew of the crazy things I had done when I had bipolar disorder. I was free to forge a new identity.

On my first day to college, without my parents as chaperone, I felt free as a bird. I almost danced all the way to the railway station. I was humming and the backpack thumping rhythmically as I walked felt like celebratory drumbeats. As I sat in the train, and the stations sped past, taking me closer to my destination, I became ebullient. A little boy got into the train and began singing the latest film song: '*Baazigar, O, baazigar,*' he sang in a shrill pitch, as he made music with two flat stones, which he used like an instrument, holding them expertly in his hand. He made eye contact with me as he sang, '*Tu hai bada jaadugar*', and broke into a little jig. I chuckled in delight as I slipped a ten-rupee note into his palm, which quickly vanished.

Churchgate was the last stop and as the train came to a grinding halt, the passengers began streaming out. It was a short walk to the college. The college – a Christian women's college – I knew would be similar to St. Agnes in Kerala, where I had done my graduation, as it was a sister institution.

Giddy with exhilaration, I entered the college building, an imposing structure – a white multi-storied building that stood like a fortress. A black-board at the entrance welcomed us – the new batch of students of the creative writing course – and directed us to the fifth floor, where our classrooms were located.

My classroom, surprisingly, had long red curtains that billowed ceiling to floor. The windows overlooked treetops, and there was nature all around. The parrots perched on branches were surely a good omen. The afternoon sun cast rainbows in the room, the light filtering in through the redness of the curtains. I loved my classroom instantly. This was even better than St. Agnes!

I had been locked away from the world for so many months. For everyone else in the classroom, all of this was not anything unusual or extraordinary. But I stared at the benches, the black-board – everything. It had been such a long time since I had seen any institution other than a mental hospital. I revelled in this atmosphere, soaking in every tiny detail.

I loved it all! It was my own personal slice of heaven.

'At last I am here,' I high-fived myself as I made my way to the back of the classroom.

I didn't want to sit right in the front, so made my way to the middle benches, my eyes scanning them quickly for an empty space.

My new life had begun and I was eager to dive in.

2

Like a Virgin

'Pssst... Come, come, sit here,' said a girl, patting the seat beside her. Though seated, it was easy to surmise that she was at least half a foot taller than me. The first thing I noticed about her after her height was her pale creamy complexion. She was so fair that she could easily be mistaken for a white person. Short brown hair framed her face, matching her deep brown eyes. She was a striking figure in her canary yellow kurti, which contrasted with her maroon pants. I found myself instantly liking her. Like the classroom, there was a warm gleam to her.

'Hi, I am Ankita,' I said as I placed my bag under the desk, sliding onto the bench.

'Parul. Nice to meet you,' she said. 'And this is Janki,' she introduced the girl next to her. Janki, much shorter than me, wore a worried look as she sifted furiously through her bag.

'Hi,' she said, barely looking up.

'Hi. Lost something?' I asked.

'Yeah, my train pass. Can't seem to find it.' She frowned.

'Has to be in your bag,' said Parul.

I noticed it under the bench then, right next to my bag.

'Is it this?' I asked as I picked it up and handed it to her.

Her eyes lit up.

'Thank you! You're a life-saver… Er… I didn't catch your name.'

'Ankita,' I said.

'So, do you two know each other from before?' I asked.

'No, we just met. I invited her to sit here too. I choose my companions carefully. They have to pass my secret test,' whispered Parul conspiratorially.

'Oh! And how did you choose? What test did we pass to qualify?' I asked.

'I can read faces. You have a kind face. So does Janki. See that girl over there?' She pointed to someone with a pointed face and straight hair in the front row. 'I can tell she is a complete bitch. Don't be friends with her,' Parul said with certainty.

Janki laughed. 'And how do you know that we are nice?' she probed.

'I told you, I have a sixth sense,' said Parul.

I noticed that Janki was dressed very fashionably in a white linen top and a knee-length paisley-printed skirt with a crocheted lace border. Her shoulder-length hair was styled professionally and she wore pale pink lipstick. Her eyelids were lined with eyeliner, accentuating the almond shape of her eyes. She looked glamorous. Compared to them, I felt very ordinary in my usual jeans and a tee, my hair pulled back in a simple ponytail. Most of the girls in the class seemed to have dressed up, and I made a mental note to step up my style quotient.

'So what is your background? Which college did you graduate from?' asked Janki.

An innocent, casual question, but I found myself stiffening up. I didn't want them to know anything about my past; I had to be careful.

'I moved here from Kerala. I graduated from a college there,' I answered after a moment.

'Oh! So you are new to Bombay!' said Parul.

'Yes,' I lied. It was not exactly a complete lie. It was a half-truth. I had indeed graduated from Kerala and moved to Bombay. There was no chance in hell I was sharing the NMHI episode with anyone, let alone people I had just met.

'What about you two?' I asked them, quickly deflecting attention away from me.

'I did my BA Literature from Xavier's,' said Parul.

'And I did my B.Com from SNDT,' said Janki

'I too did my B.Com! So we both have something in common,' I said.

'Then how is it that you both decided to do a creative writing course?' Parul asked, surprised.

'I have to do *something* till my parents find a husband for me. This course was just for a year, so it suited me. I hated-hated-hated accountancy, mercantile law and all that nonsense they taught in B.Com.' Janki wrinkled her nose comically.

'Oh! And you are okay with that?' asked Parul, her eyes widening.

I had never met anyone like Janki. She was nonchalantly declaring that she was not serious about the course and was just waiting to get married.

'I guess I am. I never really thought about it,' said Janki.

'What? Are you for real?' exclaimed Parul.

Janki just shrugged and smiled.

'And what about you? Why creative writing after B.Com? Don't tell me you are waiting to get married too?' Parul addressed me.

'Of course not. I like writing more than commerce or accountancy. I want to write for a magazine or a newspaper,' I said.

'This is what I want too. I initially thought of doing an MA. But I felt this was more practical, as we have an internship here after our course. We get work experience, which is great,' said Parul.

'God – you two are so sorted, yaar,' said Janki, as she rummaged through her bag, fished out a mirror and reapplied the lip gloss. I watched in fascination at how expertly she had done it.

'No boys here. I wish there were,' she said as she put away her lip gloss and mirror.

'Was your previous college a co-ed?' I asked.

'No! My parents won't let me to go to a co-ed college.' Janki made a face.

'It's over-rated. I went to a co-ed college, and boys are nothing but a bore,' said Parul, pretending to yawn.

'I agree,' I said, though I hadn't thought about boys for a long time.

But I desperately wanted to fit in with them, and talk about whatever they wanted to talk of.

A professor entered the class just then. She motored in fast, breathless as she placed her books on the table. She looked young and was dressed very unlike a professor, in jeans and a shirt. All the girls stood up.

'Hellooooo, girls! I am Nalini,' she said, 'You can call me Nuls.'

There were nervous giggles, as we didn't know if she was joking or not.

'Sit down, sit down,' she said. Her voice was child-like and sing-song. 'I have discovered that the students anyway give nicknames to professors. So I thought I would choose my own nickname. Nice?'

'What the hell,' muttered Parul.

Nuls declared that she would be teaching poetry. She gave a brief overview of what we would cover, and how we would be writing poetry ourselves.

'Any questions?' she asked when she finished.

A hand shot up from one of the benches at the other end of the classroom.

'Yes?' said Nuls eagerly.

'Do you always wear jeans to class, Nuls?'

The whole class laughed. Nuls laughed too.

'I couldn't find any formal wear. I was too lazy to do laundry,' she declared.

'Nuls, I have a question,' another voice piped up from the front of the class.

'Yes? And it better not be about my clothes,' Nuls warned.

'Do you have a boyfriend?' asked the girl who had raised her hand.

'Why? Are you planning to steal him?' Nuls was quick to retort.

The whole class laughed again.

She was only a few years older than us, and she seemed very casual in her approach to the course. It was evident that she had not done any preparations for her lecture. The kind of things she said was what my eighth grade English teacher had taught me. I felt a bit cheated. My expectations of the course had been very high, and Nuls, though friendly, was disappointing.

Parul and I glanced at each other and I knew instantly that Parul felt the same way. Parul shook her head. 'Nuls is nuts,' she whispered.

I fiercely nodded. Out of the corner of my eye, I caught Janki laughing along with all the others.

We had a break when Nuls's lecture finally got over. We discovered a sugarcane juice stall across the road, opposite the college, where all the girls congregated during the break. We sat on makeshift benches which the stall-owner – a middle-aged man named Maneesh – had fashioned from bricks and granite slabs. He had named the stall after himself, and the red crude letters painted on the side of the stall announcing its name were now faded.

Everyone seemed to have formed their own groups, with Parul, Janki and me forming a trio. Parul dragged us and introduced us to another group of girls. They all had varied backgrounds, and their own reasons for taking up creative writing – ranging from wanting to go the US (which mandated a four-year degree for undergrad) to wanting to be in the same city as a boyfriend, to wanting to be in South Bombay and not getting into any other course.

No one was really serious about creative writing other than Parul and me. I didn't care though! I was happy to be among all these girls, and join in the fun and laughter. I was Rip Van Winkle emerging from his slumber to join civilisation. This was something I had missed for so long. I wasn't letting *anything* get in the way of my enjoying the world I had sorely missed.

The girls were excitedly talking and discussing Nuls as they sipped their sugarcane juice.

'Do you think Nuls is a virgin?' asked one.

'She definitely is not.'

'How can you tell?'

'By the way she walks. After a woman has been fucked, she walks differently.'

'What?! Get out of here.'

'It's the truth, I swear.'

'Okay, let's all walk, and you guess which one of us is a virgin, okay?'

'Okay, I am in.'

'So am I.'

'So am I.'

'Me too.'

There were hoots of laughter as each of the girls sashayed, walking one behind the other, and the 'virgin-identifier' declared her verdict on whether each one was a virgin or not, amidst peals of laughter and wolf whistles. The girls were quite rowdy and having been in a women's college earlier, this kind of behaviour didn't shock me at all. I was used to it. When women get together without any men around, there is a different vibe, a different energy. It was a lot of silliness really, but I reveled in every little bit of the silliness.

'Your turns,' said one of the girls suddenly, pointing at Janki, Parul and me.

'Nooo!' protested Janki.

'Yes!' affirmed Parul as she pushed her in front, and asked me to line up behind her, and we walked a few steps.

The virgin-identifier declared that Parul and I were not virgins and that Janki was. Parul couldn't stop laughing, and I found it hilarious too. Janki too was wiping away her tears of laughter.

I knew what the truth was. I had only kissed, and never had sex with any guy. But these girls seemed to think that *not* being a virgin was somehow cooler. It instantly elevated your status. So I went along, and pretended she was right.

'This group is a fun group, yaar!' said Janki as we walked back to the class for the next session.

'Yes! Stupid, but fun,' Parul agreed. How could I even tell them how much this bit of ribaldry meant to me! So I said nothing and walked back to class with them, a huge grin on my face.

'We didn't learn much in Nuls's class. All we learnt was a null,' I said as we entered the classroom and took our seats.

'Yes. But then that's what the library is there for,' Parul said.

'Is it good? Have you seen it?' I asked.

'Yes, it's an excellent one. We can teach ourselves all the topics that Nuls doesn't cover properly,' Parul said.

'I hope the next lecturer is better,' I remarked.

But as it turned out, the other lecturer was even worse. Mrs Amrita Tulapurkar was a middle-aged lady with a master's degree in literature and a talent for making even interesting topics dull. She droned on in a nasal voice, mostly reading out lengthy passages from voluminous tomes as 'examples of good writing'. We weren't allowed to ask any questions in her class. During her lecture, Janki rested her head on the desk and fell asleep. Mrs Tulapurkar did not even notice.

By the time classes got over that day, the sun had already set. I wasn't used to being out this late. After my sheltered days at NMHI, this was radical.

'I wish the classes got over a little earlier. It's so dark,' I remarked.

'Why, what's with your fear of the dark? Afraid of Dracula?' laughed Parul.

'Actually, I'm afraid of losing my glass slipper,' I retorted.

'Eh? What glass slipper?' asked Janki.

'*Arrey baba*, Cinderella,' said Parul.

'What Cinderella?' Janki asked, frowning.

'What? Haven't you heard of Cinderella? The fairy tale princess? What are you made of, girl?' Parul exclaimed.

I was taken aback too. How could anyone *not* have heard of Cinderella?

'Is she famous?' asked Janki.

'It's a fairy tale, Janki. Haven't you read fairy tales?' I asked.

'We weren't allowed any story books. Only text books,' said Janki.

'What do your folks do?' asked Parul, slightly intrigued.

'Diamonds,' Janki replied. 'We own a jewellery business – mostly diamonds. We export, but we also sell here.'

'Your family must be loaded! Where do you live?' Parul asked.

We learnt that she lived in a joint family and they owned a massive house on Grant Road. Her grandfather had established the business, now run by her father and uncles. Nobody in her family believed that women should go out and work. Academics weren't important.

'What a cushy life!' marvelled Parul.

'What about you, Parul? Your turn to tell us all about yourself. Where do you live? What do your parents do?' Janki asked.

'Single child of a single mother, I live in Mahalaxmi,' said Parul.

'Are your parents divorced?' Janki probed.

'Ha ha. No. They never got married. I have never met my father. He is American. He was a part of a delegation that visited India. He stayed here for about a year when he and my mother met and fell in love. He wanted to take my mother back to the US and get married. But my mother chose to stay in India, as my Nani had been diagnosed with cancer at that time. She needed care. Nana had died while he was in the army. Nani was all my mother had, before she had me, of course,' said Parul.

'Oh, so you are half-white!' said Janki.

'Can't you make that out from how I look? I thought it was obvious. But I am one hundred percent Indian on the inside,' she said.

'So you never met your father?' Janki questioned.

'No. I think he has visited us a couple of times. But I was too little to remember,' said Parul.

'What does your mother do?' I asked, fascinated by her story. I had never met anyone like her before. I was liking her more and more. She was so honest and forthright. She was the 'coolest' friend I had ever made.

'She works in the film industry. She has been an assistant director in many movies. She has also written a script,' said Parul proudly.

'Cool yaar! Take us to film sets sometime. Make us meet all the stars!' Janki said.

'It's a drag, trust me. But, yes, will take you sometime,' Parul promised. 'What about you, Ankita? What is your story?'

'Yes, tell us about yourself,' Janki echoed.

We had reached the Churchgate station by then. There was already a fast train standing there.

'Mine is an ordinary story. Just a middle-class family. Nothing exotic or interesting,' I said.

I was happy my train was waiting, as I didn't want them asking me any more questions. They had to take the slow train, as their stations were quite close to Churchgate. The slow trains halted in every station. I took the fast train, as it would stop only at Dadar and then at Bandra.

'See you tomorrow, girls,' I said.

'See you tomorrow,' shouted Parul, as I ran towards my train, feeling light as air.

When I got back home, my parents were eagerly waiting to hear all about my first day.

'It was wonderful! It is just like my old college in Kerala. The girls are so much fun. I made new friends,' I replied, pirouetting around the drawing room, a big smile on my face.

My parents were relieved.

'Ankita, that is so good to hear,' said my father, the relief and joy in his voice ringing clear.

'Yes. How nice this is,' said my mother. 'I almost forgot – a letter came for you,' she added. She held out an envelope. I knew from the writing who it was from even before I opened it.

Heart racing, I rushed to my room with the letter.

3

Here's Your Letter

Iwas so familiar with his handwriting that I'd have identified it even after a hundred years. Though I had written to him after my discharge from NMHI, I had never expected a reply. And here he was, replying after *months*.

26th September 1993
Delhi

Dearest Ankita,

You have no idea how happy I was to get your letter after such a long time. Your mother was very sweet on the phone every time I called. She kept telling me that you were in a village in Kerala, and there were no phones there. I realised then that there was something not quite right, which was one of the reasons I kept calling. I will come to the other reason later.

I can only imagine what you must have gone through. I was deeply disturbed, and also moved, when I read about everything you had gone through. Why didn't you reach out to me? I was always there. Though submerged in my studies, had you called, Ankita, I would have dropped everything for you.

The last year in IIT is always stressful because of placements. When I went home for the summer, I discussed with my parents and weighed my options and thought about whether to go for higher studies, civil services, study management or get a job. I decided I would work in India for two years and get enough work experience, and then decide whether to go abroad or study management. I will have more clarity then.

From September onwards we had companies coming to our campus, and the application process began. They held presentations, and we had to write tests. I don't remember a single weekend I was free. Then the short-listing began. Everyone tries to get an offer in phase 1 itself.

I am happy to let you know I have two offers, and both from Bombay. I have accepted one of them and start my new job in a month! This was the other reason I kept calling you – I was so excited to be moving to your city.

From your letter it is evident that you are now very strong, and the worst is behind you. Still, I want you to know that I am always here for you. Always. All you have to do is pick up the phone and call me.

And soon we will meet.
Love,
Vaibhav

'Oh Good Lord!' I exclaimed out loud when I finished reading his letter. How could he just decide to walk back into my life? I wanted a *fresh* start. And if that meant severing all ties with my past, I would do it. After all that I had been through in NMHI, I felt I *deserved* a fresh start. But now he had got back in touch and spoilt it all.

I wasn't sure he understood th*e enormity* of what I had gone through, even though he had written that he had. It was evident he had no clue. How could he even comprehend when I myself was grappling with it? There was no question of 'reaching out' to him, like he had mentioned in the letter. It had all happened so fast, like being swept away by a gigantic tidal wave. The anguish, the rage, the sheer helplessness of being confined to a mental hospital, the fight to get back to normalcy, the trauma. I couldn't even begin to explain.

Granted that while in school, we had been in love – or maybe it was just a crush, I wasn't entirely sure. After school, he had left for Delhi to join IIT, and I had joined St. Agnes for my graduation. We had kept in touch through letters and phone calls. I remembered how thrilled I used to be to hear from him. On my eighteenth birthday, he had told me he loved me. But all of this seemed to be from another life, before I was diagnosed with bipolar disorder, before I had to go away to a hospital to heal.

When I had written to him after I was discharged, explaining my silence and mentioning how I was a different person now, I had treated it more as a closure from my side. As far as I was concerned, I was done with my old life, and perhaps the people in it too.

I had been to hell and back, and I had lived to tell the tale. And now here he was, moving to Bombay.

Why? Why? Why?

I wasn't happy about this development at all. I wasn't even sure if I wanted to meet him. But there was nothing I could do. He was moving to Bombay whether I liked it or not.

●

I put his letter out of my head as I rushed to college the next day. Parul was already in class by the time I reached.

'Tomorrow onwards, let's wait for each other at the station. It is boring to walk to college alone,' she declared.

Today she was dressed in a peacock blue peasant top, a smart black tight skirt and boots. Janki wore a yellow top with puff sleeves, and a checked ankle-length skirt with tiny bows running all around the hem.

'You guys dress up so well. I feel plain,' I admitted, as I slid in next to Parul.

Parul looked at my jeans and T-shirt.

'You're fine the way you are. But if you want to go shopping, we can go to Fashion Street tomorrow. I buy all my clothes from there; I don't mind going with you,' she offered.

'Fashion Street? What's that?' I asked.

'Oh, you don't know Fashion Street?!' both Janki and Parul said together.

'Do you also buy your clothes from there?' I asked.

'Oh, we have a *darzi* who comes home and copies all the patterns from any movie that you tell him. This one I am wearing is what Juhi Chawla wore in *Raju Ban Gaya Gentleman*,' she said.

She expected me to have not only seen the movie, but also to remember what the actress wore! I had no idea of either. But I nodded.

It was no different from my expecting her to know about Cinderella.

A professor entered the class then, and the excited chatter suddenly stopped. She was frail, in her early sixties, and walked slowly. Her bobbed white hair added to her aura of dignity. I noticed her string of pearls and pale pink dress with a matching formal jacket. She looked like the queen of England to me – distinguished, sophisticated and gentle.

She said we could address her as Mrs Hayden. She spoke about how she had taught literature in a prominent college abroad and how after retirement she had moved to Bombay and how the principal of the college was very keen to have her teach here. She said she would come in only thrice a week, and that she expected all the work she assigned us to be submitted on time. She outlined the topics she'd be covering in the first nine weeks – characteristics of good writing, figurative language, imagery, sensory details, point of view, descriptive writing and persuasive writing.

'There are some ground rules I want to lay down,' she said in her British accent, her voice so low that all of us had to be absolutely quiet to hear.

'My first rule is that you have to be on time. If you are late, not seated and ready to begin your work when the bell goes, I shall mark you absent. Be respectful to everyone in the classroom – to your peers as well as to your instructors. Procrastination is a bad habit, and if you turn in your work late, I take away credits. I shall grade all your work on a scale of A to E. E indicates that the work is full of clichés and not thoughtful; A would mean that the work is highly original, highly successful and shows informed engagement with the literary genre. May you reach your goals as writers! I wish you the very best and I look forward to reading your assignments,' she said.

With that she ended her little speech, and asked us to introduce ourselves.

There was not a single student who was not affected by her crisp manner and approach. After Nuls and Tulapurkar, she was a welcome change. We found ourselves sitting up a little straighter. After all of us in the class had introduced ourselves, she asked us what writing meant to us.

Parul's hand shot up. I ducked out of sight. I didn't want to be called out to answer this question. I wasn't ready to face the class.

Mrs Hayden pointed to a girl in the front bench and asked her to answer.

'Writing gives meaning to my life,' she said.

'How does it give meaning to your life? Could you elaborate?' Mrs Hayden asked.

'Ummm… aaah,' went the girl. She had no answer.

'Remember, you have to think about what writing actually means to *you*. Do not try and paraphrase what other literary greats have said. Also, they are people just like you who stuck at it long enough to become successful.'

Mrs Hayden then pointed to Parul.

'Writing is something that will help me pay bills and my rent, my money for my bread, and hopefully some butter too,' said Parul.

The whole class laughed. Mrs Hayden smiled.

'Now that is a practical answer,' she said.

I hunched over and scribbled in my notebook. I didn't want to look up in case I caught Mrs Hayden's eyes.

'What does writing mean to you?' I had written.

While the other girls were answering, I was thinking hard. My brain was furiously trying to find an answer. My hands were moving across the page almost on their own.

I stared at what I had just written.

Writing is what stopped me from taking my own life.

It was the truth. A truth I hugged close to my heart. A truth I buried deep within me. A truth I would never reveal.

So I shut my notebook, chewed on the tip of my pen and listened to the other girls talking about what writing meant to them, not knowing that this truth would become a noose around my neck.

4
The Visit

When Mrs Hayden gave us a break, we went to the sugarcane juice stall.

'Bhaiya, put some plastic chairs here. We come here daily! Is this the way to treat customers?' Parul admonished him as she sat on the slab, sipping her juice.

'I can't really do that. Those *Pandus* will then say it is a proper restaurant, and I will have to pay them extra *hafta*,' Maneesh said.

'Pandu? What is a Pandu?' I asked.

Maneesh guffawed. 'She doesn't know Pandu? Is she new to Bombay?' he asked.

Parul and Janki both shushed me.

'Don't ever say it loudly. It's a derogatory term for policemen. They get mad if you call them that,' Janki explained.

The moment she mentioned policemen, it rekindled a memory I thought I had long buried.

Old memories have a way of resurfacing when you least expect them to. They clutch your heart, dredging up emotions you thought you had killed. I remembered how the police had tumbled out of their jeeps in Kerala the night I had kissed Abhi all those years ago. Recalling that incident felt like a sudden stab in the gut.

If I had known at that point that he would die, would I have kissed him harder, or would I have refrained? What would have made it easier to bear what was to follow? I didn't know. All I knew is that even after all this time, it felt like someone had torn out my heart and flung it aside. Half-formed regrets came rushing to my head, clouding my brain like mist. I had not even gone to see his body that day. I heard Appachan's voice clearly in my head, breaking on the phone the day I had called him. This is the problem with life, I thought bitterly. It snatches away people who do not deserve to die. It destroys everything when you least expect it. It takes away all that you value and hold dear, leaving you with scraps of longing and regrets that gnaw at your soul.

'Hello! You have gone pale and you seem miles away. Are you okay?' Parul was snapping her fingers in front of my face.

'Yes, sorry... I am fine,' I said, as I took a deep breath and exhaled, furiously fighting my memories.

I did not want to remember the past. I had fought my way out. I tried to push it away, but it clung to me like a stubborn stain.

For the rest of that day, neither Parul's jokes nor Janki's comments and the usual chatter of the other girls had any impact on me. Outwardly, I smiled and joined in. Nobody noticed that the smile never reached my eyes.

●

I was so busy with my new course and my new friends that I had forgotten all about replying to Vaibhav. Each day brought new homework. I was very clear that I wanted to top this course. I wanted to succeed very badly. It would be my comeback, my redemption for dropping out of MBA and getting admitted to NMHI.

I was ready to do whatever it took. Anything that was assigned, anything that needed to be read, anything that the professors told us to do, I would do it meticulously, promptly and with great care.

I began frequenting the college library, with its very large collection of reference books. When I first entered it, I instantly compared it to the library at St. Agnes, its wood-panelled walls, its massive ancient ceilings and the warm welcoming feeling. This library was nothing like it. It was a modern structure on the topmost floor of our college. There were rows and rows of cold steel bookshelves. I didn't care though! It held a well of knowledge and my thirst was unquenchable.

Soon I became a fixture there. Mrs Asthana, the librarian who had a reputation of being grumpy, began recognising me and smiling at me. I would be at the library very frequently, poring over reference books, finishing my assignments. On some days, I left home early and spent the entire morning there, doing my work till it was time for classes to start.

Parul and I had now begun competing with each other to see who would earn the higher grade, and who could elicit more praise from Mrs Hayden. It was a sunny rivalry.

●

It had been almost a month since my college started. I had settled down well into the new course with great optimism. Spending time at a mental hospital changes you in ways you can't imagine. I had never thought that I would be able to read again, let alone write. I shuddered when I thought of the days I'd lost my ability to read. The time I couldn't even read a children's book seemed like a bad dream, even though it was only a few months ago. Most people take for granted that they can read. They don't think twice about it as they go about their daily business.

For me, each word I wrote, each assignment I submitted was a triumph, a victory lap. It was a joy I couldn't share with anybody. Nobody knew what it was like to be a prisoner of your mind. I had broken those shackles and, oh, how I enjoyed the freedom!

My parents were overjoyed to see me in this mode. The medications too had been stopped. I too couldn't get over it!

'I am NORMAL, I am NORMAL! I don't have to take any medications anymore. I can READ, I can WRITE. Do you realise how GOOD that feels?' I wanted to shout from the roof-tops. But, of course, nobody would understand. I would just be this fool mouthing gibberish to them. How could anyone even begin to imagine the darkness I had once been thrust into?

I ran my hands over the scar that ran across the back of my left forearm, extending right up to my wrist, a permanent reminder of my ordeals, of that bleak day I tried to slash my wrist. They were my secret badges, my medals. I applauded myself silently, celebrating on my own, inside my head.

The human mind copes with new realities, making adjustments in ways that suit it best. My mind had shut the door firmly on my past. It was the only way to move forward.

Whenever a memory from my old life came back to me, I would push it away, suppress it, till it receded. I would remind myself how fortunate I was to have this course, how good I was at all the assignments, and how lucky I was to have found new friends.

But the past has a way of catching up with you. It is not so easy to escape its clutches. I should have known.

If life was a house, then you could compartmentalise things you did not want to deal with by pushing them into a room which you never enter and forget all about. That is what I had done. I had presumed I could get by without ever opening that door. But as long as that room existed, it couldn't stay locked forever. At some point you had to deal with what was behind the door, breathe in the stale air, the dust, the neglect in that closed room.

For me, that door to my past opened up when I least expected it. I came back from college one evening, and my mother greeted me smiling. 'Ankita, there's a surprise for you. Look who is here!'

I froze as I entered my home. Sitting on the living room sofa, waiting for me with a big smile on his face, was Vaibhav.

5

With a Little Help from my Friends

I stood rooted to the spot, staring in disbelief.

'Hi, Ankita! Thought this would be a nice surprise,' said Vaibhav, his voice deeper than I remembered.

My first reaction was annoyance. How could he just turn up like this out of the blue? And why was my mother smiling at him so benignly? How did he get here?

All my life, my mother had discouraged boys from visiting home, or my going out with boys. Though I was allowed to write to anyone, I wasn't really allowed on 'dates'. If I was going out with a boy, I hid it from her. I knew that my stay at NMHI had changed my parents completely, especially my mother. But this? I never expected this. It was a drastic change. I didn't know what to make of it.

'How come you are here?' I asked. My words betrayed my displeasure, though I tried to hide it.

'Four years since we met and you ask how come I am here? A hello would be nice.' Vaibhav couldn't stop smiling.

'He called about an hour ago, and I told him the time you usually get home. He asked if he could come over and surprise you,' my mother hastened to explain.

'A nice surprise too,' I forced myself to say, looking at Vaibhav's happy face.

'Let me get dinner ready. And, Vaibhav, please join us for dinner,' my mother said, disappearing into the kitchen, not giving him a chance to refuse. It was evident my mother and he got along like a house on fire. Vaibhav was easy to like.

'You look amazing, Ankita. You have grown even more beautiful,' said Vaibhav as soon as my mother was out of earshot. His voice was low as he gazed at me with open admiration.

It took me back to the time when he had called up on my eighteenth birthday and played Jefferson Starship for me. It was a sweet enough memory and I appreciated the effort he made that day, carrying the tape-recorder in the cold Delhi winter, and waiting at the STD booth just to play that song. His words would have melted me back then. But today, they had no impact. The freshly minted me had a different perspective.

Of what use was looking beautiful? What you do with your life is everything. Beauty is not what you see on the outside. Beauty is what you are deep inside, where no one watched. My stay at the mental hospital had opened my eyes. But if I said all of it now, in response to his compliment, I'd be seen as weird. I had to filter everything that came to my head through the lens of 'normalcy' and not just blurt it out. This was something I was painfully aware of. So I did the next best thing I could. I commented on *his* looks.

'You… You look older,' I said.

'Hahaha. I should hope so! I was such a kid back then,' he said, as he ran a hand over his stubble.

Now that I had recovered from the initial shock of seeing him all of a sudden, I scrutinised his clothes. He was wearing a neatly ironed black cotton shirt and dark blue trousers. Almost six feet tall, hair stylishly cut, he now wore glasses and looked fit. We had been teenagers when we last saw each other. In the years we had been away from each other, he had transformed into a handsome young man.

There was an awkward pause, as we both didn't know what to say. I had to say something quickly to dispel this uncomfortable silence.

'So, when did you come to Bombay? Did you find a house? Tell me all the news,' I said as I sat on the single sofa opposite him, forcing myself to make conversation

'I arrived only this morning. And see my luck, I am staying close by, Ankita! It's just a ten-minute walk to my place. I was so thrilled when I discovered that. How could I not see you immediately?' he said.

Alarm bells rang in my head then. Uh-oh. Bombay was such a big city. Couldn't he have found somewhere else to live? I didn't want him so close by. Did he deliberately find a place in Bandra, knowing I was here?

'Have you rented a place here, then?'

'Oh, no. I can't afford to rent a place in this area,' he said. 'At least not yet, anyway. I just moved into an apartment the company allotted. My office is in the Bandra-Kurla complex, and all the management trainees are given accommodation in chummeries,' he explained.

'Chummery? Is it like a hostel?'

'No, just a regular flat I share with three other management trainees. The company has taken many flats on lease.'

Many of the multinationals had their offices in the Bandra-Kurla complex. So his explanation made perfect sense. What a relief to know that his moving to Bandra was not deliberate!

'So, welcome to Bombay,' I said brightly.

I didn't mean it at all, but it seemed a good-girl thing to say.

My mother called out from the kitchen just then and asked me to lay the table. Vaibhav jumped up to help.

When we were seated, he asked where my father was. 'Travelling on work,' said Ma, serving us hot rotis.

It was a homely scene and Vaibhav looked at ease. My mother was serving him the dal now, and fussing over how he should eat more. He praised her cooking, telling her how much he enjoyed it. She basked in his approval. I looked at it all and resentment stirred deep within me. I hated it. I tried to analyse why I was feeling agitated about Vaibhav being here and my mother getting along well with him. After all, he *was* a friend. I was seeing him after so long. He had made the effort to come over. He was so amiable too. I *ought* to feel joy. But I didn't. Instead, I was filled with something between mild irritation and dread. I think what irritated me was that Vaibhav had just marched back into my life like he *belonged*.

Long after Vaibhav left, the feelings of discomfort and resentment remained. Can a relationship continue when two people have had dramatically different life experiences and those experiences have changed one of them in a profound way? I wasn't sure.

But Vaibhav saw nothing amiss.

'You know, Ankita, it feels wonderful that even after so many years, and even after everything that has happened, we still have this. And you are just the same as I remember. You haven't changed at all. And it feels so good to have an old friend in a new city,' he had said as he waved goodbye.

If only he knew.

●

I was so disturbed by Vaibhav turning up unexpectedly that I skipped going to the college library the next morning. I found Janki waiting for me at the usual spot. The understanding between Parul, Janki and me was that whoever reached Churchgate first would wait for the others at the vada-pav tea stall near the exit that led to our college.

'Ah, there you are! ' said Janki.

Soon Parul too came along.

'Let's bunk today. It's only Tulapurkar. Nuls is on leave,' she said.

'How do you know that?' I asked.

'Her cousin lives in my building. They all have a family wedding at Nashik,' Parul said.

'You are top-class when it comes to all this. Let's bunk,' Janki agreed.

'Let's take Ankita to places she's nevers been before,' Parul said.

They took me to 'Khau Galli', a two-minute walk from Churchgate station. It was a street lined with food stalls on both sides. I had never seen anything like it before. As soon as we neared the place, different aromas of food hit us. There was the smell of delicious biryani spices roasting in ghee, mingling with the fragrance of the condiments used in cooking various other delicacies. At the entrance there was a nimboo pani stall, and Parul bought ice-cold nimboo pani for all of us. Right next to it was a fruit-stall in a profusion of reds, oranges and yellows; neatly cut watermelon and mangoes and muskmelons vied for attention, begging to be eaten. There were stalls for every kind of food item, ranging from 'Indian-Chinese' like hakka noodles and Schezwan fried rice to aloo tikkis, chaats, samosas. The names of these stalls too were as varied as their menus and they amused me: Nikhil Pure Veg Stall, Dream Girl Dosa Stall, Lenin Pav Bhaji Stall...

A steady stream of customers stood around the stalls, eating from plates in their hands. The food, especially the pav bhaji, looked delicious.

'God, this is making my mouth water,' I said.

'Come, follow me. I shall take you to a place where we can sit down and eat at leisure. All these places at the start of the street are crowded,' said Parul as she led us further down the street, almost to the very end.

We went inside a stall hidden behind a large peepul tree, shielded from the crowd and the noise. The stall-owner greeted her as we entered.

'Long time! Where is Freddy?' he asked.

'Will tell you another time, bhaiya. I have brought my friends today. Make the best ragda patties, okay? Don't let me down,' she said as we settled down. It was a tiny space, the walls painted a refreshing pale green. At the entrance was a picture of Lord Hanuman, right above the cash counter. Incense sticks and a lamp burning in front of it sent a peaceful vibe through the stall.

Though the furniture was Spartan – just plain white wooden benches and matching tables – the whole place was spotless. I was filled with a sense of calm.

'You're both okay with ragda patties, right? They are to die for,' Parul checked our preferences, as she had taken the liberty of placing our orders for us.

'Yes, let's try it,' Janki confirmed.

They started chatting about a movie Janki had just watched. I listened, barely participating in the conversation.

'What's wrong, Ankita? You look kind of lost,' Parul addressed me. She had noticed how quiet I'd become.

'Nothing, all okay.' I brushed her concern aside.

'You are such a bad liar, and your face is so transparent. Anything you feel is reflected instantly,' Parul said.

'Is it so obvious?' I asked.

'Yes, your face is like a movie screen,' Janki said.

I smiled at that. Even for a simile she could only think of cinema.

'So, are you going to tell us or not? Boyfriend troubles?' asked Parul. I was surprised. She was astute. Could she read my mind?

I told them about Vaibhav turning up at my place, how annoyed I was about him making himself comfortable at *my* house, and the casual way in which he had presumed he could walk back into my life.

Both of them listened raptly.

'So let me understand this – you had something going on with this guy in school? Then you guys kept in touch intermittently in college. And now he has come back?' Parul asked.

'Yes,' I confirmed.

'Do you like him?' Janki asked.

'I don't know if I like him like *that*. I used to. Now he is a friend – that's for sure,' I said.

'Just date him a few times and see how you feel. He doesn't seem like a bad guy at all. At least he isn't like how mine turned out to be,' said Parul.

'You have a boyfriend? You didn't tell us! What's his name? Tell us all the details!' Janki ordered.

'Had. Not sure if I want him back. I used to come here with Freddy. That's his name. At first I was in love with him. But now he just seems like a good-for-nothing guy. He was living with us for a few months and he got too comfortable. I kicked him out now,' said Parul.

'What? He was living with you? Was your mother okay with it?' I asked. I couldn't imagine a scenario like that. It was so far removed from my reality. I don't think my parents would *ever* be okay with a guy living in with me.

'Yeah, my mother was okay about it. She is totally open-minded. She left it to me. I took him in as he had nowhere to go. He had defaulted on his rent, so his landlord kicked him out. He was staying as a paying guest. Then he moved in with us. But the guy just can't hold down a job. He plays the guitar and thinks he is Bryan Adams. I have now given him a deadline to find a job. Hope he comes to his senses. Now your guy, Ankita – he doesn't sound anything like Freddy. He sounds like a decent guy. Give him a chance,' said Parul.

I had told them only half the truth. I had not told them about my days at NMHI. They had no idea what I had gone through. They had formed their opinion based on the inputs I had given them.

That was the problem with advice. Everyone gives advice based on the narrow prism of their own experience.

'I guess you are right,' I replied. I wasn't going to contradict her.

'Yes, maybe you will enjoy his company and fall in love with him. And we will have an Ankita-Vaibhav love story blockbuster,' Janki said.

I smiled.

Maybe I would! Maybe I would surprise myself.

Sitting there that day in that stall, munching on delicious ragda patties and talking to my friends, all of a sudden the whole Vaibhav issue seemed easy-peasy.

6
This Charming Man

Afew days later, when I reached home from college in the evening, Vaibhav was waiting for me in the lobby of our building.

'Hey, Anks!' he called out. 'Your mother invited me to dinner again.' He smiled as he joined me.

'I think you must have invited yourself,' I remarked dryly.

He laughed, treating it as a joke. 'Of course, I just call up random people and invite myself over. That is my hobby,' he quipped.

When we entered my home, both my parents welcomed him warmly. Vaibhav was a good conversationalist and he got along with my father just as he had with my mother. Going by my father's animated expression, he was genuinely pleased.

I excused myself, saying I had to wash and change. I lingered in the bathroom, taking longer than usual, foolishly thinking that the more time I spent in the bathroom, the lesser time I would have to spend with Vaibhav.

'Ankita, what are you doing?' my mother called out. I had no choice but to step out then.

The table was already laid and everyone was seated.

'Come, Ankita, we were waiting for you,' said my father.

I joined them silently, taking the chair next to Vaibhav.

I was irked that my parents seemed to be giving Vaibhav the royal treatment. Like he was their future son-in-law or something. My mother had not even thought of checking with me whether it was okay to invite Vaibhav. She had just presumed it was fine.

Then things got worse.

'You never told me Vaibhav loves badminton. I have asked him to join me in the mornings in the court. I would love to take it up again. It has been a while since I played,' my father announced.

While I knew that Dad used to be a good badminton player in his younger days and had won prizes at university level, I had never thought he would actually want to take it up again.

'Aren't the courts in our complex only for residents?' I asked coldly.

'I am entitled to bring guests. And if we pay the monthly fee, we can get a pass made for Vaibhav. He can then use the facilities as our guest whenever he wants.' My father had the solution already.

'Thank you so much, uncle. I love sports, and the place where I am currently staying has no facilities at all. In IIT, I used to play every day. I was missing that. Now this has come as a blessing. It is very kind and generous of you,' Vaibhav gushed.

'Oh, my pleasure. I too will get to play. What is the point of having all these facilities if you never use them?' my father replied.

I scowled. Then I un-scowled. I didn't want my parents catching my expression.

Vaibhav took a second helping of the vegetable curry Ma had made and praised it, making her glow.

'Why don't you join us when we play badminton, Ankita?' said Vaibhav.

'No, thanks. I have too much college work. Also, I don't like badminton.' I was quick and curt in my dismissal.

Vaibhav caught on to my mood. But he didn't say anything then, not to me. To my parents, he was the life and soul of the dinner table. My father laughed at the jokes Vaibhav cracked. My mother asked Vaibhav about his family and he was only too happy to tell her about how much he missed Madras.

'My hostel-mates became like family, aunty. But home is home. Nothing can replace that,' he said.

Ma nodded in approval. Vaibhav was definitely striking all the right chords. The conversation continued and I answered in monosyllables when asked anything. I was sulking, but my parents didn't notice. Vaibhav did though.

When I was seeing him off in the lobby of my building, he said softly, 'Hey, if I've done something to upset you, it was not my intention at all. Look, I will tell your father that I can't make it for badminton.'

It took me only a few seconds to decide. I couldn't be unfair to my father, who was eagerly looking forward to playing with Vaibhav. I had never seen such excitement in Dad's eyes for years. How absurdly petty would it be on my part to tell Vaibhav that he couldn't come because I was jealous that my father and mother liked him? That would be immature.

'Of course not! Please come. He would love it,' I said.

When I got back home, my father said, 'Good friends are a treasure, Ankita. Vaibhav seems to be a sensible young man.'

'You are only saying that because he will play badminton with you,' I replied.

My father and mother both laughed, and I joined in the laughter, even though I wasn't really joking.

I knew Vaibhav was in love with me even after all these years. But I felt nothing more than mild affection for him. Sometimes I wondered if I felt even that. I tried to reciprocate his feelings for me, I really did. But when do hearts listen? It was far from the blockbuster love story that Janki had envisaged in her head.

That's the thing about love. You cannot force it. You cannot fight it. If it comes, you gratefully accept. If it doesn't, you can't do a thing. All you do is go about your daily business, hoping it will come tomorrow, the day after, eventually.

But nothing prepared me for what happened next.

Sometimes, it is only when you lose what you had that you begin to value it.

7
Confident

'Euphoria', the annual cultural festival of my college, was upon us. The preparations had already started for this big event. Hosted by our college, this would see many colleges participate. Members of the culture club ran around like headless chickens, trying to coordinate everything – right from getting the sponsors to coming up with events, organising judges, sending out invites to various colleges, making a list of those who had accepted, arranging accommodation for them, getting the audio-visual systems installed and deciding the various venues where the events would take place. And all of it handled entirely by the students. A notice calling for volunteers for various committees was put up and many students in my class signed up. It was a celebration for the whole college. The enthusiasm was infectious.

One felt it as soon as one entered the college gates. The bustle, the colourful banners, students talking excitedly in almost all corners, buzzing like bees.

'Let's volunteer! It will be fun,' said Parul.

Janki was all for it, but I wasn't so sure I wanted to.

Parul signed up all three of us to be part of the welcoming committee. We had several meetings with the members of the culture club, where they briefed us in detail on our duties. We would be in charge of coordinating stay arrangements, making sure our guests reached whichever place they had been allotted to and ensuring that their requirements were met. We were given specific instructions on everything related to making the students of other colleges and our special guests comfortable as hosts for the three-day festival.

'They have to rave about our hospitality, please remember that,' instructed Harini, in charge of the welcome team. 'Is everything clear?'

We saluted like good soldiers.

The welcoming committee was an important one as we would be the 'face' of our college. We had to be aware of all the other arrangements as well. It was during one of these meetings that we learnt that our college had no official team for 'Dumb Charades'. I remembered my days at St. Agnes. The inter-collegiate festivals were fun.

'Come on, let's sign up for Dumb Charades,' I urged Janki and Parul.

'What? For the college team? I have never played this in my life!' said Janki.

'There's a first time for everything. I will teach you. I used to take part in school, and I was good at it,' I said.

They were reluctant, but I submitted our names anyway. If they could bulldoze me into joining the welcoming committee, they could jolly well oblige me for this one, I told them firmly.

While writing down our names, Maya, who headed the events committee, asked me if there was anyone in our class who was good at public speaking.

'You are looking at her!' The words slipped out before I could stop myself.

'Will you come for a trial then? We are choosing the college team, and we want to have representation from all courses, so that we choose the best. Come to Room 21 at 11.30 a.m. tomorrow,' she said, writing my name in a register.

I had blurted it out on a whim, but began having second thoughts almost immediately.

'Have you done public speaking before? You never told us!' said Janki.

'Yes, I have won a few prizes at college festivals earlier,' I admitted.

The memory of my last public speaking event came back then, and I felt my hands go clammy as I recalled the details. How flawlessly I had spoken at 'JAM' (Just a Minute, where one had to speak without a stutter, pause or grammatical error for one whole minute on a topic given on the spot) at the cultural festival when I was doing my MBA. I remembered how engaging my little talk was and how everyone in the room had forgotten it was only for a minute, and had let me continue for a full three minutes. I recalled the giddy exhilaration I felt and how everyone clapped. I was also painfully aware that it was during my 'highs' or the 'mania phase' that it had happened. Dr Madhusudan had meticulously explained what I had been through, during my stay at NMHI. Now I was off medication, and was 'normal'. I did not have the 'special powers' I had then. How could I hope to repeat that performance? Why had I gone and committed myself?

'You are full of surprises, Ankita. I never knew you were so clever,' said Janki.

'Why? Do I look dumb?' I asked.

'Yes, you do look a bit of a bimbo,' teased Parul.

'What?' I said, outraged. They laughed.

'We will come and cheer for you. And after that, you can teach us Dumb Charades, now that you have entered our names,' said Parul.

When I reached home that evening, I confessed my fears to my father.

'I'm really nervous about it. I don't know why I enrolled,' I fretted.

'You should think before speaking, Ankita. Then you will not get into such situations,' said my mother. Her advice didn't help. I only chewed my lower lip some more.

'Look, what's done is done. What is the worst that can happen?' asked my father.

I shuddered. 'I might freeze, I might be unable to speak,' I told him.

'So what?' he said.

'What do you mean "so what"? It will be *terrible*,' I told him.

'Terrible? Really? The sun will still rise. The earth will still spin. Thousands of people will still go to work. What will really change? Nothing.'

'Ummm,' I said, still not convinced.

'Things are only as terrible or as wonderful as you imagine them to be,' said my father. 'Always prepare for the worst, but hope for the best.'

'I think if we hope for the best, we might be disappointed,' I replied.

'In that case, do not think about the outcome. Do your best by preparing for the worst-case scenario.'

I thought about his words for a long time. I had no idea then that I would use them later in a way that would change the course of my life.

●

Despite my father's advice, I was a bundle of nerves the next day. I had read a lot of random things the previous night from my father's large collection of books. I had also memorised a few quotes from *Quips, Quotes and Anecdotes for Speakers,* which I had found in the collection. I hoped whatever I had read would come to my aid.

My friends were unwavering in their support. They comforted me and told me I would be fine. Parul made me drink some water before they called out my name.

I went up on stage, and drew a chit from a bowl for my topic. Five minutes to prepare and then I had to speak. When I opened the folded chit of paper, I heaved a sigh of relief. My topic was 'If life was an object, what object would you choose to represent it and why?'

I found it an easy topic. I quickly jotted down the points I would speak on. When I was called, I was surprised that the words flowed easily. Any nervousness I felt vanished the moment I was on stage. It was as though I had been transformed into a different person. I compared life to a coconut. I talked about how it is green on the outside, and that is what people see. I talked about how when we are young, the brown part is not yet formed, but as time goes by, how it gets formed and hardened. I compared it to the experiences that toughen us. I spoke about how we reveal only our outermost selves to strangers, the brown bits to friends, the white bits, the most vulnerable core, to only a trusted few. I spoke about how some people are so closed that they never reveal the white bits to anybody, and how it ultimately shrivels up and dies inside. I talked about how you never know what a person is till you reach the very core, and how sometimes the core turns out to be rotten, or not quite what you anticipated. I ended by speaking about how sharing our vulnerabilities help us form human connections, and how it is very important. I spoke fluently, confidently and clearly. There was a stunned silence in the room when I finished; every single person clapped or thumped their desk in appreciation.

'Oh my god, you were fantastic! You should represent our college. I am putting you in the college Public Speaking team,' said Maya. The others on the panel agreed. They patted me on the shoulder, shook my hand and said, 'well done'.

Parul and Janki were delighted. 'You are a *chhupa rustam*!' said Janki.

'No, I am not any Rustom! I am just plain old Ankita.' I smiled.

'No need to be so modest. Congratulations, girl! You made it to the college team,' said Parul.

'Now let's practice Dumb Charades, since you signed us up for that too. You said you would teach us,' Janki reminded.

'Yes, I will,' I said, wiping the beads of sweat off my forehead, and willing my heartbeat to return to normal.

Because of Euphoria, regular classes were suspended for a while. We went to an empty classroom and began our practice in earnest.

I explained the basic gestures to them. One word; two words; rhymes with; split word; name; man; woman. There were specific gestures that would make it easier for your team-mates to guess what was being mimed. Parul and Janki picked it up easily. I came up with names of movies, songs and books for them to mime and guess. Janki had a tough time not speaking out the word aloud while miming. She did it at least four times. She couldn't stop herself.

'Janki! If you do this, we get disqualified!' warned Parul.

We practised for a couple of hours every day. Soon we became very good at guessing what our team member was miming. Our teamwork was great and we all got each other quickly, within 30 seconds. Parul got a stopwatch, and we timed ourselves, constantly trying to improve our speed. After we finished our practice, we would go to Khau Galli and gorge at Parul's usual stall.

'Ankita, I think whatever they give us, we should be able to mime. We have practised so much that we have run out of names of movies and songs now,' Parul mused.

'You are right. We have practised most of the things that come to mind. But we still have a comprehensive list of books to get through. In these competitions, they always give a lot of book titles,' I said.

'We haven't practised book titles at all. Movies and songs we will be able to guess, but I am not at all familiar with any book names.' Janki grimaced.

She was right. Unless we were familiar with the names of the most famous books, we would be at a disadvantage.

I made a mental note of this, and decided we would have to practice harder.

Parul and Janki were doing it for fun, but I couldn't accept anything less than perfection.

I was playing to win. I would do whatever it took.

8
The Book

When it comes to ties between the opposite sexes, each little action can be interpreted in a hundred different ways, especially if one of them is in love with the other. It was the same with Vaibhav. I spoke to him as I would speak to an old friend. I treated him the way I would treat any friend. I could see how elated he was with small gestures of mine that I never even gave a second thought to. It didn't mean a thing to me, but that was not how he interpreted them. And yet, I couldn't do anything differently, as it would be seen as being unfriendly.

Vaibhav had started turning up each morning to play badminton with my father. Ma would greet him and serve him coffee. On some days I would open the door, and he would give me a million-watt smile and then shyly look away. I would smile back, ask him to come in. I would then disappear into my room, saying I had something to finish. Vaibhav was fine with that, as my mother would take over. She liked chatting with him while he finished his coffee.

My father treasured his time with Vaibhav. Whether Vaibhav had made progress with me or not was irrelevant; he had made great progress with my parents. Both my father as well as my mother seemed to be in love with him.

After badminton, he would go back to his flat. On some days I'd watch him leaving from my window. He had his badminton racquets in a deep brown rexine cover slung on his back. Drenched in sweat, his hair damp, he would walk away. He never saw me though.

On some days, when I got back from college, Vaibhav would be waiting for me in the lobby, Ma having invited him for dinner.

'You know, I am making palak paneer tomorrow. I think Vaibhav will enjoy it. I will invite him,' my mother would say whenever she was cooking something special. The only thing that changed was the name of the dishes she cooked. My father would nod.

'Why do you have to invite him all the time?' I asked one day in exasperation.

'He lives so far away from his home. He must be missing home food,' my mother replied.

If my parents sensed my irritation at Vaibhav coming over so often, they didn't mention it. I had become an expert at hiding my true feelings about his visits.

My parents and he never ran out of topics to chat on. Ma had a habit of devouring the newspaper, and she would discuss something new that she had read that very day with Vaibhav. Surprisingly, he would have read it too.

'Do you prepare for these discussions with my mother?' I asked him one day.

He laughed like it was the biggest joke in the world. I hadn't meant it to be funny and I didn't know what he was laughing about. But my mother laughed too.

'No, Ankita. I just read the newspaper every day,' he said when he stopped laughing.

With Dad he spoke about various policies the government was implementing and how these would affect the industry. He discussed his training schedule, he talked about his work. He spoke about how, as a management trainee, he was learning about various aspects of the job, and how his training included several weeks in various departments so as to get a feel of everything.

One evening, as I was seeing him off in the lobby downstairs, I told him about being selected for the college Public Speaking team and practising for Dumb Charades. I mentioned that I needed a comprehensive list that had names of famous books.

'That is wonderful, Ankita! I am so proud of you, and genuinely happy to hear this,' he said, his eyes shining with delight.

'Thank you,' I said.

I now felt silly about my jealousy. Here was a guy so much in love with me, and who my parents liked too. And here I was, feeling irked. It was absurd, I chided myself.

'Look up the *Manorama Yearbook* in your library,' he said, interrupting my thoughts.

'Eh?' I asked.

'The comprehensive list of books. The *Manorama Yearbook* has it. Look it up in your library,' he called over his shoulder, as he waved and walked away.

●

I was determined to find the book-list to include in our daily practice. At the library, Mrs Asthana was happy to see me.

'Hello, Ankita! You are coming here after so long. Forgot your way to the library or what?' she mock-chided.

'Ha ha. No, Mrs Asthana. We have all been practising hard for Euphoria,' I said.

'I have seen the madness of that festival for so many years now. I don't know what it is with you young people. You all go crazy at these festivals,' she said.

'Well, it is a heady mix of youth and competition. There's such a rush of adrenaline at the thought of winning,' I confessed.

'It is either the adrenaline or the testosterone in the air with all the boys coming over,' laughed Mrs Asthana.

'I guess that too,' I said, though that part of it had not even occurred to me.

My only focus was on winning the contest. I wanted to hear the applause of the crowd ringing in my ears. I had been out of all this for too long. This felt like a resurrection, a redemption of sorts for all the time I spent locked away from everybody at NMHI. I craved recognition and adulation. Winning a contest also brought so much respect. I was hungry for it.

'Mrs Asthana, I am now a part of the college Dumb Charades team, as well as the Public Speaking team. Hence, I was wondering if you could help me with some specific books,' I said.

'Oooh, that is exciting. Well done! What books do you want?'

'I needed something like a list of famous books. An all-time list of the most popular books. Would you have the *Manorama Yearbook*? My friend suggested that,' I told her.

Mrs Asthana furrowed her brows and pinched her nose. She closed her eyes as she tried to remember. 'Hmm... *Manorama Yearbook... Manorama Yearbook*,' she muttered.

'Shall I look in the encyclopaedia section?' I asked, trying to expedite her thinking process.

'Have a look if you like. But I don't think you will find it there. I know the book. It is a fat book. I am trying to remember where it is. We used to have a copy of it. But I am not sure if we still have it. I know all the books on the shelves, and I can instantly tell you where a book is likely to be.'

'I need it badly, Mrs Asthana. Our team's victory depends on practising those book names. Let me have a look, anyway,' I said as I headed over to the encyclopaedia section.

I was rummaging through it when Mrs Asthana called out to me.

'I remembered where it is,' she said when I headed over to her desk. She handed a bunch of keys to me. 'At the end of the library is the stockroom. Open it. You will find many cartons of books there. They are all books we have to dispose of. You can rummage through the cartons, it is sure to be there. We took some books off the shelves last year when we got new stock. I still haven't gotten around to sorting them out and getting rid of them.'

'Oh, thank you, Mrs Asthana! You are such a help,' I said, taking the keys from her.

'Only one thing. Please hurry and make it fast. I have got permission to close the library early today as I have to take my mother to the dentist,' she said.

When I opened the door to the stockroom, I sneezed. Dust moats danced in the sunlight streaming in through the dirty windows. The musty smell of old books permeated through the tiny room, packed to the brim with cardboard cartons of various sizes. There were at least fifteen cartons, all piled haphazardly. Some of the cartons had books spilling on to the floor. How was I going to locate the *Manorama Yearbook* in this massive pile? But I didn't have a choice. I decided I would look through each carton one by one.

I opened the first one. It was full of textbooks. I went through each title as quickly as I could. Then I pushed it to a side, leaving a dust track on the floor. The second one was full of old classics, mostly damaged. I went through all of them too. The next carton was again full of old textbooks. Going through each book in every carton was time-consuming, but what if the book was in a particular carton? So I continued my diligent search. I was on the fourth carton when Mrs Asthana peeped in.

'Ankita, I have to leave now. Have you found your book?' she asked.

'Not yet, Mrs Asthana. I am only on my fourth carton,' I said.

'Sorry, child. You can come back tomorrow then.' She glanced at her watch.

'Please, Mrs Asthana, I need that book. We have to start practising,' I said.

'What do we do? I wish I could help you, but I need to lock up the library,' she said.

An idea struck me then.

'Mrs Asthana, would you trust me to lock up the library? I can do that. I shall come early tomorrow and even open it for you. That way you can come in a bit late too,' I offered.

She considered it for a few seconds. I could see that she was tempted by the offer of my opening it the next morning as well.

'Hmmm… Will you be responsible and careful?' she asked.

'Of course, yes! You can trust me,' I said, elated that she had agreed to my suggestion.

'Alright, bolt the door then, and remain inside. I don't want anyone else walking into the library thinking it is open. When you leave, carefully lock the stockroom, as well as the main door. And tomorrow, open the library at 9.30 a.m. sharp. I shall come in around 11.00 or so,' she said. She then pointed out the key to the main door in the bunch that she had handed over earlier. I assured her that I would.

After Mrs Asthana left, I bolted the door and continued rummaging through the cartons. I found the yearbook in the eighth carton. Just as I removed the yearbook from the carton, another book caught my eye. It was the title that attracted me.

The Best Way to Go: A Handbook on Suicide for the Dying read the title. The book was by an author I had never heard of. It was a strange book.

I picked it up and turned it over.

The back blurb said that the book was at the centre of a heated controversy that sparked a national debate. It was a crucial handbook for those who wanted to end their lives due to unbearable pain because of an incurable disease or terminal illness. I flipped through the table of contents. It had a detailed manual that gave instructions on how to commit suicide in the most efficient way, a chart that listed lethal drugs, legal considerations to be aware of, letters to leave behind, among many other things. I also saw that the book had spent several weeks on the *The New York Times* bestseller list, and it was a self-help book.

My heartbeats increased as I read what it contained. I felt the muscles in my body tighten. My palms went sweaty. I wasn't aware that I was holding my breath and when I released it, it came in a shallow gasp. I couldn't believe what I was reading. What had I found here? A suicide manual?

The memories of the two times that I had tried to take my life came flooding back, drowning me. I remembered how my father had grabbed the knife from my hand the first time and how he had found me on the terrace of our building the second time; I was in the grip of the lows of bipolar disorder then. I shuddered as I recalled how close I had come to taking my own life.

I sat there clutching my head.

Calm down.

Calm down.

Calm down.

I told myself over and over.

The book was calling out to me. I had to read this book.

No, I had to *study* it. It was mine.

I slipped both the yearbook as well as this book into my bag. I closed the stockroom and then the library carefully. It felt like my backpack had grown heavy with the weight of the book. The book was all I was aware of. I was dying to read it. I felt a dark energy present in the book drawing me to it with great force. I couldn't resist it. *A suicide manual... A suicide manual... A suicide manual.* I kept thinking about it on a loop as I walked to the station.

I was impatient to get on the train and find a seat. Once I was inside the train, I took it out of my bag. When I opened the book, I got a surprise.

There was a small folded note inside the book, between the cover and the first page. I removed the note carefully. But before I could read the note, I saw that someone had inscribed something on the first page. Scrawled across the page, in large cursive letters were the words:

To my darling Ruth.
All my love,
MH

9
Killing Me Softly

The book was a gift. To someone called Ruth. Why would someone gift a suicide manual to another person? What kind of a bizarre gift was this? Then I opened the note. It was a small note folded like a card, the paper a thick ivory sheet that looked expensive.

Be strong. Don't hesitate. It's the best thing you can do. I am with you.
xx

That was what the note said, the handwriting the same as that in the book. There was no name mentioned in the note, nor was there a date. I was puzzled. What a strange note it was. What did it mean? I had no idea. I carefully put the note between the last pages of the book.

By the time I reached Bandra, I had gone through the book and got a broad overview. The author had clarified that this book was *not* for those who were depressed or suicidal. I got a jolt when I read that. As though someone had read my mind and discovered my guilty secret. The book mentioned the Hemlock Society in

America, which advocated the right to die and assisted suicide. The name was derived from the highly poisonous herbaceous flowering plant that Socrates was said to have used to take his own life. The motto of the Hemlock Society was: 'Good Life, Good Death'. The author had written elaborately on the need for compassion if someone with terminal illness and unbearable suffering did not wish to live anymore, and why we must respect that right. His own wife, diagnosed with terminal cancer, had ended her life with him by her side, with an intentional overdose. He had mixed the lethal drug in her coffee and held her hand as she died.

I read all of it with a morbid fascination. But I couldn't complete the whole book as the train had reached my station by then. I was so eager to read the rest of the book that I almost ran the whole way home. When I reached the lobby of my building, I sighed with relief to see that Vaibhav wasn't around. Today I just didn't want to talk to anyone. The book was all I could think of. It was drawing me towards it with an unfathomable pull.

I greeted my parents as usual. But I was restless throughout dinner. My parents noticed it immediately.

'Is everything okay, Ankita?' my father asked.

'Yes, all good,' I lied.

'Did something happen in college today? You seem a bit distracted.' This was my mother.

'No, Ma. I am fine. It's just that I have a lot of work to do.' I thought she would accept that explanation. But my mother frowned.

'You told me that there are no classes now because of your college festival,' she said. She was sharp, didn't miss a thing.

'There are no classes. But that doesn't mean an assignment is not due. This was given last week, and I am to submit it tomorrow,' I lied again.

I just wanted to get back to the book.

At last we were done with dinner, and I helped my mother clear the table. Then I rushed to my room and sat up long past midnight, devouring the book, my heart beating in my mouth the whole time.

As I read, I discovered that the author had repeated himself several times. He kept saying that it was for those in terrible, terrible pain. He described cases where there was no hope left at all. He spoke about how hospitals were incentivised to keep a person alive at any cost, but how that took away their dignity and, most importantly, their choice.

It was a fascinating read. I ignored all those bits where the author said the book was for people who had made a rational, voluntary choice to end their life. All I wanted to know were the best methods to kill oneself.

I learnt a lot from the book. The author had discussed each method of 'self-deliverance' in detail. While I had tried to commit suicide when I was going through the down phase, I had not thought about it so scientifically. This book helped me with just that. I now knew that plant or chemical poisons were not easily obtainable, and also that one might end up with brain damage if it didn't work. Gunshot was violent, and also, everybody would not have access to guns. It was excessively messy too. When it came to pharmaceuticals, one had to be sure of the dosages needed and also the certainty of how much dosage would prove fatal. One could never be certain about the purity of the pharmaceutical and also the calculated dosage.

The method he most recommended was also the simplest one. All one would need was a plastic bag taped at the neck. Death by asphyxiation was by far the best, provided you didn't tear it out in panic as an involuntary natural response. He recommended sleeping pills and alcohol before using the bag, so that you were fast asleep before you suffocated to death.

The author was also for leaving a suicide note behind, so that all loose ends were tied up. I kept thinking about the methods I could use to kill myself if had to. I had my doubts about using any of the methods recommended in the book. Putting a plastic bag on my head and taping it firmly around my neck was easy. I could also get alcohol easily as my father kept a couple of bottles of whiskey at home. But where could I get the sleeping pills without prescription? Also, what if I convulsed and threw up with the plastic cover around my head? These were possibilities I considered and thought about in great detail.

There were indeed no clean or comfortable ways to take one's life. It was difficult. The author had given information about the medication to use, which ones not to use, which ones would work best and what to expect with each one. But they were all American trade names. I had no idea what they were called in India. The images used in the book, the diagrams, the step-by-step guides, the various tips, etc., I read over and over, till I almost memorised them.

When I finished the book, I was in turmoil. On the one hand I felt a huge sense of relief and comfort. On the other hand I felt disturbed and terrified. It was a strange, unsettling feeling. I was so agitated after reading the book that I now wished I hadn't read it at all. What an idiot I was to have not only read it, but also studied it in depth. I wished now I could undo all that reading.

I had thought I was over that phase of my life when I had given up on wanting to live. I thought I had fought my biggest battle and won. And yet, with just one book, here I was thinking about death again. I hated myself then. How frail my mind was! How could I be this easily perturbed and swayed? Why was death drawing me towards it? Hadn't I escaped its clutches twice? And here I was flirting with death once more.

I was restless. And yet exhilarated. I felt like I had climbed a mountain, and was now on the precipice, looking down.

My mind was in a churn. Words formed of their own accord and went around in whirlpools. I was overcome with an urgent desire to write down whatever was in my head. I could sense something larger than life that I wanted to express.

I quickly took out my notebook and began writing, as though in a trance. Words formed one after the other on their own. All my conflicting emotions and feelings were pouring out through the tip of my pen. When I finished writing, I lay my head on my desk and closed my eyes. I lay like that for a while. Writing whatever I had scribbled had exhausted me. When I finally gathered the courage to look at what I had written in my state of frenzy, I realised it was a poem that had flowed out.

The Void

Looking ahead into the future,
a void stares back,
occasionally decorated by specks
of people who seem to matter,
whom you seem to need
till they let you down.
Then you are back to the beginning
where the void still stares back,
suspended, devoid, untouched by time,
unaffected by the specks,

now long forgotten,
not even a trace of memory remains.
All that exists is the void
still staring back.

I read the words again. I knew they came from a place deep within me. Whatever I had written was what my subconscious was telling me. It was not something I was consciously doing. What did this poem mean? Who were the people who had let me down? Who were the people who 'seem to matter'? Why had I written it? I contemplated on the words I had just written.

Suddenly the poem was crystal clear. I realised in that instant why I was pushing Vaibhav away.

I had built a wall around my heart. I was so terrified that what happened to Abhi might repeat itself with Vaibhav. The logical side of me told me that Vaibhav wasn't Abhi. Vaibhav was a different guy. But I also knew that when it came to love, all men were the same. They got possessive about the women they love. I wouldn't be able to bear it a second time. I simply didn't have the strength anymore.

When I was at NMHI, all my energy was focused on getting better, and be able to start reading again. The routines there had kept me busy. Now that I was on the verge of a semi-relationship (I didn't know what else to call it) with Vaibhav, I was terrified. Most people associate love with feelings of pleasant, carefree memories. For me, the word love conjured up death and the sound of an old man's wails. It was a word that strangled me. That was why I was rejecting it.

Abhi had let me down. By dying. I had fooled myself into thinking that it didn't matter anymore, though every detail of the horrifying days that followed his death was imprinted on my soul. I remembered how I met him during a youth festival in college, how crazy he'd been, the letter he wrote to me in blood, and how relentlessly he had stalked me, despite my telling him I had a boyfriend. When I got admission in a Bombay college for MBA, he acted betrayed, begging me to stay back in Cochin, accusing me of abandoning him, of being too ambitious, of not loving him back. I recalled that horrible morning my mother read out a report in the newspaper of the discovery of Abhi's body, and asked me if I knew him. I could only say that I'd known him in passing.

I would never know if Abhi had killed himself or whether it was an accident. His love had been too heavy for me to bear in the end, and perhaps the weight of it was too much for him too. We had both crumpled.

But now, he was dead. There was a big hole in my heart where love used to be. And here I was, trying to limp back to normalcy. Normal people didn't do this, a voice inside my head told me. Normal people did not read a book about suicide, memorising all the methods to take their lives. You can never be normal, the voice inside my head screamed.

Shut up… Shut up, I wanted to say. I wanted to gag the voice. I wanted it to go away. But I was helpless. The voice continued taunting me, tormenting me. What are the best methods to kill oneself, the voice asked. I answered in great detail, without any emotion, narrating everything I had just read. Good, well done, said the voice.

It did not even occur to me that I was so clinical about it. The book I had devoured was about killing oneself.

Ironically, I treated it like my life depended on it.

10

When a Man Loves a Woman

It was only in the wee hours of the morning that I remembered the *Manorama Yearbook*. I hadn't slept the whole night, as I was so engrossed in the guide to suicide (that was what I had termed it in my head). I had been lost in the labyrinth of my thoughts. I was tired and exhausted now. It was already 4.30 a.m. I crawled into bed and shut my eyes.

I was woken up from deep sleep by my mother. Her voice seemed to be coming from somewhere far away.

'Ankita, Ankita, are you okay? What happened?'

She was tapping me hard on my shoulder now, almost shaking me. I struggled to open my sleep-laden eyes.

'Yeah, Ma, I am okay. I slept late. I want to sleep for a little while more, please,' I muttered, pulling the duvet over my head.

'It is 8.00 a.m. already. You said the same thing when I woke you up an hour ago. What is happening?' asked my mother. She sounded frantic with worry.

That was the thing about having been a patient in a mental hospital. Every action, every little thing you said or did would be carefully scrutinised and measured against a degree of 'normalcy'. I had to prove to everyone that I was 'normal'. Any small deviation from the usual seemed to send my mother into a tizzy. I did not blame her. But I was groggy with sleep now, and after last night, all I wanted to do was rest my exhausted mind. I also had no recollection of her waking me up an hour earlier. I opened my eyes then.

'Ma, please don't worry like this. I am fine, really. I just want to sleep a little late today,' I said.

'After what happened....' my mother's voice trailed off.

'Ma. This is *not* like that, okay? I am *fine*. I just had a *late night*,' I said, my voice up several notches though I didn't intend to raise it. Couldn't she just let me sleep?

'Get up right now, Ankita. You have to sleep on time and also wake up on time. Else it will upset your bio-rhythm and change your body clock.' My mother was firm.

'Fine,' I said, gritting my teeth, throwing off the duvet. I reluctantly got out of bed and headed over to the bathroom. My eyes burned with a lack of sleep. But I knew my mother wouldn't let me sleep any more.

I brushed my teeth lazily, and considered what I could do with *the* book. Should I return it to the library? I wasn't sure. I had studied it in detail. There was nothing more the book could tell me, yet I wanted to hold on to it. So I hid the book under a pile of clothes in my wardrobe. It was only then I remembered that I had promised Mrs Asthana that I would be in early. That swung me into action. I shed my lethargy in a jiffy.

'Oh god, Ma. I'm late! I have to hurry,' I called out. I hurried through the morning rituals at top speed and was ready to leave in less than ten minutes.

'Wait, Ankita, aren't you eating breakfast?' my mother called out.

'No time, Ma,' I shouted.

But my mother had already made a sandwich by then and she insisted I shouldn't miss breakfast. I rushed out of the house, sandwich in hand, without even brushing my hair. I had just scooped it into an unmade bun, and piled it on top of my head. I must have looked a sight. But I didn't care. I couldn't let Mrs Asthana down. I had promised her I would open the library for her.

I was late only by about fifteen minutes. I opened the library and occupied one of the chairs that faced the door, so that I would know if anyone came in.

I hadn't even opened the *Manorama Yearbook* and now I had all the time in the world to go through it. Vaibhav was right. The book did have a section that listed the 100 greatest books of our times. I took out a pen and copied down all the names in my notebook.

Mrs Asthana arrived in about an hour. She was happy to see that I had kept my word.

'Thank you for coming early and being responsible, Ankita. I can see you have been busy,' she said, glancing at my notebook, where I had copied out the names of the famous books.

'Of course, Mrs Asthana. How could I not? Should I put this *Manorama Yearbook* back in the stockroom?' I asked.

I debated with myself whether or not to mention the suicide manual. It was not right on my part to have just taken it from the library. So I mentioned it. But I couldn't bring myself to tell her the title, even though I remembered every word of it.

'Also, Mrs Asthana, there was another book I took yesterday from the stockroom as it seemed interesting. I forgot to bring it. I shall return it soon,' I added.

But Mrs Asthana didn't seem to care about it at all.

'Oh no, no. Please feel free to keep it. You can also keep this *Manorama Yearbook*. I don't need any of the books there. They are for disposal,' she said.

'Thank you,' I said as I slipped the yearbook back into my bag.

I wished Mrs Asthana had asked for the suicide manual to be returned. Then it would have been off my hands. The dark energy in that book wouldn't pull me to it anymore, wouldn't whisper seductively to me in my ear. I could have returned it to the library and forgotten about the strange inscription in it, as well as the puzzling note. But that was not to be. I had taken something that did not belong to me, and in a strange way, I was now stuck with it. I didn't know what to do about it. One part of me wanted to throw it away. But another part of me wanted to retain it. I decided I would deal with it later. For now, I had more urgent things to do, as I knew Parul and Janki would be waiting for me.

I thanked Mrs Asthana and left the library.

'Where did you disappear yesterday, madam? You better have something good to show us,' said Janki as soon as she saw me.

'Yes, yes, I do,' I replied and I took out my list of books.

'Oh, look at this,' said Janki as she snatched it from my hands and pored over it.

'I just copied it off a book! Now come on, let's practice,' I cajoled them.

We practised most of those hundred book titles that day. We went over and over miming the names of the same books till we could guess any book title in less than ten seconds.

'We've improved so much! I dare say we are good,' said Parul.

'Yes, but we can be even better. We are competing against thirty other best teams in the country. Remember that,' I said.

I was pushing them to raise the bar. And both Parul and Janki had got the hang of it now.

'We definitely will win at this rate,' said Parul.

'We better. We have just a few days left now. Janki, you have to see that you don't slip up and mouth the words. Else, we will be disqualified,' I replied.

'Aye, aye, captain.' Janki giggled.

It irked me that she didn't seem to be taking it seriously, but I didn't say anything. She had improved a great deal. And I knew we would be one of the good teams. We had practised such a lot.

●

Vaibhav asked me for a date that evening. He was waiting for me at the start of my lane, at the tea stall by the side of the road, having a cutting chai as I walked up to him.

'Hi! Do you want chai?' he called out when he saw me approaching.

'Nah, I am good. Why did you change your waiting place?' I smiled.

'You have to move up in life. From the lobby of your building, I have now graduated to a tea stall.' He smiled back.

'Don't you ever get tired of waiting for me?' I asked.

'Not if I know I will be getting to eat your mother's delicious food later.'

'What? So you are actually not waiting to see me? It's all about the food!'

'Of course! If I didn't like the food, no way would I be hanging around your building.'

'I thought as much. I knew you had an ulterior motive,' I said.

'You know me so well, Ankita,' he replied. 'But here's what you don't know. I have planned something for the whole of Saturday. Will you go out with me? I already checked with your parents, and they were okay with it.'

That indeed took me by surprise. Vaibhav had already asked my parents, even before speaking to me. But then, he was friendly with my father and mother, and it was only natural, as I would have had to ask their permission anyway. Still, I didn't like it that he had asked them directly. He had destroyed my 'first line of defence'. He had taken away the option from me, of saying I'd have to check with my parents. He seemed to be two steps ahead of me.

'Ummm… well,' I stalled for time, not knowing what to say.

'Please say yes. Don't think so much. A lot of planning has gone into this,' he said.

'Alright, yes,' I gave in.

●

It was my first real date with Vaibhav. I felt awkward about it around my parents. During my college days, I had always talked to Vaibhav in secret. I had been comfortable with that. But now, my parents being so agreeable, I couldn't get used to it. On the days that he came home for dinner, it was a different dynamic, as my parents were always around. Here, I would be alone with him the whole day. I wasn't sure what to expect. This felt too 'real' and far too sudden. It had taken me by surprise. But I had already said I would go with him, and I knew he would be crushed if I backed out. Also, what excuse could I give?

Vaibhav did not tell me where he would be taking me. I pestered him as best as I could as we walked back home together.

'What's the point of a surprise if I tell you in advance?' he asked.

'I don't like surprises. Honestly, I don't. I like routines and I like to be in control,' I replied.

'Trust me, you will like this one,' he said. 'I will pick you up at 7.00 a.m. tomorrow. Be ready. And wear comfortable footwear,' he instructed.

'So you are off badminton duty?' I couldn't help being cheeky.

'Off the *joy* of badminton, not duty. Also, your father is playing doubles with two other people we met at the badminton courts.'

●

He rang the bell at 7.00 a.m. sharp; my mother let him in. Dad had already left for his badminton. I heard the doorbell as I was getting ready. Vaibhav had specifically told me to wear comfortable footwear. So that meant I couldn't wear heels. I could wear only clothes that went with my very comfortable walking sandals, which limited my choices. I fretted over what I could wear.

In the end, I wore knee-length khaki pants and a plain black T-shirt. I also wore a long chain with a large maroon diamond-shaped pendant with a silver dolphin carved into it. I decided my outfit was casual yet smart. I didn't want to look like I had made too much of an effort. I did put on eyeliner, a bit of mascara and a light lipstick. Since I had never bothered with makeup while going to college, I could see that even with so little, the effect was dramatic. My eyes were black shining pools, my lips parted differently. I also left my long hair loose, combing it so that it came down in waves. Ever since I had left NMHI, I hadn't cut it, and it had grown very long.

'Ankita, Vaibhav is here. Are you ready?' called out my mother.

'Yes, Ma. Coming,' I said.

Vaibhav was having his coffee, and he froze midway when he saw me. Our eyes locked. I held his gaze. The admiration in his eyes travelled all over my body, even though his eyes did not leave mine.

There were no words needed at that moment. If one could *see* love and choose a moment to embody it, then this was that moment. It was so obvious now. This was the look of a man hopelessly and completely in love. I recognised that look in his eyes.

Then I shuddered involuntarily.

It was the same look I had seen in Abhi's eyes all those years ago.

11

A Kind of Magic

'You look stunning,' said Vaibhav, the moment we were alone in the lift.

'Ha, that's just because you have never seen me dressed up,' I said, brushing his compliment aside. I did not know how to accept it gracefully.

'No, you are hardly "dressed up". It's just that you are naturally beautiful,' he said, not taking his eyes off my face.

His scrutiny was making me uncomfortable. So I changed the topic.

'Where are we going?' I asked.

'You will see!'

'Are we taking the train?'

'No, we are not! Your vehicle, m'lady,' he said, making a sweeping gesture with his hand as we stepped out of the lift.

At the driveway, a smart chauffeur in uniform saluted us. As my eyes fell on the car, a sleek black shiny BMW, I gasped. I had never seen such a car before, except in magazines.

'Good morning, ma'am,' said the chauffeur, as he opened the door for me. With quick steps, he was at the other side and held the door open for Vaibhav too.

The soft black leather seats were so plush that I drowned in them. A lovely fresh citrus smell wafted over us. I was completely overwhelmed by all of this.

'Do you like it?' Vaibhav grinned.

I couldn't get over the lavish interiors. I had never sat in a luxury car before.

'This is beyond words!' I said

'Let's go, Kumar,' he told the chauffeur without mentioning the location.

The car soon joined the traffic on the main road.

'Kumar, can you switch on the music, please?' Vaibhav asked.

'Oh, you planned music too?' I raised an eyebrow.

'Yes, I did!' Vaibhav looked pleased. 'Now close your eyes, sit back, and listen to this.'

'Why should I close my eyes?' I asked.

'How many questions you ask! Just do as I say,' he said.

I felt weird as I leaned back in the seat and closed my eyes. I had no idea what to expect.

The speakers of the car reverberated with Jefferson Starship. It was the same song that Vaibhav had played for me on my eighteenth birthday.

People always talk about how music transports them back in time, back to happy memories they associate with a particular song. But whenever I looked back at my happy memories, I was also reminded of what came afterwards. Little had I known at that time how coldly and cruelly life would smash me, break me down, trample upon everything that meant the world to me, destroy me completely and then spit me out. I was so innocent back then, I had no idea what was in store. In some ways, I was still picking up the pieces of my life, even though externally it seemed as though everything was fine. My parents were happy that I was 'okay' and attending regular college. But deep down, I was struggling. I coped by studying hard, and drowning myself in college activities. It took my mind off... a lot.

In NMHI, I had learnt to focus on the present moment to get through each day. I had learnt how to do that painstakingly, by consciously directing my attention to only what mattered, that moment that day. Whenever my mind flew back to the past, I had to rein it in. Now Vaibhav was rekindling an old unwanted memory by playing this song.

I opened my eyes. I had outgrown this. I didn't know how to react or what to say.

Vaibhav was looking at me expectantly.

'Nice?' he asked.

What could I even say? He was trying so hard to make me happy. How could I take that away from him?

'Perfect,' I said, wishing desperately that I could be genuinely happy. But a wave of sadness engulfed me.

The songs continued to play. He had chosen all the songs we used to listen to back then, and had thrown in some classics as well. There was Bryan Adams, George Michael, Madonna, Sting, Bon Jovi and Michael Bolton along with Elvis Presley and the Beatles. All romantic songs. Unfortunately, they took me right back to NMHI, when my co-inmates had gifted me the cassettes of 'The World's Greatest Love Songs' just before my discharge from there. The last thing I wanted was to be reminded of my time in NMHI. I had shut that part of my life away in a trunk of *Bad Memories* and pushed it down deep within me. I wasn't ready to open that trunk. But this music was doing just that. It was pounding on that locked trunk of bad memories, trying to force it open. The songs were painful. Each lyric pierced my eardrum. It hurt so much! I remembered the time when I was helpless, struggling to read. I remembered every single excruciating detail of my early days at the hospital. I remembered how abandoned I felt, how frightened, how helpless. A tsunami of thoughts rose inside my head. I was struggling to breathe, struggling to stay afloat. I was being swept away by the intensity of the pain. I couldn't listen to this anymore. I wanted it to stop.

I shut my eyes tightly and tried to block out the memories. I tried to stop my thoughts. I clenched my fists, my fingernails digging into my palms. I was holding my breath.

Calm down, calm down.

Stop.

I don't want this.

Not this.

Never this.

Suddenly the music stopped, and I felt Vaibhav's hand on my shoulder. He looked frightened and concerned.

'Ankita... Ankita – are you okay? What just happened? Oh my god, you are so pale,' he said.

I opened my eyes. My body felt like it was not mine.

It was only then that I remembered to breathe. I swallowed, trying to speak.

'I... I don't know. I am sorry,' I whispered.

'Please don't apologise. Is anything wrong? You look so tense. It's okay,' he said.

It occurred to me then that I must have spoken out loud.

I sat still, trying to calm down. I couldn't speak.

'Here, have some water.' Vaibhav handed me a bottle.

I drank it in large gulps, and sat very quietly, willing my heart rate back to normal. Vaibhav watched me anxiously.

The car was weaving its way through Worli now.

'Why did you stop the music? Did I say something? I am sorry, I didn't mean to,' I said after a while.

'Yes, you said you didn't want this, and shouted "stop". And it is okay, Ankita; you don't have to apologise. I already told you.'

I felt miserable then. I thought about how much trouble Vaibhav must have taken to create this playlist. He had rented a car, planned the day, and spent a small fortune. For me.

The voice inside my head laughed at me. Why are you pretending to be normal? You will only cause pain to anyone who tries to make you happy, it said. I tried to drown the voice out. But I couldn't. It rang loud and clear in my head.

You are worthless, that's what you are.

What are you? the voice asked.

Worthless, I replied.

I sat quietly for a while, not having anything to say. Vaibhav didn't know what to do. I felt so bad looking at his anxious face. He didn't deserve this. I wanted to make him feel better. I felt I owed him an explanation. I didn't want to speak in the car, as I did not want Kumar to hear me. So my only option was to wait till we were alone.

'So, are you still not going to tell me where we are headed?' I forced a smile.

'Almost there, Anks! Just a few minutes more,' he said.

I looked outside; we had reached a part of Bombay I had never been to before. I wondered where he was taking me. Kumar stopped the car then, by the side of the road.

He was about to get out to open the door when Vaibhav stopped him. Then he turned to me.

'Listen, will you be okay if I blindfold you and walk you from here?' asked Vaibhav, as he took out a scarf from his backpack.

My first reaction was panic. I hated not being in control. I didn't know how I would feel. But then, I had already messed up once in the car by asking him to stop the music. I knew this surprise, whatever it was, meant a great deal to Vaibhav. He had even got a scarf. I didn't have the heart to refuse.

I nodded.

'Alright, thank you, Kumar,' said Vaibhav as he came to my side of the car, opened the door for me, and neatly tied the scarf around my eyes.

'Allow me, m'lady,' he said as he took my hand.

I was frightened. But I was not out of control. I was relieved that I could keep my fear in check.

Vaibhav put an arm around my shoulder and expertly guided me. I walked for about what seemed like 50 metres. There was no way of telling how much I walked, as my sense of distance was lost with my eyes closed. It is strange how taking away one sense organ makes you feel completely disoriented. I felt comforted by Vaibhav's hand on my shoulder, and I felt excited too. His voice soothed me. He kept assuring me every step of the way that we would soon be there. 'A few more steps. Careful now... Slow down,' he repeated over and over. I smiled at the care and concern in his voice.

'And now, ready?' he asked.

I nodded again.

He removed the blindfold.

I gasped as I saw the Gateway of India rising up large in front of me. It was a sight I would never forget. Framed against the bright blue sky with white fluffy clouds, the sea in the background, and thousands of pigeons flying about, the colossal arch made of basalt and concrete stood majestically right in front of me. It was about 85 feet in height. I had only seen pictures of it before, and seen it in some movies. Seeing it up close took my breath away.

'Wow, Vaibhav. This is amazing!' I said. I forgot my fright, my anxiety and all the unease I'd felt in the car a little earlier. All that mattered was this towering structure, the smell of salt from the sea, the wind blowing my hair wildly in all directions, and Vaibhav's hand still around me. I loved it.

We both stood there staring at it in awe and joy.

'You know, I too have never seen this. Ever since I came to Bombay, I wanted to. And now I am happy to have seen this with you,' said Vaibhav.

'Thanks. It was a good choice.' I smiled.

'Want to feed those pigeons?' asked Vaibhav.

'I would love to,' I replied.

Vaibhav bought a bag of seeds from a cute little boy who was selling the packets. He grinned impishly at me and said, 'Tell bhaiya to buy one more, didi.'

I chuckled. The little boy knew it would work, and Vaibhav ended up buying two packets. Both of us walked to where the pigeons were gathered. We squatted to feed the birds that evidently were used to this. They seemed tame, and two of them pecked the grains right out of my open palm.

'Look at these greedy pigeons,' I laughed as I felt their beaks on my hands.

'See? I told you, you would like it!' said Vaibhav.

For breakfast we had bhel puri and poha from the numerous vendors selling them around the area. It was delicious. We sat by one of the platforms on the side of the Gateway of India, and ate our breakfast off paper plates with plastic spoons, engrossed in the magnificence of the structure.

'Imagine, Ankita, this was built in 1911 to welcome King George V and the Queen on their maiden visit to India. This was the first thing he would see when his ship sailed in.'

'How grand it would have been,' I mused.

'And what about King Shivaji there? That couldn't have been made during British rule,' I said, pointing to the statue opposite the Gateway of India.

'I think that was made around 1961. It was unveiled on Republic Day,' said Vaibhav.

'Wow! You do know your history,' I said.

'I read up about it, Ankita. I wasn't kidding when I said a lot of planning went into this,' smirked Vaibhav.

'What next?' I asked him.

'Are you okay with a fifteen-minute walk?'

'Yes! See, I did wear comfortable footwear,' I said pointing to my sandals.

'Good, good. Come, let's go!'

'What about the car?' I asked him.

'You know, I have booked just a pick-up and a drop. Else I would have to pay for a full day and that was too expensive. We can take a local cab if you don't want to walk,' Vaibhav said. He looked apologetic.

'Vaibhav! I was okay to travel by train too! Hiring cars is a luxury I am not used to,' I said.

'Come on then, there's something I want to show you. And I promise you will love this too,' said Vaibhav, as he led the way.

I felt light-hearted and happy. Even though this date had started badly, I was now enjoying myself. Vaibhav looked happy too. We walked side by side, making our way from Gateway of India.

I couldn't wait to see where he would take me next.

12

Total Eclipse of the Heart

After walking for about five or six minutes, Vaibhav stopped at a fountain.

'Our next stop, Wellington Fountain. This was built in 1865, and named after Arthur Wellesley, the Duke of Wellington, as he visited Bombay frequently,' said Vaibhav.

'My goodness. You have memorised all these details!' I exclaimed.

'Yes, I believe in meticulous preparation.'

'I am impressed,' I said and I genuinely was.

'Thank you,' said Vaibhav with a gesture that was a cross between a bow and a curtsey.

It was a grand fountain. It comprised of a two-tiered octagonal structure made of basalt in a neo-classical style, and around it, at each point of the octagon, stood a marble statue, eight in total. The top layer was made of metal and had cast iron leaves. There were some Latin inscriptions and Vaibhav told me they described the Duke's achievements.

'You know what amazes me about this city?' asked Vaibhav.

'What? The spirit of Bombay? How it went back to normal within a day, after the bomb blasts?' I asked.

'Oh, that goes without saying. But look at where we are right now. We are standing here, at a magnificent historic site, and all around it life goes on. All these people going about their daily business probably don't look twice at it. I love how the historic structures here have become an integral part of the busy life in this city,' said Vaibhav.

'So right! I had never looked at it that way.' I appreciated Vaibhav's detailed explanation and insights.

'Shall we walk on?' he asked.

'Yes, please,' I replied.

This part of Bombay was unique. Full of beautiful, ancient Victorian buildings with decorative arches built during the British era. I loved the walk. We had nimboo pani from the roadside. The cool lemonade refreshed us and we walked for a few minutes more.

'Next stop Flora Fountain, which you see in front of us, to the right,' announced Vaibhav, exactly like a tour guide.

I gawked at the exquisitely sculpted architectural monument. Right on top of it stood a magnificent statue of a Roman goddess. Around this too were beautiful statues.

'Isn't this something?' Vaibhav asked smitten.

'It is, it is! And what is the history behind this one? Did you memorise that too?'

'Of course. This one was commissioned in 1864 by the Agri-horticultural Society of Western India. It took five years to complete. The main statue was sculpted from imported Portland stone. James Forsythe was the sculptor. It is the Roman goddess Flora who you see at the top. Hence, it is called Flora Fountain,' Vaibhav was ready with the explanations.

'But this was just a fringe benefit. The real place I want you to see is just a few steps ahead over there. Come with me,' he said, holding out his hand. He held my hand as we crossed the road.

I stared in surprise at the sight that stretched before me. The expansive curve of the footpath was filled with thousands and thousands of books piled high, stretching from one end to the other! It was a tower of books we were both looking at.

'I had only heard of this. I never expected it to be this huge!' said Vaibhav.

We made our way into the turret of books. I looked in wonder at the books piled higher than ten feet atop each other. I was Aladdin and this was my cave of treasures. There were all kinds of books – management textbooks, medical books, art books, coffee table books. Then there were tonnes and tonnes of paperback and hardbound novels. The sellers were sharp. The moment I showed interest in an author, the vendor immediately produced all the books by that author. He knew exactly where to rummage in the massive pile to pull out a specific title.

He said he had new books as well as second-hand ones and asked me which I would prefer.

'Madam, pirated *nahi*, original *hai*,' he assured me.

I noticed a little girl about eight or nine years old squealing in delight as she had found *Tintin in America*.

'Mom, please, please, can I have this?' she asked her mother who was busy browsing through some art books.

Vaibhav was going through some engineering textbooks.

'These are so cheap! You know I paid a fortune for some of these,' he said.

'We have a buy-back scheme also, sir. You can take these, and return after you are done. We will pay you fifty percent of the cost,' said a vendor.

We spent a good hour there, just browsing through all the books. I picked up two *Calvin and Hobbes* books, and also a book of assorted poems that I discovered. I loved the illustrations and

Bill Watterson's imagination. At a bookstore I would have paid much more than what I paid here. Though Vaibhav insisted on paying for them, I did not let him.

'No, no. You have paid enough for all of this. I can get this for myself,' I said as I paid for the books. 'What a place!' I sighed happily as we walked away

We passed the statue of Dadabhai Naoroji, the intellectual and thinker after whom this road was named. He stared down at us with a book in his hand.

'You think he bought his book from these stalls?' I quipped.

'Must have. He would have got a bargain for sure,' Vaibhav joked back.

'Where to next?' I asked.

'Wait and see!' he said.

'You are the king of surprises today,' I said.

'As long as my queen is happy, I am,' he replied.

'Your queen?' I laughed.

'I love you, Ankita. I have been in love with you since our school days. But then, you already know that,' he said. He said it so casually, in the middle of a busy Bombay road, as we walked together. He didn't even look at me when he said it.

If I hadn't heard it so clearly, and if he hadn't elaborated on the 'school days' bit, I could have laughed it off, pretending it was a joke. But I knew he was dead serious.

He didn't even expect me to say anything. I didn't know what to say either. So I just squeezed his elbow in response and we walked on.

If I had known what was to come next, I would have ended the date right there and asked him to take me home. But I didn't. This was turning out to be so much fun, and I was greedy for more. It had been very long since I had gone out on a date like this. In

NMHI, my days and nights were about carefully curated routines. There was no 'enjoyment'. It was a regimented existence. After I came back from the hospital, I was focused on getting back to college, and trying to make a career path, trying to regain what I had lost by dropping out. I had worked hard, and never taken a break. Roaming around Bombay like this, with Vaibhav giving me so much of attention, made me feel… normal. Like anybody else. I was elated. After the hard time I had been through, little moments like these meant a great deal to me. I cherished this.

Vaibhav took me to a rooftop restaurant that faced the ocean on Marine Drive, the terrace of an eighteen-storied building on the sea-front, and the table he booked was in a private dining area, with a floor-to-ceiling window with a magnificent view. The whole place was full of trees in giant containers. Everywhere I looked, there was deep green foliage juxtaposed against a bright blue sky. Sunlight shimmered on the deep blue waters, the waves brighter than diamonds. It felt like we were dining in the sky. Even though it was a terrace restaurant, there was some sort of a glass cover, and I guessed that the giant vents that ran along the top of the walls, carefully integrated into the design of the restaurant, were for air-conditioning. It was cool inside.

'You like?' Vaibhav asked.

'I like. How can I not?'

His face lit up like a lantern.

We sank into our leather chairs, facing each other. I could see the sea hit its fists against the rocks. How relentless were the tides. They receded and they came back, again and again. It was mesmerising to watch the waves. Then an uninvited thought crept into my head. I wondered if Abhi had watched such waves the same way and thought the same things that I did just before he drowned.

I pushed the thought away. I was here with Vaibhav now. I should *not* be thinking about Abhi. He was dead and gone. But memories have a strange way of creeping up on you, even when you don't want them to. I remembered how I had read the newspaper report with horror and dread when my mother told me that the papers that day carried a news item about the body of a young guy washed ashore. I remembered how I had told my mother casually that I knew him in passing. Abhi's words rang in my ears then.

'*Keep in touch, Ankita. That is all I ask of you.*'

'*Pride has gone to your head, Miss Bombay.*'

'*I am willing to wait a lifetime for you if you say yes.*'

Abhi had asked the impossible of me. To give up my dreams of doing an MBA. And then, just as it was within my grasp, life had snatched it from me.

'Hello! You are a million miles away! What happened? You look so sad,' Vaibhav spoke, interrupting my thoughts.

That snapped me back into the present moment.

'I'm so sorry,' I said.

'Oh, please don't keep apologising. Just tell me where you went to.'

I took a deep breath. 'There' so much that has happened, Vaibhav. There is a lot I haven't told you,' I said.

'So tell me now. We have all the time in the world. I know you have been through some really hard times. But I don't know any details.' He was earnest and sincere.

'It is just so terrible, Vaibhav. I am afraid I will cry if I speak about it.'

He took both my hands in his.

'Look, Ankita, I saw this morning in the car that the music I played stirred something deep within you. I must admit I was a bit freaked by how you reacted. But you know what? I am here for you. Unless you share what is happening to you, how will I ever know in what way to help?' Vaibhav looked at me with so much tenderness.

I felt I owed him an explanation. He deserved to know. Not just the bare minimum I had mentioned in my letter after I left NMHI. That letter had been written in a state of joyousness at having finally left NMHI. But now, here I was, fighting a battle with my mind on a daily basis. I needed a friend I could trust. I needed someone on my side. I needed someone who made me happy, like he did today.

Which was why I made the mistake of telling him all that had happened in my life, after we left school and he had gone to IIT. I left out no detail.

I told him everything that had happened ever since we parted and I joined St. Agnes. I told him about the election and how I had won. I told him about how I met Abhi, and how he had given me a ride home. I told him about Abhi's letter written in blood, and how I had gone to Abhi's house, and then evaded him when he kept declaring his love for me, a love I did not return. I told him about Abhi's senseless death in a fit of pique that haunts me till today.

I asked him if he remembered the sixteen-page letter I wrote him. He did. I explained to him how bipolar disorder worked – and how that letter was written during my highs. I told him about how I had come crashing down when the lows took over. I told him in detail about the psychiatrists I had seen, how I had felt like a rat in a laboratory. I explained my fears, my sadness, my obsessive thoughts, my hatred, my suicide attempts. I told him how I had struggled to read and my routine at NMHI and about Dr Madhusudan. I held back nothing.

Tears were pouring down my face as I spoke. This was not something I had ever shared with anyone. It was not easy to talk about. I couldn't meet Vaibhav's eye. I looked down and told him how after facing all of that, what fun this day had been and how much it had helped me see the lighter side of life, which I had almost forgotten. Today meant a lot to me, in more ways than he could imagine, and I thanked him for it.

I realised only then that Vaibhav had gone completely quiet. When I looked up at his face, I was taken aback. His expression was grim. His lips were pursed, and his eyes were blazing.

All he said was, 'You cheated on me.'

'What?' I asked in shock. Of all the things I told Vaibhav, this was what he picked up on? How was it cheating? I never slept with Abhi. It was Abhi who had kept chasing me.

But Vaibhav was furious. He did not want to listen to my explanations or anything I said. He had made up his mind.

'You never told me you were this involved with another guy.' His voice was soft, almost fragile. It was a statement he made, not an accusation. I could feel the pain in his words.

Sometimes people become bridges between your past and your present. My life was neatly divided into sections. There was a 'before Abhi' and an 'after Abhi'. Then there was a 'before NMHI' and an 'after NMHI'. Whenever I looked back at my life, all these divisions I had made in my head helped me make sense of it. They were clear and distinct to me. They were not connected. I had compartmentalised these sections and kept them separate. Once a section was lived, I burnt the bridge down and started a new life, on the other side. It was the only way I knew to cope and to retain my sanity. It was the only way to escape the clutches of my past and move forward.

But now Vaibhav had come into my life, resurrected as one of the bridges. With that, a little bit of my past had caught up with me. And now, by mentioning Abhi to Vaibhav, I had reconstructed yet another bridge to my past. By speaking about Abhi to Vaibhav,

I had jumbled up the bridges and dragged them messily into my present life.

I had expected Vaibhav to understand. But he exploded in a range of emotions. I had never seen him like this.

'If he wasn't dead, I would have killed him myself.'

'Am I competing with a dead guy?'

'Why didn't you tell me then?'

'You cheated on me!'

'How could you do this?'

'Did you sleep with him?'

I answered all his questions patiently. But Vaibhav wasn't listening. He was stewing in the juices of what he perceived as betrayal.

'All this while I was thinking *only* about you. Ankita. In IIT, thoughts about you kept me going. And all this while, you were ... fucking hell.' I was aghast at his reaction.

The sudden outburst and the coldness in his voice filled me with dread.

What the hell had I done? Why had I told him everything? Of what use was it? It was my past. That was where it should have stayed. I had forgotten everything that was taught to me at NMHI. I was such a fool. I wished I could retract everything I had said.

I learnt that day that there *is* such a thing as too much honesty. I wished I had kept it all to myself. I wished I could go back to before I narrated everything in detail to Vaibhav. I wished I hadn't mentioned Abhi at all. I wished I could turn back the clock to just a few hours ago, when we were at the Gateway of India or to the time when we were buying books.

Whatever happened to his promise of being there for me forever? I wanted to ask him that. But he was so angry and hurt, and I was afraid I would enrage him further.

'Vaibhav, it was a different time. It was a different me,' I pleaded. I hated myself for pleading with him.

'You haven't gotten over him,' was all he said.

Vaibhav seemed to detest me now. I kicked myself for raking up bygones. I beat myself up for over-estimating Vaibhav's love for me. I felt let down, as I thought he, of all people, would *understand*. But he had not.

'It was way back in the past, Vaibhav!' My voice was almost a whine.

I wanted his love back. I wanted him to look at me the way he had looked earlier this morning. But his eyes had turned to marbles.

'Make no excuses, Ankita. This was before your mania or whatever the hell you had. You knew what you were doing. Don't use your illness as an excuse,' Vaibhav spat.

His words felt like a punch in my gut. I hadn't used whatever I had been through as an excuse. I had merely explained. I wanted Vaibhav to be my strength. I wanted him to understand me. If he had not asked, I would never have revealed this. It would have stayed in my past, in my neatly slotted sections, tucked away deep inside, never to be opened.

But I had jumbled up the sections now. Vaibhav's words crushed me in ways I never imagined.

What was worse, I had no one to blame for it, but me.

13
When You're Gone

The ride back home with Vaibhav was completed in silence. The mood had changed dramatically. In the morning we were buoyant, excited. Now we both sat without uttering a word, enveloped in a cloud of our own thoughts. I do not know what Vaibhav was going through. All I knew is that I just wanted to curl up into a ball and vanish from the face of earth. I wished this ride would end. If the chauffeur sensed the mood, he was sensitive and too well-trained to mention anything. He just drove on, pretending nothing was amiss.

I kept thinking about how badly this day had ended. What would Vaibhav do now? Would he break up with me?

The thought was unbearable. I could not imagine *not* having him in my life. When he had been coming over on his own, I did not value his visits much. But now that this had happened, I was terrified of losing him.

We don't realise the value of what we have till it is taken away.

I thought of what it would mean if he vanished from my life. What would happen to his badminton sessions with my father? What about his conversations with my mother? How badly I had messed this up. How I wished and wished I had said nothing. How

85

much I lamented telling him my story. What in the world was I hoping for? The look in Vaibhav's eyes haunted me. He did not deserve that. I should have dealt with my own stupid mess, instead of dragging him into it with my big fat great confessional. How could I hurt him like this?

You always hurt those who love you. That's all you are capable of.

You killed a good friendship.

You killed Abhi.

You hurt people.

You disappoint your parents.

You are worthless.

The thoughts kept going round in my head, tormenting me. I endured them silently. I was afraid to close my eyes, in case I spoke out aloud like I had in the morning. I bit my lip, clenched my fists, and bore it. Bore the words.

At last we reached Bandra. It was the longest car ride of my life.

'Thank you for all of this, and... I am sorry, Vaibhav. I never meant to hurt you,' I said as I got out.

'I don't even know what to say, Ankita,' he said.

'I... I have a request. Whatever you feel towards me, please, please, don't stop the badminton you have going with my father. And the chats with my mother. It would be so unfair to them. I have caused them so much pain already. They are so glad when you come over. They look forward to your visits. It is a request from my side, Vaibhav.' I swallowed my pride, put aside my ego, and begged him.

Vaibhav said nothing. He just shook his head, and asked the chauffeur to drop him home.

My parents were waiting for me in the living room.

Dad looked up in surprise as I entered. 'Where is Vaibhav? I thought he would be having dinner with us.'

'He had some work-related thing to complete. He asked me to apologise to you and Ma,' I said without even hesitating. I sounded convincing. I knew my father would ask this, and had decided in the elevator that this was what I would tell him.

'Such a pity. I had made his favourite poori and bhaji,' my mother said.

'Ah, good! I will have it,' I said like I meant it.

This was easy. I actually sounded cheerful.

'So how was your day? What did you do?' asked my father.

'It was great!' I replied.

Over dinner, I went into a detailed explanation of all the sights we saw, the historic details that Vaibhav narrated, how impressed I was by all of it and how much I had enjoyed myself. I only left out the last bit when everything had gone wrong.

I was surprised that I could pretend so well that things were great and that I was happy. I was dying inside, yet I concealed it so well.

After we finished dinner, I took out the poetry book, as well as *Calvin and Hobbes*, and showed them to my father. He gave a cursory glance at the *Calvin and Hobbes* book. My father wasn't much into cartoons. He was curious about the poetry book though. He wore his glasses, opened it and began going through the contents.

'*We grow accustomed to the dark* by Emily Dickinson; *The Wound* by Ruth Stone; *Alone* by Edgar Allan Poe; *Solitude* by Ella Wheeler Wilcox,' he read out loud. 'Why are all these poems sad?'

'Dad, it is a book with a theme of sadness and pain. All the poems are chosen that way,' I replied.

I loved the poems. I could connect with them deeply. I felt as if the poets understood my pain and expressed it beautifully. There was beauty in pain too. But I knew my father wouldn't understand it.

'Read some inspirational poetry, Ankita. Stay away from such depressing stuff,' said my father as he handed the book back to me.

'Ankita, you've had a long day. Go and sleep now,' said my mother.

'Ma, you are my sleep monitor. Do you count even the seconds I sleep?' I teased her.

'Yes, of course. I use a stopwatch to check. Now go,' she joked and cajoled.

'Oh, one more thing, Dad. Vaibhav may not come for badminton tomorrow. He asked me to tell you, but I forgot. He said that he has some training module to complete urgently,' I told my father.

'I see. That is fine then. We have some regulars there whom we play doubles with. One of them can take Vaibhav's place,' said my father.

When I went to my room, the pain of Vaibhav's words came flooding back. I decided to read my book of poems.

Among all the poems in the book, *The Wound* by Ruth Stone caught my eye.

The shock comes slowly
as an afterthought.
First you hear the words.

It was a very short poem, which began with these lines. The words struck an instant connect. I read the entire poem and felt the truth of each word. I felt it was written just for me. I wondered who this Ruth Stone was. I turned to the back of the book, and there were a few lines written about her. She seemed to be a renowned poet with many books. I froze when I read the next line. Ruth Stone was quoted to have said that all her poems were 'love poems written to a dead man'. Her husband had committed suicide and she had raised their three daughters alone.

Something clicked in my brain then. I rushed to my cupboard and rummaged among my clothes for the suicide manual. I opened it and read the inscription again.

To my darling Ruth.
All my love,
MH

Was this a sign from the universe? The suicide manual was gifted to Ruth, and the poem I had just read was by Ruth. What a strange coincidence! Both had something to do with death and dying. I couldn't quite wrap my head around it. I felt I was groping in the dark for something – but what I was searching for, I did not know.

I read the other poems in the book too. They all spoke to me. They matched the melancholy I felt inside. The sadness at being misunderstood by Vaibhav was unbearable. Had I cheated him? What was cheating? How was it cheating? Had I promised him I would tell him every bit of my life? He wasn't around anyway when I was in St. Agnes. We wrote a few letters and talked on the phone sometimes. How did that make me obliged to tell him about Abhi? More importantly, if I had, would he have understood?

Thoughts began whirling in my head. I didn't know where one ended and the other began. It was happening again. Things inside my head were racing around at a terrifying speed. Fragments flew in all directions. I was losing control. I didn't know what to do. I needed to do something. I needed to write.

I grabbed my notebook.

I began writing:

Love is not a contract you sign, where you commit to telling everything to each other. Love is when you feel understood without saying a thing. When you love someone, you accept them in their entirety. The bad bits along with the good bits. You learn to control your jealousy. You put their happiness above yours. You want the best for them. You wish them well. You tell them things that you believe are your absolute truth. You share your vulnerabilities with them. You show them your weakest side. You bank on their compassion. You never expect love to be unkind.

And when you lose love, it feels like you have lost a part of yourself. Forever.

I started crying at this point. Tears clouded my eyes and I couldn't see anymore. A tear fell on the page I was writing on, and landed on the word 'love'. The ink blotted, and the word faded.

I picked up my pen again. Then I wrote:

Love dies, and there is nothing you can do except endure the loss. It is the most painful feeling in the world.

I felt better after I wrote. The fragments in my head, the words flying around, the disjointed thoughts, all of it had come together like the pieces of a jigsaw puzzle on paper. A long time ago I had come across a book, *Notes to Myself*. I decided that is what I would do too.

Whenever I felt my brain being 'churned', I would write a note to myself.

On the cover of the book, I wrote: *LIFE'S LITTLE NOTES*.

Then on top of the page of the piece I had just written, I wrote **Note 1**.

I read it again. It made perfect sense to me. It was an epiphany. While the pain of Vaibhav's words did not go away, writing all this took some of the edge off it and made it easier to bear.

I went to bed after that. As I fell asleep, my last thoughts were whether Vaibhav would turn up the next day. I desperately hoped he would.

14
Wishing, Waiting, Hoping

Vaibhav didn't turn up the next day. My heart sank. I had pleaded with him so much, I had apologised so many times. How could he be so unrelenting? I wanted to call him up. But then, I hadn't bothered to take down his phone number.

My parents did not see anything amiss. They had believed me when I said that Vaibhav had a training module to complete. It was a Sunday and my father was at home. That meant we had our usual routine of watching a movie that was playing on television and sometimes we went out for ice creams.

I stayed in my room most of the day. I pretended to be working, but I could hardly focus on anything. I grew restless with each hour that passed. I didn't know what to do. I wanted to stop thinking about Vaibhav, but couldn't. I was obsessing over this. Any time the doorbell rang, I went rushing out, hoping it would be Vaibhav. But each time I was disappointed. It turned out to be the housekeeping staff, the dhobi who had come to collect the clothes, and on one occasion the next-door neighbour who had come to borrow a tomato (of all things).

'Why do you come rushing out of your room each time? I will get the door. Focus on your studies. I thought you were studying,' said my mother.

If only she knew. I couldn't even read a book, let alone study. All I could do was think about Vaibhav's words and the look on his face. I couldn't bear it. So I comforted myself in the only way I knew. I wrote.

I opened my newly created *LIFE'S LITTLE NOTES* and wrote **Note 2.**

When you are waiting to hear from someone, each minute, each second somehow stretches and becomes longer. The needles on the hands of the clock move slower. You obsess over the person you are waiting for. If only they called. If only they came home. If only you saw them. Your time becomes a series of 'if onlys'. We seek our happiness from the actions of others that we have no control over. All it brings is expectations and then disappointments when those expectations are not met. How do we let go when it is the only thing that matters?

Is waiting for someone a sign of love? Or is it a sign of unmet expectations? If someone loved you truly, they would be there for you, no matter what. They wouldn't make you wait. If they cared for you, they would keep you informed. Not keep you in the dark. Love does not mean waiting for the phone to ring or waiting for them to appear. Love is the quiet knowledge that they aren't going anywhere, and will always be there for you.

'Ankita, there's a call for you,' said my father, peeping into my room.

He called! He called! He called! My heart sang.

But when I rushed to the phone, it wasn't Vaibhav. It was Parul.

'Don't you think we need to practice today too? Euphoria is starting tomorrow. As it is, we lost one day yesterday,' she said.

In my obsessing over Vaibhav not calling me or turning up, I had almost forgotten that. How could I? I was glad Parul called.

'Please come home na. My mother is on the sets today, and we will have the whole house to ourselves,' Parul said.

'Sounds like a plan. Give me your address, and the directions. I will be there in an hour,' I said.

I was happy for the distraction. At least for a brief period I wouldn't be thinking about Vaibhav. I told my parents that I was going to Parul's house as Euphoria was starting the next day.

'I am so glad you have made friends, and it feels wonderful to see you going out,' said my mother.

'Stop, Ma. You don't have to mention it each time,' I said.

'I can't help it. I know what I went through when you refused to move from your bed for days,' my mother reminded me.

'Ma, *stop it*! I told you once. Please don't keep reminding me. I am trying to forget it,' I said.

My father said nothing. But I saw him giving my mother that look, which meant he was in agreement with me. I don't know what twisted pleasure my mother got out of reminding me each time. As though I needed reminders. Perhaps it was her way of getting it out of her system. I knew my parents had suffered along with me, and so I let it go.

I got off at Mahalaxmi and found Parul's house easily. It was a two-bedroom apartment on the twenty-sixth floor, and was about a six-minute walk from the railway station. Parul greeted me with a big smile and a hug. The view from her balcony made me swoon.

'Look at that!' I exclaimed. 'Look at all those cars rushing, and, hey, you can also see the railway station,' I said.

'Don't you have cars in Bandra? And is there no railway station there?' Parul sounded bored.

'No, Bandra is a village. We travel in bullock carts,' I said and she smiled.

Parul gave me a tour of their small home. Her mother had done it up nicely in pastel shades, Buddha statues and indoor plants.

Parul's room was very colourful, with an entire wall of graffiti.

'Go ahead, add your work to it,' said Parul, handing me some markers and spray paint.

'For real?' I asked.

'Of course, why would I give you the paints otherwise?' she asked.

I had fun spray-painting her wall. I made a red heart, and it bled downwards.

'Bleeding heart,' I wrote with a black marker.

'Oooh, angsty art! I like it,' said Parul.

'So when Freddy stayed with you, where would he sleep?' I asked.

'He used my room. I shared my mom's room. But then I would creep into bed with him after my mother went to sleep,' Parul said.

I smiled. I couldn't imagine a bohemian life like Parul's. Graffiti on wall, boyfriend in bed. I remembered Vaibhav again, and a sharp pain shot through me.

Fortunately, I was distracted by Parul's non-stop chatter. Soon Janki arrived. We practised hard for about an hour and a half. After that, Parul made onion pakodas and tea for us.

'You cook so well, yaar!' said Janki as she bit into one.

'Yeah, I learnt to cook when I was a kid. My mother was busy on the sets all the time. Some days I would even keep dinner ready for her,' said Parul.

'Who would let you in?' asked Janki.

'When Nani was alive, it was fun. But after she passed away, I would just let myself in,' said Parul.

We sat on her balcony munching pakodas and sipping the tea she made.

'So, how is Freddy in bed?' asked Janki.

I almost choked on the pakoda I was munching. How could Janki ask that!

But Parul was unfazed.

'He is good. Really, really good. I have multiple orgasms,' she said, her eyes lighting up.

'Really? What does he do?' asked Janki.

Parul then went into a detailed explanation about how caring Freddy was, how he took time with foreplay, how he whispered sweet nothings in her ear, and how he held himself back till she came. I sat listening quietly.

On my way back home, I thought about how Parul looked self-assured and confident. Janki looked splendid and stylish. They were both so light, so carefree. Why couldn't I be more like them, content with life and so sure of what my goals were? They seemed to breeze through life like a couple of kites.

My life was about fighting my thoughts. Every day.

●

The next morning too, there was no sign of Vaibhav. I felt miserable about his absence. My father was getting ready to leave for his badminton.

'Er... Dad, did Vaibhav call?' I asked him. Maybe Vaibhav had informed him that he couldn't make it?

My father looked up in surprise, as he tied his shoelaces.

'Oh, didn't Vaibhav tell you?' he asked.

'What?'

'He is going to be out of town for about two weeks or so. He has a training stint in Malegaon, at the factory.'

'I see. When did he tell you this?'

'He called yesterday, Ankita. He spoke to me as well as your mother when you were at Parul's house.'

'Did he… did he ask for me?'

'Umm no. That is why I presumed you already knew. He called just to tell us that he won't be around for a few days and that he will see us after he returns.'

My heart leapt up when I heard that. I did not mind that he hadn't asked for me. What was important was that he had said he would see us. I saw a sliver of hope. At least he still cared. If he was breaking up with me, he would not have bothered with the phone call to my father. I felt as if a big burden had been lifted off my shoulders. I was humming as I made my way to college. We had all been asked to report early in the morning. Time for Euphoria!

●

The first day of Euphoria turned out to be great fun. As soon as we reached college, we were given the official 'Euphoria' T-shirts with the logo of our college printed on it. We were also given badges that said 'Student Volunteer', which we pinned on to the T-shirts. Parul, Janki and I, as part of the welcoming committee, were on our feet the whole day, taking guests to their places of accommodation, arranging cars, coordinating, making everyone feel at home. The competitions started right on time. Our duties also included guiding the students from other colleges to the right venues. We could hear the boisterous noise from the auditoriums as the various colleges cheered for their respective teams. Both Public Speaking as well as Dumb Charades were scheduled one after the other on the final day of the festival.

We were told that while we were taking part in competitions, some other volunteers would take over from us. But once we finished our bit, we were to get right back to the welcoming committee duties.

'And yes, do well! We're counting on you, Ankita, to get us a few prizes. We haven't done too well today. Our teams didn't even make it past the semi-finals in most events,' Maya said.

'Don't worry. Ankita has made us practice so hard. We will be among the best teams in Dumb Charades, and we hope to win,' Parul said.

'And in Public Speaking too I think we might get a prize. I have seen Ankita speak.' Maya winked.

We had indeed worked hard, and I knew we would definitely be among the best teams. I was exhausted by the end of the day, and so were Parul and Janki.

'Do you want to go to Khau Galli?' Parul asked us.

'No, yaar, my feet are killing me. I can't walk a step,' Janki said.

'But I am so hungry!' wailed Parul.

'Don't worry, girls. We have ordered food from the pav bhaji stall. It has all been arranged in room 8, next to the office room,' Maya told us.

All of us rushed there and feasted on the pav bhaji. It was the best food I ever ate.

As we left for the day, Maya called out, 'Rest up well, girls! We need to be fighting-fit tomorrow!'

'Yes, yes. You can count on us,' grinned Parul.

I went to sleep that night dreaming of trophies, medals and thank-you speeches on stage.

15

One Moment in Time

'**G**ood luck, Ankita!'
'Do well! Win, okay?'
'Make us proud, girl'
'You are awesome. You will win for sure.'

Maya, Parul, Janki and a few other girls wished me luck as I went into the classroom that was the venue for the qualifying round for Public Speaking. There were three rounds in total. Since there were over sixty registered contestants, there was to be a first round, a quarter-final, where twenty people would be selected. In the next round, which was the semi-finals, eight people would be selected, who would then compete in the finals where there would be a winner and a runner-up. Only the finals would be held in the auditorium. Rest of the rounds would be in classrooms.

The Public Speaking trophy was a prestigious one instituted by the Goenka family, and it came with a cash prize too, apart from the trophy itself. It received a lot of attention each year as every participating college waited to see who would take the trophy home. The two students who won this would also get a chance to compete in an international contest. The rules were simple. The participants would be assigned their topics through a draw of lots, and given six minutes to prepare. They would then have to speak for six minutes. It was coordinated in such a fashion that when one participant was on stage, the next person to speak would draw up their topic. You had to think on your feet.

Since I had some experience at JAM, and knew I was good at this, I wasn't too nervous. Being selected to represent the college had given my confidence a tremendous boost. It also helped that the quarter-finals were held in a classroom with only the participants as audience, as there were sixty of us. Speaking in a classroom was not as stressful as speaking on a stage in the auditorium. For the quarter-finals, we also had to speak for only two minutes, as the number of participants were too many. The three judges sat right in the front and wrote down the marks of each participant in their little clipboards. I was the forty-eighth to speak. I just hoped I would not get a topic that had anything to do with politics. If you did not know about it, you couldn't make up stuff. But all the topics they gave were ones that did not require factual knowledge. Mostly they were humorous and light topics, and I was happy about that.

The topic I drew was a very easy one: 'What not to wear on a first date'. The moment I got it, I felt it was serendipitous. I made up a funny story about a girl who couldn't decide what to wear, and ended up wearing pyjamas to her first date. It was a ridiculous story, and I could see the audience laughing, which kept me going. At the end of two minutes, the buzzer sounded, and I stopped. I was one of the few participants who managed to get some claps.

When everyone finished speaking, the student volunteer said that the results would be announced in fifteen minutes. I could see the three judges and the student volunteers huddled over the desk, adding up the marks. They announced the results. I had made it to the semi-finals. They also announced that the semi-finals would start in two hours, and the participants would have to speak for four minutes each.

Parul and Janki treated me like a boxer who was resting between bouts.

'Do you want water?'

'Shall I get some juice for you?'

'Are you hungry?'

They fussed over me till Maya reminded them that they were still to do the welcoming committee duties. She excused me from this, saying she didn't want me to be exhausted.

The semi-finals turned out exactly like the quarter-finals, but with fewer contestants. For this round too, there wasn't a big audience, even though anyone could attend it. There were many finals of other competitions happening in the auditorium and most students were engrossed in them. Parul and Janki came, of course. The topic I got this time was: 'You are an ant. Convince an anteater to not eat you'. I found this very easy to speak on too. There was a lot of scope for fantasy as well as humour, and I made up a tale about how I was an ant cursed with depression and a grave illness, which would be ingested by anyone who ate me, and that was the only way I would be free. I created a scenario where, as an ant, I plead with the anteater to eat me to release me from the curse, and the anteater refusing and running away in horror. I also modified my voice and spoke as the anteater as well as the ant. I was so enjoying this. Every single person in the room clapped when I finished my story. I reveled in the attention.

Since I had sailed through the semi-finals, I would be one of the eight contestants for the finals on the following day, the last day of the festival.

Maya was ecstatic. So were the others in the culture committee. 'Well done, Ankita! You have quite the imagination, and you speak so well,' Maya said.

'You have absolutely no stage-fright at all,' marveled Janki.

If only Janki knew what went on inside my head. Deep down, one part of me was acutely aware of the mania phase of my illness, when I had my highs. My mind ran on wheels then. I remembered how I had struggled to rein in my thoughts and how chaotically they had scattered, taking a life of their own. I was afraid of it happening again.

A thin line separates creativity from insanity. I was tiptoeing that line every single day, in constant fear of whether my actions would be considered normal or abnormal. My mother monitored my sleep, down to minutes. My father kept a hawk-eye on my moods.

Yes, I was not afraid of being on stage, but I was terrified of losing my mental balance, and going back to the psychiatrists where every action of mine would be analysed and dissected in medical terms. Janki had no clue. This was my cross to bear, and I bore it in silence. Yes, I was not afraid to be on stage, but then, my fears play hide and seek even with me.

How would anyone ever understand any of this? I did not want to be labeled a weirdo. So I said, 'Yes, I am comfortable on stage.'

'So lucky, yaar,' Janki remarked and I managed a wry smile in response.

'Girls, tomorrow you are excused from the welcoming committee duties as you have your Dumb Charades. And Ankita has her Public Speaking finals. And, by the way, we have just twelve college teams that registered for Dumb Charades this year. So you guys are through to the finals there too,' said Maya.

•

The third and final day was an important day and I wanted to sleep well so I was ready for it. My father was overjoyed to hear about how I had spoken that day. He made me narrate the anteater story twice, and he laughed each time. My mother just listened to me, and did not comment.

'Ma, isn't it great that I cleared the semi-finals?' I asked her. I wanted her to praise me. I wanted her to encourage and acknowledge my victory. I wanted her to see my triumphs, especially after how I had struggled at NMHI. But I think deep down my mother was terrified of my imagination and what it could do to me.

'Be careful. Don't get carried away,' she said.

'What do you mean don't get carried away? Can't you be happy for me?' I was angry now. Couldn't my mother see how *much* this victory meant to me?

'What do you want me to say, Ankita? I don't find these things amusing like your father does. What curse and what anteater? What kind of a silly story is that? And your father is encouraging you, and laughing like it is the greatest story in the world. I'm sorry, I can't pretend to be happy when I am not. I am telling you to just be wary so we all don't have to run to the psychiatrist again,' she said.

I felt terribly hurt at her sharp words. A simple 'well done, Ankita' would have satisfied me. Instead, she had voiced my very fears. By speaking about it, what was in my head was now out in the open. It was the elephant in the room, and she had acknowledged it.

It crushed me and angered me at the same time. Wasn't anything I did good enough? Out of *sixty* people, I was in the final *eight*. Did that not mean anything? I wanted to yell at my mother; I was so angry I was shaking. But if I had yelled, it would have been seen as losing control. So I clenched my jaw tight and kept my mouth shut.

That day I realised that no matter what I did, it would forever be viewed through the prism of the symptoms of a mental illness.

All my little victories would be tinged with the fear of my mind going out of control. My happiness would forever carry that little bit of sadness, a reminder of my past when I had lost my balance. Whatever I achieved, my mother would never be happy. She would be terrified. I knew my mother was being practical and wary. Yet, her words angered me.

'Don't worry about it. I will ensure you all don't have to take me to a psychiatrist again,' I told her through gritted teeth. It was my pride speaking. I took off for my room, my anger boiling over like hot lava. I slammed the door shut with all my might. The loud bang rang through the whole house.

In my room, I yanked the pillows off the bed and threw them on the floor.

Then I picked one of them up and buried my face in it.

'AAAAAAARGH…. AAAAAAARGH…. AAAARGH,' I screamed into the pillow. I didn't want the sound to be heard outside my room. I did not want my mother or father to know how enraged I was. I had to hide it.

Hide it. Hide it. Hide it. Hide it. If you don't, they will find you and drag you to a doctor. Don't show your emotions.

I took deep breaths like I had seen some patients do in NMHI when they felt an anxiety attack coming. After a few minutes, the intensity came down. The disappointment at my mother's reaction grew inside me and I didn't know what to do about it. When anger had evaporated, the intense sadness at what my mother had stated jabbed my insides. I was sad at not being good enough, sad that I had to be cautious all the time, and mostly I was sad that my mother did not appreciate my imagination anymore.

LIFE'S LITTLE NOTES had become the only friend I could turn to. I opened it then and wrote **Note 3**.

Live life according to how your parents want you to, and you might end up frustrated. The norms they lay down, the things they tell you to do – these are things they have been told by their parents. Your parents come from a different generation, a different time. Though their love for you is unquestionable, their methods are not. What worked for them may not work for you. The only way to get over this hurdle is to prove to them that you were right. How can you do that? By your actions. You have to act, and SHOW it. There is no use arguing with them. They won't get you. But actions – those cannot be ignored.

Writing that down helped me crystallise my thoughts and I made up my mind firmly after that. I would win the Goenka trophy; I would bring it home, and *gift* it to my mother. She could show it off proudly to whoever came home. She could tell them that her daughter won it. Maybe it would erase her fears then. Maybe she would be proud of me. Maybe she would finally acknowledge my imagination.

●

It was in this state of mind that I went backstage the next day for the grand finals of the Public Speaking event. The entire auditorium had filled up. Parul and Janki were in the third row. My whole college was there to cheer for me.

I was to speak second. I heard the first contestant begin speaking and the auditorium grow silent.

'Your turn to draw the chits,' said one of the volunteers. I drew my topic and read what was on the chit. This was easy! I could speak so well on this.

My topic was: 'The strangest stranger I ever met'.

I formed the story in my head. I would speak of an old man who was a wizard, and who spoke in rhymes. I would say that he lived in the land of upside down, where he wore his shoes on his head and supped in bed, and slept standing up, and ate lying down. This was a cakewalk.

I went up on stage with a confident step. The auditorium was full to maximum capacity. There were even people standing. The spotlight shone on me.

'AN – KI – TA… AN – KI – TA… AN – KI – TA – thud thud thud…' Someone started the chant, by saying my name thrice and then making a thud sound by cupping a fist and hitting the other palm. The chant, like a war cry, was picked up by the others and soon the whole auditorium was reverberating with this. I had to wait for the roar to die down before I began to speak. I was certain I had nailed it. But life has a way of pulling out the rug from right under your feet when you least expect it.

I began my speech well, and the audience lapped it up. But then, I stopped mid-sentence. I had spotted someone I never expected to see. Every single person and every single thing around me seemed to fade. I froze. My stomach somersaulted, my mouth went dry. I felt the air being sucked out from my lungs.

This was another bridge I thought I had burnt. But I had not. The bridge had come back to taunt me. Was I imagining it or was this real? I stood there on the stage, opening and closing my mouth. No words came out. I couldn't think. I couldn't speak.

Sitting in the second row, next to Parul and Janki, staring at me with a big smile across his face was Joseph.

16

The Winner Takes it All

Ilost my train of thought then. I blinked several times. I was vaguely aware of the murmurs among the audience as they waited for me to resume speaking. Seconds ticked by. Five. Ten. Nobody knew what was happening. Someone from the back of the audience booed. I knew I had to resume speaking, but I didn't even remember what the topic was now. My heartbeats were getting louder and louder. My palms dripped sweat.

Was this real? How did he come here? How was he sitting next to Parul and Janki? What was going on? Was I hallucinating? I felt the colour drain from my face. Had I seen a ghost? Had I imagined Joseph? I wasn't sure if I could trust my mind. I looked again, and there he was, looking straight at me. I couldn't control my panic, my fright and, the worst, my thoughts. Memories resurfaced, rising in waves, submerging me. I remembered my highs. What I had done just before getting admitted into NMHI came back to me in vivid detail. Images flashed in front of my eyes: Joseph and me in a cab, Joseph asking to see my book of poems, Joseph kissing my hands, Joseph apologising, and then with a sinking feeling, I recalled how I had kissed him on the lips in the cab, my tear-soaked face against his stubble, and how he had said he loved me. I had lied blatantly when I told him I loved him, all because I had seen Abhi in him, and I had remembered Abhi's grandfather's voice in my head. I recalled the poem I wrote that day. I felt sick and repulsed with myself, as I remembered all of it. And then I felt the bile rise. My stomach tightened; I could feel it swirling, swirling. Frozen in horror, like a deer caught in the headlights, I tasted it then at the back of my mouth. Before I could react, I buckled over. To my utter disgust, a clouded yellow semi-solid gush of vomit spilled from my mouth and splattered over the wooden floor of the stage, some of it splashing on my legs. My face burned with shame, as I stood there horrified, in shocked silence. I couldn't believe this was happening. I had thrown up in front of an entire auditorium of a thousand-plus people.

The whole auditorium went silent.

I could only remember hazily what happened after that. I think Maya rushed to the stage and helped me out. I think Parul came too. I was dying of shame thinking about how the housekeeping staff would have to clean it up. I could smell the pungent stench of the vomit.

'Please… can I have a mop?' I asked, but I felt the bile rise up again.

I ran out of the auditorium and threw up in the mud, by the flower-beds.

I remember turning around and Maya handing me tissues. Parul held a bottle of water, and accompanied me to the toilets.

'Are you okay? Wash your face,' someone said. I think it was Parul. Everything was foggy. Like I was in a bad nightmare.

'Sorry, I am sorry,' I kept repeating till Parul told me to shut up.

'Look, it was an accident, and you felt sick. It could happen to anyone,' she said.

Except, it hadn't. It had happened only to me. In front of an entire auditorium, in front of students from other colleges, in front of my professors, in front of every damn person I knew.

I had failed. And failed miserably at that. I had let down every single person who depended on me. The Goenka cup – it was gone now, along with my dignity.

You are worthless.

You let down anyone who depends on you.

You are a failure.

You are not normal. Not normal. Not normal.

This is all you are capable of.

You can't even control your thoughts.

I washed up, wanting to disappear from the face of earth. How could I even look at anyone in college again? I couldn't even look Parul in the eye, even though she was trying to reassure me.

'Had you eaten something unusual?' asked Parul, as we emerged from the restrooms.

Nobody knew the reason for what had just happened. They presumed I was unwell, and it was something I had eaten.

I shook my head.

I wanted to go home. I couldn't face anybody. I wanted to retreat into my shell and hide in the safety of my room. I didn't want to stay even a second longer in college. I looked down, my cheeks still burning with shame and humiliation.

'Ankita, are you okay? What happened?'

I recognised his voice, even as I stood there wishing to die.

It *was* Joseph. Along with him was a thin short guy in a denim jacket with messy hair and a snake tattoo on his arm. Janki was with them.

'Wait, you two know each other?' asked Parul, saving me from having to answer.

I stood there, numb, not knowing what to say.

'We used to be in the same class,' Joseph answered.

'Oh, the world is so small! And how strangely we're all connected. And look at me! I haven't even introduced you to Freddy. Ankita, meet Freddy. He is Joseph's cousin,' she said.

Freddy extended his hand.

I took it without meeting his eye and offered him a limp, brief handshake.

'You know, I had thrown up once just like you did. It was in Essel World after I took a roller-coaster ride,' Freddy chuckled.

My toes curled. Someone talking about it, *joking* about it was even worse than what had happened.

'Shut up, Freddy. That's not a thing to joke about.' Parul nudged him with her elbow.

'All I am saying is it's no big deal,' said Freddy.

I wished he would shut up.

'I have to go. Sorry...' I said, my voice quivering. I was shaking so much, I could hardly speak. I fled, half-walking, half-running.

I had left my bag in one of the classrooms and I went in to get it. I ran into Maya just as I was walking out.

'Hey, Ankita, are you okay now? Where are you off to? You have Dumb Charades in the evening, remember?' she said.

'Sorry, Maya, I feel sick. I have to go home,' I said and walked away, leaving her staring after me.

Just as I reached the entrance, I ran into Mrs Hayden. I tried to duck into a classroom to avoid bumping into her, but she had already seen me. 'Ankita, I was looking for you.'

I had no choice but to walk up to her. 'I saw what happened. Please don't berate yourself. It happens sometimes. I just wanted to tell you to not let this affect you. You will see that in the larger scheme of things, this is just a minor bump,' she said gently, her eyes full of kindness.

I couldn't take it any more then. Till then, I had controlled myself. But now, my tears burst forth. I was crying in front of Mrs Hayden. Would my humiliation never end? I tried to stop the tears from flowing and my nose from running. I wiped my face with the back of my palm, desperately trying to get a grip over my feelings.

'Here, here now. Don't cry, my dear, it is okay,' said Mrs Hayden.

'Sorry, Mrs Hayden. I have to go,' I said between sniffles.

'Don't let this get you down. Your essay is due day after tomorrow, let's not forget that,' she called out as I walked away.

I don't know if Mrs Hayden was trying to distract me by reminding me of the essay or not, but at that moment, I was too devastated to care. I felt sick to the pit of my stomach. What was worse, after practising so hard for Dumb Charades, I had left my team-mates and fled. I couldn't bear to face Joseph. Of all the things, him turning out to be Freddy's cousin! When had Parul even made up with Freddy? Why did he have to come? Why did he have to bring his cousin? Why did I have to see him? Why why why – the questions were on a merry-go-round in my head.

When I reached home burning with guilt and shame, my mother opened the door. She was frantic with worry. Parul had already called home and told my mother that I was to call her back on the college phone the moment I reached home.

'What happened, Ankita? Is everything fine?' she asked.

'I don't know, Ma. I feel sick. I am going to lie down,' I said and went straight to my room.

My mother wouldn't let me be. She followed me inside.

'Did you get nervous?'

'Did you eat something at college that didn't agree with you?'

'Why did you throw up?'

'Aren't you going to call Parul back?'

My mother bombarded me with questions.

'*Leave me alone*, Ma,' I snapped at her. I was taking out all my frustration and anger on her for no fault of hers.

'Sorry, Ma. I didn't mean to yell,' I said the next instant. But it was too late. I saw that wary look in my mother's eyes. She was putting me under a microscope, looking for the first sign of the disorder returning. I knew it. I had seen that look before.

I was filled with regret about how I had behaved. A million other laments came into my head and made a place for themselves in my brain. I tried to dislodge them, chuck them out with logic. The doctors at NMHI had explained my weird behaviour in the time leading up to my being admitted there. It was mania. When I had kissed Joseph, it was the illness acting, not me. They had explained this to me in detail. They had talked about how it was not 'my fault' or 'my mistake' and how I had no control over it, any more than I had control over a common cold. I knew all of that, but why did these feelings refuse to go away? Why was I feeling like it *was* all my fault?

The phone rang just then. It was Parul again. My mother forced me to talk.

'Ankita, you can't just leave a person hanging like that. Go explain to her,' insisted my mother.

I sighed and walked to the phone.

'How are you feeling? Are you really sick?' asked Parul

'I don't feel too good,' I replied honestly.

'Physically, I mean. Are you still throwing up?' she persisted.

'No… no, I am not throwing up. Why?'

'Listen, you silly goose. We need you back here. Our *team* needs you. You cannot run away like that, do you hear me? We still have two hours left for Dumb Charades. Now get your ass back here on the next train,' said Parul.

'I can't,' I said.

'You can't? Or you won't? Stop being *selfish*, Ankita. You made us practice hard for this. Now just because you threw up on stage, you are giving up and running away? So not done! Why the fuck did you waste my time and Janki's time then?' Parul was angry.

She was right. No matter how I felt, it wasn't okay to abandon the team. I would have to go back. I would have to participate. I couldn't let them down like this. I would have to swallow my shame and face my worst fears. I would have to bear all the hushed whispers. I knew everyone would be talking about me as the girl who threw up on stage. I felt sick even thinking of it. One part of me just wanted to run away screaming. But the sane part of me took over. I had just one question for Parul.

'Are Joseph and Freddy still around?' I asked.

'Ha! Knew it! I knew that was why you left. Because of Joseph!' Parul said. I had confirmed her suspicion with my question.

'Tell me if they are there or not,' I said.

'No, Ankita. They have gone. I didn't know myself that Joseph would turn up. I wasn't even expecting Freddy. He decided to surprise me. He came to tell me that he had turned over a new leaf, picked up a job and had been working for the last two months. Joseph came with him, to vouch for him, as his moral support. Anyway, why am I telling you all this? Just get back here, and hurry. Don't let us down,' Parul said and hung up.

There was nothing left to do but go back to college, and try and salvage what was left of my pride. My mother said it was the right thing to do.

'Don't let your friends down if they are depending on you,' she said.

I hurried back to college with trepidation at how to handle this. I had to face the music. When I entered, I saw a group of girls turning to look at me and I could hear the hushed whispers. My ears burned with shame. Parul whisked me away backstage.

'Listen, we have practised hard. Now forget about everything and focus, okay?' she said.

My hands shook as I went up on stage. I looked at the spot where I had puked. There was no trace of it left now. Since I was in an agitated state of mind, I couldn't perform well. Parul and Janki were the stars. They saved the day. We finished third.

They were happy. So was Maya and the whole culture committee.

'Well done, girls,' Maya told us after the event.

'Ankita, if you were in full form, we could have finished first,' said Janki.

'I tried,' I said wanly.

'Don't worry, you did well. You came back despite not feeling up to it, that was what was important,' said Maya, putting her arm around me.

But I was not satisfied at all. I had messed up everything.

Euphoria was finally over and all the girls were going out to celebrate. They were going to party at a restaurant nearby. Apparently this was the grand tradition on the final day of the festival each year, especially as the next day was a holiday. Everyone stayed out late dancing.

'We have worked so hard, we deserve it,' Maya told all of us.

'Come with us, Ankita. Stay over at my place. It will be too late for you to travel back alone,' Parul offered.

But I refused. I felt I didn't deserve it. I knew I could have done better. I knew I could have won the trophy. I wished we had at least come second or first in Dumb Charades. Then it would have been some consolation. Third place was no good.

'Sorry, I really don't feel good,' I said as I headed home.

The excited chatter and laughter of the girls faded as I walked away. But it still played in my head.

17

I Took a Pill in Ibiza

My parents were waiting for me at home. My mother had narrated the day's events to my father. I think they were scared I had taken it badly and rushed to comfort me.

'It is okay, Ankita. What is important is for us to face our fears. You faced your worst fear today. That makes you brave,' my father said as I plopped down on the sofa.

I was quiet for a minute. Then I said, 'I don't know, Dad. I wish I had won.'

'You *have* won, Ankita. Who is a winner anyway? Are winners decided by three people who are appointed judges? Isn't that a narrow definition of a victory?' My father was philosophic.

'It's easy for you to say that. You don't have to face the sniggers, the whispers, the talks,' my voice trembled even as I said it.

'Let people talk. They will tire of it,' my mother was matter-of-fact.

'You will never get it, Ma. You have not faced it. Do you have any idea what it is like to be the abnormal one? *Always*? Do you know this was one reason I did *not* want to go back to MBA. All my classmates would have been ahead of me. I wanted a fresh start. And now, even that is *ruined*.' I found it hard to control myself.

Couldn't she *see* for herself what it meant? Were they blind?

Their words were of little consolation. They were just trying to make me feel better about this whole thing.

'Why is it all "ruined"?' asked my mother.

'It is, Ma. How many times do I have to say it? You just don't get it. I have lost face in front of the *entire* college.'

'Do you think everyone in the college will be talking only about this? Let me tell you something – humans are inherently selfish. For each person, a tiny headache they have is more important than, say, even a death in another person's family. That is how it is. For each one, their own problem will seem the biggest, the most consequential. We're all supremely self-focused, and that's just what you are doing too.'

'Anyway, your mother tells me you went back to college after that. I am glad you didn't let your friends down. How did that go?' My father's voice was gentle.

'Well, we came third in Dumb Charades. If the whole public speaking fiasco hadn't happened, we would have probably come first. We had really prepared,' I said bitterly.

'You should learn to be content with what you get, Ankita. You are always wanting more. That is the problem with you,' my mother stated.

That got my goat. Why was my mother saying such things? And that dismissive tone! Implying it was no big deal, that I was making a fuss instead of just moving on.

'What *problem*, Ma? What is wrong with ambition? I think that is what makes us grow as people,' I said angrily. 'Everyone can't hide in the kitchen like you and cook all day!'

'Control your temper, Ankita,' my father's voice was still calm.

'Leave me alone,' I said and marched to my room.

I resisted the strong urge to bang the door shut again. My parents just didn't get it. I had wanted to win the trophy as a comeback. It was to have been my victory march. It was to have been my 'look-at-me-now' moment. It was my *reward* for all the months I was at NMHI – struggling to read, struggling to do everything that other people did unthinkingly. My triumph over how I had been relegated to the sidelines of the society while at NMHI. It was my big chance to show what I was capable of – in a way it was my 'revenge'.

You are not capable of revenge.

You are not even capable of controlling your thoughts.

The ugly reminder of the morning's event now reared its head, taunting me. I replayed the scene in my head. Each time I replayed it, the hushed silence and the booing that I heard got louder. I knew I was fixating over this, tormenting myself, yet I couldn't stop. I wished there was a switch in my head to turn it off.

A gentle knock on the door, and I looked up to see my father peering in.

'Leave all of that, Ankita. Come, have dinner,' he coaxed.

I joined them for dinner. My mother had made my favourite vegetable cutlets.

'Cutlets for dinner?' I asked surprised. She usually served them only with evening tea.

'These are small joys we can give ourselves.' She smiled.

I felt a bit silly then to have lost my temper. I knew cooking my favourite food was her way of trying to comfort me, make me feel better.

'Ma, I am sorry for snapping today. Just now as well as in the afternoon. I was just stressed,' I said.

'I know, Ankita. You have been through a lot. That is why I am scared, and I try to look out for you,' she said.

'We might be a bit over-protective now. But it is only because we want you to be so strong that nothing can affect you,' my father said.

I was grateful for their love and support. When I was with them, I was able to push back the memories a little further. But once I went back to my room, the shame and humiliation came back to swallow me up again.

I opened *LIFE'S LITTLE NOTES* and then wrote **Note 4.**

Often when we think we have got it all sorted, life plays a trick on us. It takes away what we expect. There might be no apparent meaning to it. Life doesn't care if you have worked hard for it or not. Life doesn't play fair. Life doesn't play by the rules you make. Life has its own way of doing things. Life is not a science experiment in controlled laboratory settings where you can study cause and effect. Life is so much more.

Our defeats are magnified in our own heads, because we focus on what we have lost rather than on what we actually have. If we have the love of our parents, if we have people who care for us, if we have a hot meal on the table, then we are blessed.

Often it is the small things we overlook. I think that is what life is trying to teach us. That little things matter. That we have to be grateful for them. We have to notice them.

And sometimes we notice them only when the big things are taken away from us.

I read what I had written. Then I added:

Life is also a great teacher. Life gives you the exams, but doesn't tell you the syllabus. It is up to us to set our own lessons.

Writing made me feel better, helped me cope with the shame and pain. I thought I had dealt with that. I thought it was the end of the matter, and I could go on. But I was wrong. I never anticipated what was to follow. Life was not done giving me exams yet. There was more to learn.

But I went to sleep that night, blissfully unaware of what life had in store.

●

The next morning, I was woken up by my mother's hand on my forehead. When I opened my eyes, I saw the frightened faces of both my parents looking at me anxiously.

My hair was damp with sweat and so was my pillow. My heart was pounding and my breath came out in shallow rasps. I had been having a nightmare, and I was thankful to have been woken up.

I hadn't slept well at all. Had tossed and turned. Only in the wee hours of the morning, when I could see the faint light of sunrise in the morning sky, had I finally fallen asleep. It was a horrible feeling to lie in bed awake, with thoughts of shame and humiliation going round and round in your head. I couldn't control them, I couldn't fight them, and in the end, I just surrendered to their torture as they ransacked my brain.

And when I fell asleep, I was plagued by frightening nightmares. It seemed like my thoughts were reluctant to leave me alone even when I slept. The nightmare felt terrifyingly real; I was up on stage and my mouth was stitched up. When I tried to speak, I was petrified as no words came out. I couldn't even scream. I heard Joseph's voice calling out to me, telling me that I was worthless. In the very next moment, I was on the edge of a parapet, with Joseph taunting me that I had no courage to jump. I decided I would show him. Just as I decided that, a black large grotesque monster with the head of a toad and limbs like those of an octopus called out to me, opening its mouth. Its skin was like a reptile's – full of warts, and pores that oozed pus and blood.

'Come… come into my darkness,' it called out as its tentacles wrapped themselves around me. I let out a blood-curdling scream in pure terror.

It was at this point that I felt my mother's hand on my forehead.

'Ankita, are you okay?' my mother asked.

My father gave me a bottle of water, and I sat up, drinking straight from the bottle, some of it flowing down the corners of my mouth, dribbling on to my T-shirt.

'What happened? You were screaming,' my father said.

'I was having a nightmare. I barely slept, then this horrible dream,' I said.

My mother and father exchanged meaningful looks. They didn't say anything just then.

'Okay, wash your face, and come along. Let's go out for lunch today. You have a holiday, right?' asked my father.

'Yes, Dad, I do, but I also have an essay to turn in tomorrow,' I said as I got out of bed, thankful to be woken up.

The lack of sleep was affecting my mind. I was unfocused, and my thoughts kept wandering. These were only small indications that something was not right. I was pretty sure I had everything under control. But my parents were frantic with worry. If your loved one has survived a mental ordeal, you become extra-cautious, and alert to anything unusual.

It was at the ice cream place that my father gingerly broached the topic. He knew I was touchy about it.

'Listen, Ankita. There's something we need to tell you,' he said.

The way he spoke immediately made me sit up and take notice. 'What is it?' I asked.

'We called up NMHI and spoke to Dr Madhusudan. He is leaving for Australia next week and will be gone for a few years. But he has assigned your files to another doctor here in Bombay, and he knows all the details,' he said.

'Oh. But how does it matter? My treatment is done. I am fine,' I said.

My father cleared his throat. 'Ankita, after you were discharged, we tapered off the medications, and had completely stopped, right?'

'Yes. And I am fine now, Dad,' I repeated.

'See, that's the thing. We had a detailed chat on the phone. Dr Madhusudan highly recommends you restart the medication. Only one tablet just before you sleep to help you reduce the cyclical thoughts, and for your anxiety,' my father said.

'What? I am coping well... I am fine,' I insisted.

'We know that. But this is just a preventive. If you don't take them, you will become increasingly worse,' my mother said.

'But why should I take a preventive? What am I trying to prevent here? I said I am fine, did I not?' I was curt.

'Look, Ankita, you are sleeping lesser. You are irritable, and you have to acknowledge that you are thinking obsessively, aren't you? Also, wasn't it because of anxiety that you threw up on stage?' Dad asked.

'I am not really that anxious or obsessive. Come on,' I protested. But my father wouldn't hear of it. He was convinced it was anxiety that made me throw up.

I hadn't told them about Joseph. I couldn't. I was too ashamed of what had happened during my mania phase. They would be shocked if they knew what I had done then. Hell, I myself did not understand the whole Joseph episode. How could I make my parents understand?

'Look, Ankita, let's do this as a trial. You take it for fifteen days, and see if you feel better. If you don't feel better, you don't have to take them, okay?' my father bargained.

I did not want to take the medication. There wasn't anything that I could *not* control. I had my LIFE'S LITTLE NOTES. That was the only therapy I needed.

Medication was a crutch. Unless I discarded it, how would I learn to walk? Not only that, I wasn't content with just walking, I wanted to fly.

I *knew* the cause for my meltdown. I had let panic get the better of me when I saw Joseph suddenly. But my parents didn't know what had triggered it. They presumed it was anxiety for no reason.

An idea struck me then. I would pretend to take the medication. I would fool my parents. That way they would leave me alone. So I agreed.

My mother came to my room that night after dinner to give me the medication.

I pretended to pop the pill in my mouth, after which I drank water. But the pill had never left my hand. I had wedged it tightly between my thumb and forefinger, and after I pretended to swallow it, I concealed it in the pockets of my shorts. When she left, I took it out and put it in my pen stand on the desk.

Then I sat down to work on the essay I had to submit the next day. I couldn't concentrate. My thoughts kept going back to what had happened on the stage. I remembered Joseph. I was angry that I had suddenly seen him in the audience like that. But then, who knows, perhaps it was a surprise for him too. After I had dropped out of MBA, I hadn't kept in touch with anybody from my class. Nobody knew that I had been admitted to NMHI. My mother had handled the phone calls whenever anyone had called. I had not bothered or worried about it.

I also thought about Vaibhav. I missed him badly now. I hoped he would be back at some point. His presence had been comforting. Then another thought struck me. Vaibhav didn't know about Joseph. He had reacted so badly when I had told him about Abhi, how could I even mention Joseph? How?

I was caught between the devil and the deep blue sea.

18
Coming Back to Life

When I went back to college, I knew people were still talking about what happened on stage that day. Walking into college was like walking around naked. I felt vulnerable, exposed, ashamed. It had been three days since the festival had ended and people were still not tired of discussing it. It was becoming increasingly hard for me to endure this. Each time I walked past a group, I could hear the whispers, and then the sudden silence as I got closer. I didn't know how long this would go on. I wondered at times if I was imagining it. Was my mind playing tricks on me? Maybe no one was talking about it, and my humiliation had been so much that now I had started imagining slights where there were none. But when I saw Parul's and Janki's reactions, I knew it was real. Not imagined. Not inside my head. It was happening, and they were aware of it.

Parul and Janki tried to make me feel better. They would talk loudly to try and distract me whenever we passed groups of people. But nothing could mask the venom of the chatter about me.

It was Janki who finally addressed them. She lost her cool when it happened the fourth time that day. She walked up to the gang we had just passed.

'What were you talking about? Why don't you tell it to our face?' she asked.

'What? We were not talking about you,' a girl said. But she was shifty and avoided looking Janki in the eye.

I pulled Janki's arm. 'Let's go,' I said. I was embarrassed beyond words. I did not want Janki to fight my battles for me. But she wouldn't let it go.

'*Dekh, jyada shani mat ban,*' she said in true filmi style, wagging her index finger at them. 'And remember one thing, Ankita at least had the guts to *go up* on stage and *face* such a big crowd. You should have heard her speak in the semi-finals and quarter-finals. Maybe you would not be this stupid then,' she said.

The group of girls was stunned. So was Parul. I was taken aback too. I had no idea Janki had it in her to confront someone like this.

Then Janki shouted, 'This is no way to behave! Gossiping about someone's accident. Shame on you, girls. If we don't support our own college-mates, who will?' Her voice rang loud and clear across the college corridors. Everyone who was standing there that day heard her. It must have struck a chord, because the whispers stopped after that.

'Thanks, Janki. But you didn't have to do that,' I told her later.

'Arrey! How could I not? They don't know how good you are. The fools. And talking behind your back! At least they should have the guts to say it to your face.'

Secretly I was grateful to Janki, of course. Over the next few days, things almost returned to normal. *Almost.*

'Listen, Ankita, what is the deal with you and Joseph?' Parul asked me out of the blue while sipping sugarcane juice.

I choked on the juice I was sipping. I didn't expect such a direct question, that too from Parul. I had thought meeting Joseph that day outside the auditorium would be the end of that, and we could move on.

'What?' I asked when I managed to regain my composure.

'There is *something*. I can see that,' Parul said.

'Why? Why do you say that?' I asked, hoping her answer would be innocuous. Something casual I could brush aside easily, and then carry on as though she had never asked the question. But it was not. She was very serious when she spoke.

'Ankita, I saw the way you reacted when you met Joseph that day outside the auditorium. And he says he knows you from before. You are acting very strange!' she said.

'Yes, I do know him. But there is nothing between him and me,' I said.

My heart jumped into my mouth at what she said next.

'Why then does he want to meet you so badly?' she asked. 'He is really desperate to meet you.'

'How do you know?'

'He has been pestering Freddy to ask me to ask you. He says he just wants to meet one time.'

Hell. This was the last thing I needed. I did not want to meet Joseph. I just wanted him to vanish from my life and leave me in peace.

'I am involved... with someone,' I said lamely, not knowing how to finish the sentence.

'That same guy you asked our advice on? That irritating guy who keeps coming to your house?' Janki said.

'He isn't irritating. I think he is rather sweet,' I found myself defending Vaibhav.

'Oho! From "irritating" to "rather sweet"! You made up with him, didn't you? You took the first step towards the Ankita-Vaibhav blockbuster. Admit it,' Janki said.

'No, nothing like that! It's been days since I saw him,' I said truthfully.

'Then what's the problem in meeting Joseph? The guy is very keen, Ankita. Meet him once please. At least Freddy will leave me in peace then.'

'I don't have anything to tell him,' I tried protesting.

But Parul wouldn't let go.

'Okay, then meet him and tell him to fuck off, and leave you alone. Once he hears it from you, he will have closure. Just go your separate ways after that,' Parul said.

And so I agreed to meet Joseph. It was another mistake I was making. But I thought if I refused, Parul would dig deeper. I didn't want to tell her what happened. I didn't want anything from my past to be revealed. If I met Joseph, I could quickly close it.

'Alright then. I will meet him. But where?' I asked Parul.

'He said he would wait for you outside college tomorrow, before class starts. He suggested you meet at around 11.00,' said Parul.

I told her I would be there.

'New love story?' asked Janki, raising her eyebrows.

'*No* love story,' I retorted.

●

Back in class, Mrs Hayden was handing out our essays. She had graded them and written her comments in the margins. My heart sank when I got my essay back. I had got an E, the lowest I ever got. Ever since the course started, I had got nothing less than A or A+. The lowest I had got was B+. My grade came as a shocker. What was worse, Mrs Hayden had scribbled in the margin that I was to meet her in the staffroom after class.

I had thought that I had written the essay quite well. I hadn't expected such a low grade at all. I was so distraught over my marks that I couldn't focus on the lecture that day. I found my mind wandering. The taunting voice inside my head started its usual cacophony.

You are a failure.

You can't even write.

Your essay is rubbish.

You will fail.

You will be laughed at.

My thoughts had come back to maul my brain. They played on a loop, shutting out Mrs Hayden's voice, shutting out the classroom, shutting out everything else. It was a frightening place to be trapped in. I wanted to get out. I wanted to stop the thoughts. I wanted to focus on what Mrs Hayden was saying. But. I. Couldn't. My brain had started to churn again. I felt helpless in the grip of it. I was carrying my *LIFE'S LITTLE NOTES* with me in my bag. I took it out and opened it. I needed it. I *needed* to write in it.

So sitting in the class, surrounded by my classmates, with Mrs Hayden's voice in the background lecturing us, I wrote **Note 5**.

Failure hurts. Failure is people judging you, and telling you that you are not good enough for whatever standards they have set. Failure in exams means you were not able to retain the information asked in the question paper. Does it mean you are stupid in some way? NO. But that exactly is the problem. Our parents, our teachers and our friends judge us by these failures. We absorb that subconsciously and start thinking of our worth in terms of the marks we get, and later on by the money we make. If we get great marks, we are successful. If we have a big house, a fancy car, we are successful. If not, we are failures.

The real danger, however, is when we buy into all of it and begin to judge ourselves by these so-called failures of ours.

Don't let these failures define you. You are beyond that. You are much more than the times you have failed. You are more than the grades you are given. You may have failed multiple times. So what?

There are no grades given for how sensitive a person is. There are no grades given for how kind a person is, or how helpful or how funny. There are no grades for the degree of friendship you carefully cultivate over years. No grades for loving. No grades for laughing.

And yet, friendship, laughter, love, kindness, hope, joy, generosity – these are the most important things in life. And there is not a single grade to measure that.

There are no grades given for LIFE.

Parul peeped into my notebook where I was scribbling furiously.

'What are you writing so intently?' she asked.

'Nothing,' I said and shut my notebook.

'Listen, what grade did you get for the essay?' I asked her.

'It was a difficult assignment. I got only a C+. What about you?' asked Parul.

'See!' I said and showed her my paper.

'Oh, no,' Parul said.

Mrs Hayden was staring at us now, as we were whispering. That was definitely not acceptable in her class. So we quickly shut up and focused on the lecture for the rest of the time.

After the lecture ended, I met Mrs Hayden in the staffroom.

'Hello, Ankita. Come, have a seat!' She indicated a chair opposite her. 'Do you know why I wanted to see you?' she asked.

'Does it have something to do with my essay?' I asked her.

'Well, yes and no,' said Mrs Hayden as she removed her glasses and wiped them with a cloth.

Her deep-set eyes seemed to pierce my very soul. I had never realised that her eyes were a sable brown, and they shone with wisdom and understanding. I waited for her to go on.

'I can sense from your essay that you were very disturbed when you wrote it. Ankita, usually your work is exemplary. Is there something troubling you?'

There is such a lot troubling me.

I struggle every day to control my thoughts.

I am fighting a daily battle with my mind.

I shook my head. 'No, Mrs Hayden,' I said.

'The incident on the stage perhaps?' she prodded gently.

'I was upset then. But I don't think I would let that affect the quality of my work,' I said.

'Ankita, why in the world then did you turn in such shoddy work? I expected more from you. Nothing in this essay is original. You are merely echoing someone else's thoughts. I thought I would check with you if you copied this from somewhere.'

I was aghast at the question.

'No, Mrs Hayden, these are my own words.'

'You haven't mentioned a citation. There is no indication whatsoever of your source materials. I do not see any examples or original observations. Also, the information that is presented here is not organised. It is just a jumbled mess. Would you like to tell me what happened?'

'I'm sorry, I guess I was distracted,' I mumbled.

'Do you want to tell me what is troubling you? I used to be a student counsellor in an earlier avatar and hold a master's degree in counselling and human psychology. When a student is troubled, I can usually tell. That's why I asked you to see me,' Mrs Hayden said. Her voice calmed my nerves.

For a second, I was tempted to open up and tell her all my troubles. She seemed concerned and willing to help. But I knew I had to keep it all to myself. What could Mrs Hayden tell me that I didn't already know? I had all the answers really. They were right there in my notebook, which was in my bag, even as I spoke to her. I also didn't want my disorder or what I had gone through to be my excuse for *not* doing well. I wanted to succeed despite that. So I just told her I would focus more the next time, and try harder. I said that nothing really was troubling me.

Was it sadness I saw in Mrs Hayden's eyes or did I imagine it? I wasn't sure. But I walked out, hugging my notebook and my secrets to myself.

19

Somebody that I Used to Know

Once again, I couldn't sleep the whole night. Once again, I tossed and turned. The talk with Mrs Hayden had disturbed me. I also knew I must meet Joseph and I dreaded it. Both these things stole the sleep from my eyes.

It struck me then that perhaps I should have taken the medication my mother brought me faithfully every night. My pen-stand was now full of the pills I'd been depositing in it every night after I pretended to pop them. Maybe they would help me to sleep. It was too late for that now. I had to make do with the measly amount of sleep that I got. The last time I had glanced at the clock, it had said 4.30 a.m., which meant I had slept for barely two-and-a-half hours.

The moment my bedside clock rang its alarm, I jumped out of bed. I did not want my parents to worry about the duration of my sleep. I decided I wouldn't tell them about my insomnia, lest they insist on more medication. I wanted to be in control of it. I would take it when I felt I needed it, not when my mother forced me to.

'Slept well, Ankita?' my father asked as we ate breakfast.

'Yes, really well,' I lied.

'You look a little tired. Do you feel thirstier than usual or do you have loose motions or anything like that? Notice anything unusual?' my mother asked.

'No, nothing. I feel great!' I lied smoothly and gave a big smile.

'Your mood seems to have improved too. I think the medication is working.' My father was happy. I think my mother was convinced too.

'If you notice any side-effects, let us know, Ankita. Dr Neeraj specifically said to make a note of any side-effects,' my mother said.

'Dr Neeraj ?'

'Dr Neeraj Ramiah is the local doctor here in Bombay referred to by Dr Madhusudan. He is very well-qualified,' my mother said.

The familiar way in which she spoke of him made me instantly alert.

'You went and met him?' I asked.

'Yes, we had to discuss the present situation,' my father said.

I felt terribly betrayed. My parents had gone and met a psychiatrist and discussed my 'case' without even informing me. How could they do that? At the very least, they should have checked with me. Here they were 'reporting' my behaviour to him, and there he was 'assessing' me without even meeting me. I felt it was not right. I did not want to sound angry in case my parents thought I was losing control again. 'Why didn't either of you check with me first?' I asked, trying to keep the hurt out of my voice.

'Oh, do you want to meet him?' my mother asked.

'Ma, it is not that I want to meet him. But I feel I ought to have been given the choice,' I said.

'Ankita, Dr Madhusudan briefed him in detail, and it is Dr Madhusudan who was conferring with him as he was leaving the country. We met him because we wanted to see who we were dealing with, and also because Dr Madhusudan had spoken highly of him. I felt there was no need for you to come in for a consultation, as I did not want to create stress for you. After what you have been through, we thought a follow-up with a new doctor might be stressful,' my father explained.

His explanation made sense. But I still got a distinct feeling of being 'spied on' or 'watched' by my own parents for the first signs of psychiatric trouble. It made me feel violated.

I knew they were doing it for my own good, because they loved me deeply and because they were watching out for me. Yet it made me feel like an animal in captivity being closely watched by the caregivers. I detested it. I also knew that there was no way around it, and no easy solution. It depressed me though to think about it, adding to my growing sense of despondency. Nothing in my life was going well. I was trying in every possible way. I was fighting as hard as I could. But nothing I did seemed to be adequate. I was losing hope and becoming disillusioned. Life stretched out in front of me like a vast barren desert that I would have to cross on my own.

I told my parents that I would have to reach college in the morning that day as I had to look up some books in the library. Since they were used to my going to the library regularly, they nodded without a second thought.

•

I glanced at my watch as I walked towards the college from Churchgate station. I was early. I had a good fifteen minutes before Joseph met me at 11.00. I also wondered what I would do in case he was late. I would have even more time to kill then. I decided I would wait in the library, and come downstairs at 11.00.

But I need not have worried. True to his word, Joseph was waiting outside the college when I reached. He was early. He broke into a big smile when he saw me.

'Hey! So good to see you,' he greeted me. He had dressed up smartly in a white formal shirt, and even tucked it into his jeans.

He wore light brown suede leather shoes. His hair was still a curly mop, just the way it had always been. He looked delighted to see me, his eyes crinkling as he smiled.

'Hi,' I replied, my voice tired. I was wary of what he wanted from me.

He noticed my lack of enthusiasm straightaway.

'I am sorry if I forced you to meet me like this. I just... just had to meet you, Ankita,' he said.

'It's fine,' I replied.

'There's a new café which has opened near Rustom's. Shall we go there? Or do you want to eat ice cream at Rustom's?'

I shrugged. It made no difference to me. I just wanted to get it over with. My eyes were burning due to the lack of sleep. My head was beginning to hurt too.

'You look like you are studying too much, Ankita. Your eyes have bags under them! Are you fine?' asked Joseph.

'Yes, but thank you for that magnificent compliment,' I said, sullen and sarcastic.

Joseph missed the sarcasm and laughed. 'You still look gorgeous, Ankita,' he said.

'Thanks,' I replied listlessly.

We walked to the new café that Joseph had suggested. He was chatty as we walked, telling me about a movie he'd seen, and asking me if I had seen any movies. I listened to all that he had to say, and then said that I didn't get time to watch movies.

We reached the café. The tables were bright yellow with colourful abstract geometric designs stencilled on them. The lime green wrought iron chairs added to the fun, trendy ambience. Instantly, I felt old and jaded.

'What will you have?' asked Joseph as the waiter approached us.

'You order for me,' I said. I didn't care.

Joseph ordered two cold coffees for us.

Then he asked me the question I knew he had wanted to ask ever since he saw me on stage.

'So, what happened?' he said simply.

I pretended not to understand, even though I knew very well what he was talking about. I was stalling for time, forming the answers in my own head, and carefully considering what and how much I should share with him. The waiter served us our coffees. I stirred mine. The ice cubes clinked against each other.

'What do you mean "what happened"? Nothing happened,' I replied, as I sipped my coffee and looked him in the eye.

That flustered him a bit. Serves him right, I thought. He had no business forcing me to meet him like this.

'I mean, why did you drop out of MBA?' Joseph wasn't willing to let it go.

'Got bored of it,' I replied.

'So, just like that, you dropped out?'

'Yes, Joseph, just like that,'

'Come on, I don't believe that even for a second.' Joseph shook his head.

'That's up to you. I hated the course. I decided to pursue another one,' I said.

'But… you left me high and dry,' he accused.

That angered me.

'What do you mean high and dry? Did I have sex with you?'

'Er… no… But—'

'But what?' I interrupted him, challenging him to finish that sentence. I did not like his line of questioning. I just wanted to close this for good.

'Come on, Ankita. You know what we shared. Why are you refusing to acknowledge it?' Joseph persisted.

'We shared nothing! A car ride. That's all we shared.'

'How can you forget? You were dancing on the parapet. Remember?'

Joseph was dredging up every past memory he could and was dangling it in front of me like bait. I refused to bite.

'So? What are you implying? That I owe you my life?' I countered.

'No. No... Of course not. I thought... well, I thought we had something. You kissed me in the cab. You told me you loved me. And then without a warning, you disappeared. I went mad trying to contact you. I must have spoken to your mother at least twenty times. I even came to your home. I found your address from the college office records. I bribed the peon. But then I found your door locked. I came back three more times. The last time I went there, they told me you all had shifted out. I tried so hard, Ankita. At least tell me the truth. Please don't pretend that whatever was there never existed.'

I had to tell him then. The look of bewilderment and hurt on his face was too much to shoulder. I could see the anguish there. I had not done right by telling him nothing. If someone had done the same to me, I would have found it hard to bear it. I felt guilty for what I had put him through, even though it was inadvertent. He needed closure as much as I did. So I braced myself and decided to tell him the truth.

'Listen, I am terribly sorry about disappearing from your life like that,' I began. Then I explained to him about bipolar disorder, just like how Dr Madhusudan had explained it to me. I told him about the mania, and how it was my condition at that time, and that was what made me behave so bizarrely. I told him about Abhi and how the guilt still ate me up after all this while. I told him about how I had seen Abhi in him that day. I told him how my panic attacks had started soon after and how frightened I was. I told him about the psychiatrists we consulted. I told him about the hopelessness that had engulfed me. I also told him about the suicide attempts.

But this time, I did not cry. I had already narrated all of this to Vaibhav. Now saying it all a second time to Joseph, I discovered, was not so hard. I narrated it like it was somebody else's story. I had learnt to distance myself from it.

Joseph looked shocked when I finished.

Then he said, 'So you felt nothing for me?' He looked like a child then.

But I couldn't lie to him.

'Joseph, I am really sorry I hurt you. I wasn't myself. It didn't mean anything. I am so sorry,' I said.

His shoulders slumped when he heard that. He looked away and blinked. We both sat quietly for a while. He was perhaps taking in all that I had said. For him, it was all sudden, whereas I had months and months to process all of this. Then he said, 'I am so, so sorry you had to go through all of this. I feel so bad for you.'

The last thing I wanted was his pity. I didn't need that. I didn't want him to feel sorry for me.

'Don't feel bad for me. It made me stronger. What happened, happened. If that had not, I would have never joined the creative writing course,' I said.

'That's true. You know that's what is amazing about you, Ankita. You take every adversity and turn it on its head. You are a winner,' he said.

If only he knew. If he only he knew how much I battled with myself on a daily basis. If only he knew how difficult it was. If only he knew how I was filled with self-doubt, how I lie awake at nights worrying too much and sleeping too little.

I didn't tell him any of it. He only saw my outer self.

'Thanks,' I said simply.

'Listen, I want you to know that I am always here for you. Call me anytime, okay? I mean it. Day or night, just reach out, and I shall come wherever you are,' he said. He scribbled his number on a piece of paper and handed it to me.

I took it and put it in my bag.

'Don't lose it, okay? And can I have your number? I would very much like to take you out again,' he said.

Uh-oh. This wasn't going the way I expected at all. He was now asking me for a second date. He had considered this meeting of ours a date. Now that I had told him all of this, I thought I had closed the loop. It was a relief for me to explain why I had kissed him and how I hadn't meant it. I thought I had made it clear where I stood.

But it looked like Joseph had missed the point entirely. He took my long explanation as a sign that I trusted him. I think he even appointed himself my 'protector' and 'guardian'. I didn't need that at all.

'Joseph, I know you mean well. But I am sorry, I can't go on a date with you,' I said.

'And, if I may, can I ask why? ' he said.

I told him the same line I had told Abhi all those years ago. At that time too, I was talking about Vaibhav. And ironically, I was talking about Vaibhav again.

'I already have a boyfriend,' I said.

20
Where's the Party

When I got back to college, I tore the paper with Joseph's number into tiny bits and threw it into the trash. I had a full-blown headache now. The Joseph encounter had been very stressful. It felt as though a tiny person was inside my skull, hitting it with a hammer. I wished I could just run back home and rest. But since it was the last day of college, I couldn't miss it. If we missed college on the re-opening day after holidays, or on the day just before the vacation started, there was a hefty fine to pay. Our term was ending and our holidays were starting the next day. Therefore, I was forced to attend.

Both Parul and Janki wanted to know how my meeting with Joseph went.

'It was okay. I now have a headache,' I said.

Parul laughed. 'Not tonight dear, I have a headache. Only married couples say that, you know.'

'I really do, Parul. My head is pounding,' I said.

'Here, have this,' said Janki rummaging in her bag and producing a pill.

'Janki carries an entire first-aid kit in that bag of hers. Ask for anything and she will produce it. Her bag is a magic box,' Parul commented.

I was grateful for the pill, and took it immediately.

'Thanks, you are a life-saver,' I told her.

They wouldn't let it go though.

'So now tell us, what did Joseph say?' asked Janki.

How could I tell them what I had told Joseph? How would they ever understand what a messed-up situation it was? This was not really a date as far as I was concerned. I didn't see it the way they saw it. But they wouldn't get that. For them, and for most people, if a guy and girl met at a coffee shop alone, it was a date. So I told them what they wanted to hear.

'The usual – that I look pretty and he wants a second date with me,' I said giving them a choice tidbit. It was the truth, but only a part of it. He had indeed said both of those things. I was pleased with myself for thinking of a clever reply to Janki's question.

'So did you say yes then?' Parul asked.

'No. I said I couldn't.'

'Why not?' Janki persisted.

'He isn't my type,' I said, hoping they would stop this.

'What is your type? Specify in five hundred words and elucidate your writing with examples to support your arguments,' said Parul, imitating Mrs Hayden.

'Ha! And will you grade it?' I asked, smiling in genuine amusement for the first time that day.

'Arrey, for this question, we need practicals, not theory. There is no use of grades for this. You just tell your specifications, and we will produce the guy for you to date,' said Janki.

Parul laughed at that. I managed a smile.

'Tell us what you seek in a guy,' Janki insisted.

I had no idea really. I hadn't thought of what I wanted in a guy. I could think of a hundred things I *didn't* want. And right now all I wanted was for Joseph to stay away from me. I didn't want another

Abhi-like situation waiting to explode in my face. That single one had scarred me for a lifetime and I still carried the weight inside of me.

Fortunately for me, Mrs Hayden walked into our classroom just then and I was saved from the trouble of answering.

'Greetings, everyone,' Mrs Hayden began in her soft voice. There was complete silence as soon as she walked in. She kept her file of papers on the table and sat down. Then she said, 'I am very disappointed by the quality of work that has been turned in for the last few assignments. When you write, you must remember to write effectively. You have to voice *your* opinions. There has to be originality. That can come only when you spend time with yourselves. As we go on with the course, the topics are going to get harder. I expect each of you to step up. Think about what made you take this course in the first place. Think about why you want to be a writer. You don't have to use bombastic language or big words. That is not what grabs the reader. It is saying exactly what you mean, narrating your truth, in the best possible way only you can.'

She then handed the papers to the girl sitting on the front bench and asked her to pass them around.

'This is your holiday homework. I want you all to reflect on this and write from your hearts,' she said. Each student took a paper and passed the bundle to the others. I wanted to get good grades again. Mrs Hayden's assessment of my last essay had come as a big blow to my confidence in my abilities regarding this course. 'Uninspired', 'Not original', 'Not what I expected', 'Jumbled mess': these were the terms she used. Even though I had performed well till now, this one assessment had thrown me off-balance. If there was one thing that I was on top of, it had been Mrs Hayden's class. I submitted the assignments on time, read up on everything assigned, worked hard. I had indeed toiled over the last essay too. But after the talk with Mrs Hayden, I began doubting myself.

All the other assignments for which you got good grades were a fluke.

You don't have any talent as a writer.

You are a sham, a masquerader.

You are capable of nothing.

Worthless... worthless... worthless.

My inner voice started its chorus again.

The terrible thing was I began believing it. Perhaps all the submissions I had done so far were just a stroke of luck. My confidence was shaken. For a course like Creative Writing, it was a death-knell. The bundle of papers had reached our desk now. Parul took three sheets and handed the rest to the bench behind us. She gave me and Janki our assignments. When I read it, my immediate reaction was panic.

If you could go back in time, what would you change about your life?

We were to write a three thousand-word essay on this. I sat with my head in my hands. What could I write? I definitely couldn't write the truth. The truth was: I wanted to change everything from the day I joined that college in Kerala. I wouldn't have met Abhi then. I wouldn't then see Abhi in every guy who liked me. I would not have this baggage to carry, whose weight sometimes was unbearable. I would not have told Joseph I loved him when I didn't. I would have stopped my mania. I would change that I got bipolar disorder, and had been admitted in a mental hospital to recover. I would change the fact that my parents put me there and *left*.

I fought on my own. I was given electric shocks. I was an aberration, a freak. I would change all of that.

But life doesn't really give us choices, does it? We make do with what we are given. And sometimes even that is taken away.

I don't know for how long I sat like that. I was lost in my thoughts. But suddenly, Parul nudged me.

'What happened, Ankita? Are you alright? Why are you sitting with your head in your hands?' Mrs Hayden was standing next to our desk now. I flushed when I heard her say my name. I hated being called out like this. Everyone in the class turned to look at me.

'I am sorry, Mrs Hayden. I have a terrible headache today,' I said.

'Oh, dear. Do you want to go to the college dispensary and take something?' she asked.

'No, Mrs Hayden. I will be fine. I took a medicine just now,' I said.

By the end of the lecture my headache had subsided, but the sinking feeling the thought of the new assignment had brought on did not.

Everyone was in a mood to celebrate as Mrs Hayden had let us off early.

'Let's go somewhere and have fun. We won't be meeting for at least three weeks now,' Janki said. The assignment didn't seem to bother anyone but me.

'Come on, let's go shopping,' Parul said.

Janki agreed.

'By the way, I am throwing a party on Friday. A surprise birthday party for Freddy. I want you both to come. Don't say no. We will have the whole house to ourselves, as my mom is travelling on a shoot out of town,' Parul said.

'I will not miss it! I need new clothes. Let's go to Fashion Street,' Janki declared.

'I thought your darzi comes home and makes clothes for you?' Parul asked.

'He does. But this is too short a notice for my darzi. Parul, you sprung this one all of a sudden,' Janki said.

'I too didn't know till last evening. Mom told me then that she was going. That was when I thought of the surprise party,' Parul said as we walked out of the classroom.

I didn't want to go shopping with them, nor did I want to attend the party Parul was throwing. I had had enough excitement for the day with the whole Joseph thing; I just wanted to go home. I was tired, exhausted. So I excused myself. I told them I wanted to go to the library and borrow some books, so I would have enough books for the term holidays.

Parul and Janki tried to convince me to go along with them.

'You are already doing so well. How much more will you study? How many more books will you read?' Janki tried to persuade me.

But I told them my headache had come back and I needed to rest.

'So I will see you at my party then? Don't miss it, okay?' said Parul. She didn't let me go till she extricated a promise from me that I would make it. I wasn't sure, even though I told her I would, just to get her off my back.

Mrs Asthana was happy to see me. She asked how I was doing and how Euphoria went. She seemed to be the only one in the college who hadn't witnessed my humiliation that day.

'I am fine, Mrs Asthana. Euphoria was fantastic,' I said. I told her I wanted to borrow some books for the holidays.

I went through all the bookshelves in the non-fiction section, rummaging for books about dreams and sleeping. I found a dream dictionary. I wanted to know what my nightmares meant. I also borrowed a book on sleep disorders. I wanted to know why I wasn't sleeping at all these days, and how I could sleep better. I combed the library shelves, found some fiction books that looked interesting, and a couple on effective writing.

'Happy holidays to you!' I said as I placed all the books on the counter for Mrs Asthana to issue.

'I guess you know the library stays open throughout the holidays,' she said, looking at the number of books I had borrowed. I usually borrowed two. But today I had borrowed eight books, two fiction and the rest reference books, which was the full quota that we were allowed to.

'Oh, I didn't know that! ' I said. 'So, don't you get any holidays then?'

'The staff is working. They have a training programme going on. We get only the usual Saturdays and Sundays off.'

'So does that mean I can come to the library if I want to?'

'Of course. You are welcome anytime,' said Mrs Asthana. 'Are you sure you want them all? Aren't they a bit heavy to lug around?'

I had spent at least a good half hour finding these books. I also wasn't sure if I would actually be coming to college during the holidays. So I told her I wanted to borrow them and that I would take all of them. The books did not fit into my college backpack. Mrs Asthana put them into a plastic cover and handed them to me.

I went home with a feeling of exhaustion and sadness. I couldn't say whether one was the cause of the other. I didn't know what to write for the essay Mrs Hayden had assigned. I did not know what to tell Vaibhav about the whole Joseph incident. I also felt bad that I had hurt Joseph for no fault of his, by telling him I did not have any feelings for him.

You always hurt the ones who love you.

You let people down.

You are not a writer.

The voices in my head were only too happy to agree with me.

Nothing in my life was going according to plan. When I had walked out of NMHI, it was with hope in my heart, a song on my lips. The song was only a distant memory now and I had long forgotten the words of the song. Hell, I did not even remember the tune. Hope was slowly dying too. The business of daily life had sucked it all out of me, and left me bereft. This was so much harder than I expected. The thoughts engulfed me like black smoke now, and I couldn't see beyond them.

I took great care to hide my real feelings from my parents. I ate with them, I discussed the TV shows, I asked my father about his work, I talked to my mother about the voluntary residents' association she was a part of, and I chatted easily about everything under the sun. They had no idea what I felt inside. I wore masks; if you removed one mask, you'd just find another.

I was terrified that if I didn't pretend to be normal, they would drag me back to the psychiatrist. That was the last thing I wanted. I'd had enough of mental hospitals and psychiatrists and medication.

I just wanted to live an ordinary life, with no complications. I didn't want a 'perfect life'. Somewhere halfway was okay too.

After dinner that night, when I retreated to the safety of my room, I opened *LIFE'S LITTLE NOTES* and wrote **Note 6**.

Often we are forced to do what we do not want to do. We are forced to go to places we do not want to go to. We are forced to smile when we feel like screaming. These are social obligations we perform for the sake of others. We want to fit in. We want to be accepted by others. We want to be liked. We want to be loved. So we put our wishes aside and perform what's expected. They aren't big things. They are little things. Little things that bring joy to others.

When it comes to the big things, it is important to speak the truth, no matter how hard it is, how unpleasant it is. If we do not speak the truth in the big things, then we end up hurting ourselves.

The small things and the big things are what make up life. We need to be wise enough to make a distinction between what is a small thing and what is a big thing. Sometimes a small thing to us is a big thing to others. At other times, a big thing to us is a small thing to others.

If we have people in our life who treat our big things as their big things, and who understand how big are our small things to us, then we are fortunate. I think when people are on the same wavelength, they completely get each other.

Big or small, it doesn't matter as long you have each other. You know that the other person will be there for you – to see you through the big and small things in life. And that you will be there for them too.

It is rare, but if you have it, you are blessed. If you have it, you are the richest person on earth.

I read the note. Then I decided I would attend Parul's party. It meant a lot to her. It was a big thing for her, but a small thing for me, and I would do it.

21

Falling Off

Sometimes, no matter how hard you try, you fail. If what you attempt to achieve is something concrete – for instance, getting a certain percent of marks in an exam – then there is a measurable goal before you. You take certain steps such as making a study time-table, planning your free time and solving question papers, which will ensure a better rate of success. But if your goal is something abstract and not so clearly defined, your task becomes that much tougher.

I was trying hard to shake off the feelings of extreme sadness I was now wearing as a cloak around me. No matter how hard I tried, I kept failing.

Every morning I would wake up determined to seize the day, determined to be happy. I would tell myself that I was fortunate to be out of NMHI, I was blessed to have loving parents, I was lucky to be doing a course I wanted to do. But none of that helped. The harder I tried to fight the blanket of hopelessness that engulfed me, the more I got caught in the misery of it. Like trying to crawl out of quicksand. I was trapped, and no matter what I did, I was sinking. I had no interest in anything. I didn't want to touch my course work. I was afraid of Mrs Hayden's assignment. I tried to read the novels I had borrowed from the library, but the words made no sense. I gave up after about 50-60 pages. I had no idea where the plot was headed or what the characters were up to. I tried to watch movies with my parents, and fake-laughed along with them at all the right places. But only I was privy to what consumed me. A veil had dropped between me and the world.

I pretended so well though. My parents were elated that everything was finally going well. They were relieved that my days of psychiatric care were far behind. I let them believe it, not wanting to burst their bubble.

●

Sleep was elusive. However tightly I shut my eyes, it just wouldn't come. It had been like this for the past many nights. I was now tired of trying. Instead of praying for sleep, I decided I would read. I took out the book about sleep disorders, which I had borrowed from the library, and began to read. I learnt that lack of sleep could slow down the cognitive process – making us testy, irritable and short-tempered. One wouldn't be alert. It would impair attention, concentration and focus. It would also cause umpteen health problems like heart disease, heart attack and even diabetes, as the human body's reaction to sleep loss caused insulin resistance. It made me sit up and take notice. I read on, finishing the book in a few hours.

Even a single night's lack of sleep set us up to react more strongly and impulsively to negative situations. And if we operated on a chronic sleep-debt, then we fell prey to heightened emotional reactivity. I learnt that sleep-deprivation increased the activity in the amygdala, which was a part of the brain that controlled our immediate emotional reactions. If we slept less, then amygdala went into overdrive, and hampered communication with the prefrontal cortex – the part of the brain that handled a lot of complex tasks and also handled impulsiveness. I absorbed it all.

No wonder I was feeling the way I did! It was all down to my amygdala. Sleep-deprivation, I read, led to repetitive negative thinking. The mind gets stuck in a negative place, going back to it over and over again. A difficult cycle to break.

It was a moment of enlightenment for me. All I had to do was fix my sleep, and perhaps I would feel better. But the problem was I did not know how to fix this. I knew the cause now, but not the solution.

There were some suggestions in the book: stopping caffeine after 6.00 p.m., going to bed at the same time every night, creating a routine, relaxation techniques, using essential oils like lavender. I tried some of the techniques, but they did not work for me. I still couldn't sleep, and with each passing night, it was slowly getting out of hand.

I had been careful to leap out of bed each morning when the alarm rang, and this led to further sleep loss. If I had been honest and told my parents, perhaps they would have let me sleep for a while longer, but I was terrified of the psychiatric implications they were sure to drag into it. I was also resisting the medication strongly. The last time I had taken it, it had numbed my senses to such an extent that *all* my thoughts had vanished. I had been trapped in a thoughtless, wordless world and it was the most terrifying thing I had ever experienced. It was worse than hell. I did not want to go back there at any cost. If sleep-deprivation was the price I had to pay for it, I would pay it.

My parents did not notice anything unusual about my sleep patterns at all. They would ask how I was doing, and I would lie, every single day. The dark circles under my eyes were carefully concealed with makeup. I applied it cleverly, hiding the smudged blue under my eyes. It was only when I washed my face at night before going to bed that I saw how frayed my face was. I looked haunted. The spark had gone out of my eyes.

●

When I got ready for Parul's party for Freddy, I put on two layers of concealer under my eyes, plus mascara and eyeliner. By the time I had put on the whole makeup, my face actually looked radiant. I had a knee-length deep brown flowing chiffon dress from the pre-NMHI era. It had been a long time since I wore anything other than my usual jeans. I tried it on, and it still fit well. So I decided to wear it, and left my hair loose. The last time I had made this much effort was when I had gone on that date with Vaibhav. I remembered him with a pang; we weren't even on talking terms now.

'Is that really you, Ankita?' my father praised when I emerged from my room.

'Around what time can we expect you back? And can you leave Parul's number with us?' asked my mother, ever-practical, always expecting the worst.

'Ma, don't worry. I will be home by 11.30 p.m. latest. Here is the number.' I wrote down the number and left it beside the phone.

'Listen, if it is that late, I can come and pick you up,' Dad offered.

'I will find my way home. I will call you if I need anything. I have the house key. Both of you please go to sleep, and I shall let myself in,' I said.

I had expected my mother to be concerned about my travelling alone late at night, but surprisingly, she wasn't too worried. The daughters of many of the women in the building worked late, and came home past midnight. My mother had discussed it with them, and they had all assured her that Bombay was a wonderful city that way, and there would still be people travelling at that time in the night in the trains. It was not a city that slept.

It was around 8.30 p.m. that I got off the train and made my way to Parul's place. The party was in full swing by the time I got there; I could hear the music pulsate in the elevator itself. When I rang the bell, Parul opened the door with a drink in her hand and hugged me like she hadn't seen me for years.

'Ankita, my friend! I knew you would not let me down. Welcome!' she yelled over the din of the music. The music was so loud, it made my ears tingle. It was a catchy number and I recognised the band as well as the song – *All that she wants* by Ace of Base. I could hear people talking too, despite the music, also their laughter. The atmosphere was charged with the energy of the young. So many were smoking inside, and I could make out that it wasn't just tobacco. The smell of marijuana hung in the air. I was certain there were other drugs too. Parul had also put up colourful lights and set up a bar in the drawing room.

Janki was already there. She greeted me and pulled me to Parul's bedroom.

'I have news for you!' she said, her face shiny with joy.

'What?' I asked.

'I am getting engaged next week! I met him today. My parents know the family and we really liked each other,' she said.

'Oh, wow! Congratulations,' I said and shook her hand.

'I am leaving now. He is picking me up!'

I was genuinely pleased for her. She had got what she wanted from life.

'See you, Ankita! Have fun!' she said as she left.

'You too,' I said and meant it.

I looked around for the birthday boy in whose honour Parul had thrown this party. At last I spotted him. Freddy was walking around wearing some kind of a bowler hat and suspenders. He had a drink in his hand, but looked already drunk.

'Happy birthday, Freddy,' I greeted him.

'Hey, Ankita! Thank you. If you are planning to throw up, use the loo, okay?' he said and guffawed at his own joke.

'You know what? I think your hat will hold the puke well. I shall use that,' I retorted. I was tired of his stupid jokes.

'No need to get prickly. I was only kidding,' he said.

'So was I.' I smiled sweetly at him and walked away.

I hated the party. Everyone was drinking and talking animatedly. Some were dancing too. I couldn't stand the smoke, the noise, the crowd. I didn't drink either. Apart from Parul and Janki, I didn't know anyone here. I wondered what would be the polite duration that I could stay and then escape. I went to Parul's balcony. I could hear the music even from the balcony. The song *Now and Forever* by Richard Marx had started playing. I liked Parul's choice of music, and I stood on the balcony inhaling the cool night air. The lights of the city were glittering and the view was a million-dollar one.

Richard Marx's voice came floating out of the windows. The words of the song seemed to be speaking to me.

'Whenever I'm weary
from the battles that rage in my head
you make sense of madness
when my sanity hangs by a thread.'

I thought of Vaibhav as each note of the song rang loud and clear. I felt very alone. Everyone at the party seemed to be with someone. Parul had her Freddy, no matter how obnoxious he was. Janki had also found her Prince Charming. I began missing Vaibhav intensely that very moment. I wished he would talk to me. I wished I could turn back the clock.

Someone tapped me on the shoulder. When I turned around, I froze. It was Joseph. I had completely overlooked the possibility that he could be here.

'So good to see you,' he said as he came closer. His eyes were bloodshot, his hair tousled.

I stepped back, away from the railing, towards the wall.

'Please don't look so frightened. I love you, you know,' he said, as he came towards me and placed both his hands on the wall, imprisoning me between them.

His breath smelled of alcohol and his hair reeked of smoke.

'Joseph, please move. I need to go,' I said.

'I won't hurt you. I just want to talk to you,' he said.

I was scared now. He was clearly not in his senses. I didn't know what to do. I stood very still, my arms hanging limp. My heart pounding.

Calm down... calm down... calm down.

I was too terrified to even close my eyes.

'Look, I have already told you all there is to be told, Joseph,' I said.

'Come on, Ankita! Don't be so hard-hearted. Give me a chance, please...' he whined.

I think he leaned in for a kiss. My head exploded in anger, outrage and fright.

I stretched both my hands and shoved him hard. He went flying across the balcony. I shut my eyes then. I couldn't bear to look.

I was so frightened at the thought that I had pushed him off the balcony.

Murderer... Murderer... Murderer...

The chants started up inside my head. I was too terrified to even scream. First Abhi, then Joseph. This was my worst nightmare coming true.

But then I heard the crash and opened my eyes. Joseph was sprawled opposite me, one hand clutching the railing in fright, and the other outstretched. Behind him, a flowerpot lay shattered.

It had all happened in a flash of a second.

The music stopped then. People had heard the sound and crowded around us. I was breathing hard, too frightened to move.

'It's okay… It's okay… All good, guys,' said Freddy, as he made his way to the balcony and helped Joseph up.

'You are nothing but trouble, aren't you?' Freddy spat the words at me.

'She is a psycho bitch! Tried to push me over the balcony!' Joseph screamed. There was a stunned silence.

But he was not done.

'She has a mental disorder… Just back from a mental asylum! Bloody psycho!' he shouted.

I have no words to describe what happened to me at that instant. I stood there in shocked silence and disbelief. Joseph had just told them my deepest, darkest secret. That which I had told him in confidence was now public knowledge. I felt like I had been raped in front of a crowd. I stood there shaking in fright.

'Deny it, I dare you to. You know you can't. You admitted it yourself!' he roared.

I willed my lips to move. I wanted to laugh it off, to deny it. I wanted to tell them that Joseph was drunk and didn't know what he was saying. But I stood rooted to the spot, my mind a blank.

Freddy spoke then. He killed me with the words he uttered.

'I knew it!' he said. 'She has that unmistakable look of insanity.'

For years afterwards, I would wonder if I looked insane each time I looked in the mirror.

There was a clear note of triumph in his voice as everyone walked away from me, leaving me alone on the balcony.

I was too devastated to react then. I was numb with pain and shock.

But later what would hurt even more than Freddy's words was the fact that Parul too had chosen to walk away with them.

22
Rock Bottom

The pain is debilitating. It sears through every cell, every pore in my body. I cannot bear this. It cuts deep. It cuts slow. It cuts thorough. My heart feels so heavy; it is like I am carrying a lead cannon inside my chest. It is with this pain that I slowly make my way home in a complete state of stupor. I am not aware of leaving the party, walking to the station, getting on the train or walking home. I am not even aware of how I let myself in.

I hear my father calling out from the bedroom, 'Oh, so you reached back early, Ankita?'

I hear myself answering that I did. It sounds like someone else speaking. It sounds as though my voice is coming from far away.

Everything is dark inside my home and I don't switch on the lights. I walk to my room and lie in my bed. The pain has taken over everything. What is worse, it doesn't abate. It keeps growing inside me, engulfing me, swallowing me.

I want to stop this. But even as I try, those words coil themselves around my insides and tighten their hold, till I cannot breathe anymore. I want to stop hurting. I wish I had never gone to that damn party. I wish I had never met any of them – Parul, Freddy, Joseph. I wish I had stayed at home.

This is unbearable. Being me hurts.

Then my thoughts come to torment me a bit more.

Failure.

Freak.

Psycho bitch.

Asylum.

Look of insanity.

They go around in circles. I cannot stop them. I am a failure and a freak and was a mental patient as well. Maybe I still have mental issues. Maybe people looking at me notice it immediately. Maybe there *is* a look of insanity about me. I am filled with self-doubts. I am not sure of anything anymore. There is only one thing I am certain of – that I have failed in every area of my life.

I think about my course. The course work, which once gave me pleasure, now seems like drudgery. It came to me easily earlier. But now I struggle. My professor herself said that my work was unoriginal, uninspired. I do not know how to tackle the new assignment. How can I ever hope to become a writer if I cannot complete one simple writing task? Maybe this course is not for me.

Then I think of Vaibhav. I need him. I need him *now*. Where is he when I need him this badly? One person who promised to be there for me, no matter what. One person who I thought I could depend on. But I had thought wrong. How does someone become so important in your life that your entire physical and emotional well-being depends on their actions? I have failed there too.

I beat myself up over how I handled Vaibhav. At first I was resentful that he was coming home. Then I got carried away with just one date. I should have never given him this much power over me. I should not have depended on him. I should not have shown him my vulnerabilities. By not calling or talking to me and completely ignoring me, he has kicked me where it hurts the most. I don't know what is worse – his distancing words or my foolishness in trusting him.

I feel betrayed as I think about how he charmed his way into my heart. The visits home, the mingling with my parents, the date, the sweet nothings. My parents couldn't have enough of him. Why make promises he couldn't keep?

I want him to come back and tell me that he made a mistake. That he didn't mean to walk away. I think about his words. I want him to tell me that he spoke in anger. I would gladly welcome him back in my life.

But he has done no such thing. My hopes are now crashing, unleashing a fresh wave of pain. I am drowning in the intensity of it all. This is excruciating agony.

'Never belittle love,' Abhi's grandfather's words come back to me. I had never belittled love. I had *believed* it. And now it has come back to strike me so badly that I do not think I can recover.

'Never trust love' – this is what makes sense. If you trust love, you will be hurt sooner or later. It is only a matter of time before the very person you love lets you down. I think about my time in Cochin. No matter how much I had given, it had never been enough for Abhi.

From Vaibhav, all I wanted were just two soothing words: 'I understand'. But, no. Instead, he has withdrawn from me. He won't even look at me anymore.

I curl up into a tight ball on the bed. I want to disappear. I don't want to exist with this pain. Oh, it hurts. And it hurts and it hurts. The funny thing about pain is how quickly it spreads. Like cancer. It begins with a dull thud of the heart when I think about the incident at the party. Then it spreads as I think about the other areas of my life where things are not going right. Even as I think about the other things, the pain tours my body. I now feel it in the pit of my stomach. I feel it in my arms. I feel it in my toes, and I feel it in my neck. How is it possible? There is nothing physically wrong with me. No doctor examining me would find any physical symptoms. Yet, pain is all I am, pain.

I have been going around carrying this feeling of hollowness inside me for a while now. My heart is heavy. But I am empty. It is strange to feel heavy and hollow at the same time.

I cannot move as all of this goes through my head and body. I am immobile. Frozen. For how much more time do I have to bear this? This agony that is tearing me inside out? I have no idea.

The hours tick by. I hear the sounds of the night. The silence, the occasional noise of a vehicle as it makes its way across the empty roads. I stare at the moonless sky. Tonight there's not a single star in the sky.

I feel as empty as the landscape outside.

I very badly want to sleep. To escape. I want a respite.

Why don't you sleep forever? All of this will end then.

The thought slithers in like a hangman's noose and settles around my neck.

Sleep.

Forever.

It will end.

My father's words, what he had said a long time back, come back to me. 'Prepare for the worst, but expect the best.'

What was the worst here? That I take my own life and it ends. Wasn't that also in a way the best?

For the first time since I left the party, I feel a frisson of excitement, a purpose. It is calling out to me now.

I walk to my cupboard and quickly rummage through my clothes. There it is, the suicide manual. I open the pages and read the description of the plastic cover method.

I think of the pills that have been piling up inside my pen-stand. They were supposed to stop the cyclical thoughts and help me to relax. What if I took the pills and used a plastic cover?

I help myself to a handful of pills. I take two, then place them back on my table. What if the pills don't work and instead my stomach has to be pumped? It will be back to the mental hospital then. Even in this strange frenzied state, I know I don't want to go back there again.

I look at the plastic cover in which Mrs Asthana gave me the library books. I take out the books, and touch the cover tenderly. Can this small innocuous thing snuff out a life? How can it?

These thoughts are zooming through my head now. They are whirling, gyrating, driving me insane. The pain, the thoughts, the sense of hopelessness, the failure, the insults I just faced, the sound of silence in the auditorium that day, Vaibhav's angry words – all of them grow in magnitude and attack me now. I want a respite. I just want it all to stop.

So I take two pills and crawl into bed.

Maybe I should use the plastic cover now? But I can't think straight.

So I just place it over my head and shut my eyes.

I can feel all thoughts slowly recede. They don't seem so terrible anymore. They are gentle, like waves in a faraway sea.

I feel sleepy now.

This is bliss.

23

Falling Apart

If there is a term called the 'sleep of the dead', I understood it that night. I slept like I hadn't slept for months. Deep, dreamless. Nothing tormented me, nothing troubled me; for the first time, I was free of pain. I have no idea how many hours I slept. I was rudely jolted awake by my mother's cry of horror.

'*Ankita! Ankita! What have you done?*' she was screaming.

Her voice sounded far off. Like I was deep inside a well, and she was shouting from somewhere above.

'Ankita, wake up, dear!' That was my father's voice. Controlled, yet on the edge.

I tried to open my eyes, but gave up. I just wanted to sleep some more.

'What are you waiting for? Just call the ambulance!' my mother yelled.

That set off an alarm in my brain, and I opened my eyes somehow.

My parents stood there staring at me.

My mother's face was pale with fright. My father looked grim.

'Oh my god, my baby, are you okay?' My mother hugged me.

She had never called me 'baby' before and she had never hugged me like this. Why were they behaving like this? I was confused.

Then it all came rushing back and I sat up with a start.

Good lord! The suicide manual, the pills, the plastic cover. OH NO… OH NO… OH NO... I had to put them away before my parents jumped to the wrong conclusion.

But too late.

They had already seen it all. The telltale pills lay on my table, where I had left them last night. The plastic cover was on the table now, and so was the suicide manual.

I was mortified to be found out like this. It was evident that they thought I had tried to kill myself.

My father stared at me with so much hurt in his eyes.

'Dad, Ma… I didn't. I didn't… it is not what it looks like… I… ca… can explain,' I stammered.

'Oh, Ankita,' said my mother and began crying softly.

'Ma, please,' I said.

She was sobbing and I hated myself for causing her pain.

'I just had two tablets. I didn't try to kill myself,' I said. I wanted them to believe me so badly. But after everything I had put them through, there was no credibility in my words anymore.

'Ankita, you have no idea how *worried* we got. For the past fifteen minutes, we have been trying to wake you up,' my father said.

'I am really, really sorry. I didn't mean to sleep like this. The thing is, I haven't been sleeping too well for the past few days,' I started to explain.

Dad said, 'Get ready and join us for breakfast. We will talk about it later.' I knew he was making a great effort to control his emotions.

I kicked myself mentally. I had succeeded in giving them a proper fright. It was the last thing I wanted to do. I was a prize idiot to have left all of this in plain sight.

I washed my face quickly, and brushed my teeth. Last night's mascara was still on my eyelashes, and I rinsed it off. I thought about the events of yesterday, and was filled with horror. How would I ever face my classmates again?

But the sleep had done me some amount of good. The most important thing was that the obsessive negative thinking had now receded a bit, even though it had not completely stopped. It was astonishing what a single night's proper sleep could do.

My parents had not gotten over the shock. Ma kept looking at me as she served me breakfast. She had made upma and she spooned it carefully into my plate, and told me to eat. She had never treated me this gently before. Dad said nothing. We sat in silence and finished our breakfast.

'Don't you have to go to work?' I asked my father, when he showed no signs of moving even after breakfast was done.

'He has taken leave today,' my mother answered.

'Why?' I asked.

Dad lost his composure then. 'What do you mean why? After what happened, how do you think I can go to work?' he asked.

'Nothing happened. I already told you. I just took two tablets. I wanted... I just wanted to sleep.'

'Permanently?' asked my father, deadpan. His face was grave.

'Dad, Ma, I assure you, I wasn't trying to kill myself,' I said.

'How do you explain the book then, Ankita? The pills? The plastic cover? *What in the world were you thinking*?' My father banged the table with his fist and I shuddered. 'I will speak to Dr Neeraj, and then we will decide a future course of action,' he said. There was a ring of finality to his tone. He hadn't even waited for me to *explain*.

I did not want him to speak to Dr Neeraj. I just wanted my parents to believe me. This was *not* a suicide attempt. If he spoke to Dr Neeraj, he would be giving him false information. Dr Neeraj would then prescribe the medication according to that. I did *not* want to take it.

I rose quietly and left the table. I shut myself in my room. How could I convince them now? How messed up this was. Yes, I did feel sad. I did feel upset. I was having a bit of trouble controlling my thoughts. But I was coping. I wanted to scream at them that I was handling it. I would be fine. But who will believe me now?

●

I sit on the windowsill, staring out at the parking lot, so utterly alone as I watch people going about their daily lives. How I dread waking up in the morning and facing another day!

The book I'm attempting to read lies next to me. I don't know what I'm doing anymore. The hours stretch on endlessly. I've been trying hard to finish an assignment, due when college reopens. But I am unable to focus. I feel inadequate, worthless, inferior. I should have never joined this creative writing course. I have no original ideas, really. Even my professor said so. I am just a sham. A pretender. Someone who couldn't do her MBA and joined this course as an escape. All of this is so pointless and painful. Today is a holiday, but soon I will have to go back to college. And face them. I don't want to. I want to stay where I am.

A thought hisses and spits in my head like a snake:

Drop out of this course. This is not for you.

The more I think about it, the surer I am. I am considering how to tell my parents that I want to drop out. *A second time.*

That's when I hear the door to my room open. I know it is my father.

I sit up straight. Not the medication again. I am unable to think because of the damn medicines. My parents insist I take them. But my head feels heavy when I do so. My tongue becomes so thick that I am unable to talk. I am unable to think.

'Please go away, I don't want to take it,' I say before he can open his mouth.

'Look, I spoke to Dr Neeraj and he says you can take these. They helped you earlier, didn't they? It was all good, remember?' said my father, standing there with the pills in his hand.

'It was good, not because of the medicines, but because I tried hard,' I reply.

'Of course you tried hard. Now be a good girl and take these,' says my father as he extends his hand.

'*No, no, no.*' My fists are clenched into tight balls and I refuse to meet my father's eye. I don't want to look at him. Or at my mother who is right behind him. I can't stand the helpless expression on their faces, the pleading looks, their panic. But mostly, it's the depth of their love that I can't bear. They don't deserve this. I have had enough. I cannot face them anymore. I don't want to be a part of any of this. I have given them enough pain in the last one year, when I had to be admitted to a mental hospital.

'Please, Ankita,' my father pleads. I detest the whine in his voice.

'*Don't... Don't say anything. Don't enter my room... Get out!* I yell, my eyes blazing, my voice high-pitched.

It is as though there is another person speaking from within me.

'Listen, Ankita, if you don't take the medication, you will become worse. Don't you remember what happened?' my father says in a calm voice.

I remember. I remember every single thing.

'Please, Ankita... Just this one tablet. Take it, please?' My father refuses to give up.

'*Get the fuck out. Now!*' I scream.

'*Watch your words,*' my mother yells at me. If there is one thing she cannot stand, it is my talking back, and refusing to do as I am told.

'*You... You shut up!*' I yell back louder. I am shaking in rage now.

I pick up a paperweight and fling it at my father. It catches him by surprise, and hits him on the forehead. He drops the pills he is carrying, his hand going up instinctively to his forehead. I watch impassively as blood gushes out from the skin split open. His face contorts in pain.

'You witch! Look at what you have done!' my mother screams, as she rushes forward to help him.

He has backed off now, wincing in pain, and is clutching the handle of the door.

My mother rushes to the fridge to get some ice.

I am still standing there, rooted to the spot, staring at him. I cannot believe I did this.

I watch as he leaves my room.

Then I shut the door.

I fling myself on the bed and weep loudly, my wails smothered by the pillow. I don't want them to hear me cry. My body heaves as I shout into the pillow, crying, sobbing. I don't recognise the primeval noises coming from deep within me. I clutch the pillow hard. I hate what I am doing to my parents. I want this to end.

How much more do I have to endure? How much more? Weren't all those months at the hospital enough? This is UNFAIR... UNFAIR... UNFAIR. I recall the months at the hospital, the electric shock treatments, the occupational therapy, my life there and how I struggled to read, to get back to normalcy. I thought I had won. I thought I had succeeded. I thought I had conquered my mind.

I thought all this was behind me. I thought I had overcome all of it. But how wrong I was! The monster I presumed to have defeated has come back with a vengeance.

The pills my father dropped are lying by the door. I hate them. I have had enough of medication, doctors, psychiatrists. I don't want any more of it.

A small voice of reason in my head speaks up. 'Take the tablets. Take them,' it says. I know that if I don't take them, I will probably have to be admitted once more. My father is right.

But the medication takes away everything. Makes me numb, drowsy, not myself. Wipes away my thoughts, empties my imagination. It is supposed to help me. But all it does is kill me. Kill me from inside.

I am frightened now. If I could lose control like that and hurt my father, there is no telling what I will do next.

I pick up the pills and walk out of the room. My father is sitting on the sofa with an ice pack to his head. My mother glares at me.

'I... I am sorry, Dad. I will take the medication,' I choke on my words . 'Are you hurt?'

'It's nothing, Ankita. Just a small cut,' he says.

I start crying again then.

I know there is no escape now. I have been getting progressively worse.

'Please make an appointment. Take me to the doctor,' I say. 'But before you do that, will you please hear me out?'

24

We Have No Secrets

My parents sat across me in the living room, ready to listen to what I had to say. I felt terrible looking at the gash on my father's head. Fortunately, the cut wasn't too deep, and had stopped bleeding. I had lost control for a moment, and ironically, it had taken that for them to hear me out.

'Dad, I am so sorry,' I began, very remorseful.

My father silenced me by raising his hand. 'It's fine, I already told you,' he said. The way he so readily said it made me feel that he was treating me like I was mentally ill. But I *had* to control myself now. I couldn't let my anger show. If I lost control one more time, it would only confirm their worst suspicions. I was walking a tightrope, the most difficult thing I'd ever done in my life.

'Alright,' I said.

'Now what was it that you wanted to tell us?' my mother asked.

'I want to tell you everything that I have hidden from you so far. I couldn't speak about it because I was ashamed till now. But last night at the party, something happened, and it changed everything. Please allow me to explain, and you will see why I behaved that way. I am not justifying what I did. There are no excuses. But I am hoping you will understand,' I said.

Then I told my parents about Joseph. I died with shame as I narrated the way I had kissed him when I had the mania. There was a lump in my throat as I went into the details of what had happened. My cheeks burned as I narrated. I could barely speak. But I was desperate. If I didn't make them understand, they would insist on taking me to the psychiatrist, and I couldn't go through that. I had to prevent it at any cost. They listened quietly as I explained. 'I didn't know what I was doing. It was the disorder acting, not me,' I said in a small voice.

'It's okay, Ankita. It is not your fault,' my father reassured me. That lone sentence gave me the courage to go on.

I told them how well I had spoken in the quarter-final and the semi-final of my public speaking event and how I had set my heart on winning the Goenka cup, and how I wanted to prove it to the world that I was worth being looked up to. It would win me respect. I wanted to win it for *them*, for my father and my mother. I could see Ma blinking away tears as I said this. Then I told them about how I reached the finals, but then faltered at seeing Joseph in the audience. At all those memories coming rushing back, I had felt sick to the core and thrown up.

'So, you see, Dad, it wasn't anxiety that caused me to throw up on stage. It was his presence,' I said.

'The bastard!' My father's jaw was clenched.

'I guess he didn't know I would be on stage,' I said. 'But that's not all. I would have forgiven him for that.'

My parents looked at me questioningly.

I told them how he wanted to meet me, and what happened after that. I also told them that I had specifically told him I had absolutely no feelings for him and didn't want to see him again. It was so hard talking about all of this to my parents. Only the extreme desperation and distress of what would come if I didn't explain kept me going. If my parents felt uncomfortable listening to any of this, they didn't show it. They nodded and listened.

I told them all the painful, excruciating details about the previous night's party. I told them about Freddy's insensitive comment after I had thrown up on stage, and how he had needled me at the party. I described every single thing that had occurred – Joseph coming over when I was standing on the balcony and me pushing him. Him screaming *mental patient* and *psycho bitch* at me, and everyone believing him when he said I had tried to push him off the balcony. As much as I tried to hold back my tears, I couldn't. I started crying when I told them about Freddy's comment – that I looked insane.

'You know what hurt most?' I asked, my voice breaking. 'That Parul walked away. She took *their* side,' I said and then I broke down completely. Tears flowed freely down my cheeks.

My mother was immediately by my side. She rubbed my back like she used to when I was a child. 'It's okay… It's okay,' she said, and I felt the childish urge to hide my face in her lap again.

My father exploded with rage. I had never seen him this angry. He gritted his teeth. 'The bastard!' he said. 'You should have pushed him over. He deserves to die. Do you know where the bastard lives?'

In that moment, when my own father took my side and said that I should have pushed Joseph over, something in me shifted. Up till then I had in a weird way, perhaps subconsciously, blamed myself for letting Joseph down, by telling him I didn't love him. But my father so strongly supporting *me* made me rethink. For the first time, I actually began believing that there was an alternative perspective to this. *That perhaps it was not my fault.* I shook my head. 'I don't know where he lives.'

'Can you find out? Where does this Parul girl live?' The veins on my father's temples were bulging. He was so angry he was ready to burst.

'Shh... Leave it. What has happened has happened,' my mother said, trying to pacify him.

But my father wasn't ready to leave it at all.

'I want to have a word with that asshole. Please give me that girl's address. Maybe she will know where he lives,' my father bellowed.

I had never heard my father swear like this.

'Look here, I am telling you to leave it. Just think about this. Ankita will be shunned in college if word gets around that her father went to a student's house and created a scene. Let's just forget it happened,' my mother said. She was insightful and sensitive about it.

My father thought a bit and perhaps he saw sense in what my mother said. He paced up and down the drawing room to calm himself down. Then he came and sat down with us.

'See, Dad, this is why I did not want to take that medication which you both insisted I take. I didn't know how to convince you. I am sorry I pretended to take it,' I said.

Both my parents considered this.

'It is only after you took the medication that you slept, isn't it?' my mother said. She was astute. She had caught on to something that had not struck me at all.

'Yes, true,' I admitted.

'So maybe it helps you reduce the cyclical thoughts, and hence it helps you sleep. So I think what we can do is check with Dr Neeraj,' she said.

'But it is also possible that I was simply exhausted as I hadn't slept for many days. I felt refreshed when I woke up this morning,' I said.

'Yes, it is possible. I think it is best if we meet him once. Let's check with him. You have been fighting this thing on your own. You have forgotten that we are with you. We are with you, Ankita, and you have been incredibly brave. But if we need medical help, we must seek it,' my father said.

One part of me did *not want* to seek medical help. I was okay. I was managing. I could do it on my own.

But the other part of me screamed at me.

You hurt your own father.

You put a plastic cover on your head.

You will hurt the people who love you.

You need help. You need help. You need help.

I started crying then.

I knew there was no escape now.

'Please make an appointment. Take me to the doctor,' I said.

The nightmare has started once again. Trapped in my body, trapped in my head, I am my own prisoner.

'Ankita, what happened? Do you *not* want to see the doctor?' Ma asked, stroking my back again.

'I am afraid. I am tired of psychiatrists and medication. I don't want to be admitted in the hospital again,' I could barely speak. The very thought of seeing Dr Neeraj was stirring up the old tsunami inside me. I wanted to escape it, yet I knew I couldn't.

'You have no idea how bad we felt leaving you there. It killed us. We felt so guilty, even though we knew we were doing it for your good. And the worst part was we did not know whether you would get better or not. There were simply no guarantees,' my father said. There was so much anguish in his voice.

'It was the toughest decision we took. But do you remember how things were? There was no other choice, Ankita,' my mother said gently.

'See, we are just telling you to meet Dr Neeraj so that things don't get worse. What you have now is very different from what you had earlier. You have not had a single episode of mania after you were discharged from NMHI. Have you noticed that?' my father said. 'Look, we have been keeping a close watch on your behaviour. I don't think you realize how much better you are, Ankita.'

That was the first time I actually thought about it. I went back to everything that had happened every since my new course had started. And how I had behaved when I was enrolled for MBA earlier. My father was right. There was a very clear difference between the two. Before NMHI, at the peak of my disorder, I had mania. I once danced on the parapet with no care or concern for my life. I had kissed Joseph. Behaved wild, out of control. I thought of the time I had cut myself, the time I had tried to kill myself. Twice.

Now, after I'd been discharged, there had been no such incident. Whatever I felt was all inside my own head. Yes, there had been external triggers too – like failing on stage, what happened at the party. But then, perhaps a 'normal' person too would have reacted the way I did.

'Let's just rule out any possibility of it occurring again. Maybe you don't need any medication at all. If we have to fight it with medication, we will fight it. Don't worry. This is not at all like last time. But we should meet him, just to be sure that the steps we are taking are right.'

'Alright, Dad. I shall meet Dr Neeraj,' I said. I grasped my own hands tightly to prevent them from shaking.

Calm down.

Calm down.

Calm down.

'You are an incredibly brave girl,' my father said.

If we were a family that displayed physical affection, I would have hugged him then. But I didn't. We didn't do things like that. So I just sat there nodding and feeling grateful to my parents. It was a massive relief to have told them everything. The only thing I had kept from them was the misunderstanding I had with Vaibhav. I didn't want to raise that with them. A girl has the right to keep a few secrets from her parents.

'I have one more question for you,' my father said. 'Where in the world did you get that book from? The one lying by your bed?'

I knew he was referring to the suicide manual.

'I am sorry, Dad… I was just curious. Honest, I wasn't going to kill myself,' I emphasised once again.

'That doesn't answer my question.' He raised an eyebrow.

I had to tell them then. About finding the book in the library. I didn't tell them about the note, though.

'You got it from your own college? I need to go and meet this librarian of yours,' said my father. 'And give me the book.'

'No, please don't meet her. I will return the book when the college reopens,' I pleaded.

'You told me not to hunt down that bastard, I listened. But this, I will not agree to. How can a college library endorse such a book? I went through the book. What a horrible book!' he said.

'It is for those with terminal illness who want to end their lives,' I tried explaining.

'I know what it is about. I flipped through the contents. Which is why I want to have a word with her.'

'Please, Dad. The book was in the stockroom, not on the shelves.'

'I don't care where it was. Students should not have access to such a book.

'Do you even realise what you put us through? I *died* this morning when I saw you like that. Imagine if something had happened to you? It was this close a call, Ankita, this close.' He held his thumb and index finger together.

I wanted to tell him that I hadn't taped the plastic cover around my neck. I had merely held it over my head. But I knew any explanation from me would only make it worse.

'I have made up my mind on this. You cannot stop me, Ankita,' my father said. 'Now go and get the book and give it to me. I am taking it back to the college.'

I apologised, pleaded and begged. But Dad wouldn't listen. He was hell-bent on speaking to Mrs Asthana. I knew I had no choice then. I walked to my room. I quickly turned to the last page and retrieved the note I had found in the book. Something told me to hold on to the note. I was worried that if I gave the book to my father and the note fell out, it would be lost forever.

I put the book in the same plastic cover that got me into so much trouble. Then I came out and handed it to my father.

25
Everybody Hurts

Fifteen minutes since my father left and I was already restless. I knew it would take him at least a couple of hours to go to my college and come back.

'Ma, what was the need for him to go to college to speak to Mrs Asthana? Why didn't you stop him?' I asked my mother.

She had made a cup of tea for me, and we both sat across each other at our dining table.

'He wouldn't have listened to me. You saw how angry he was,' she said.

'I've never seen him this angry,' I confessed.

'You are his world, Ankita. He doesn't always show it, but he is fiercely protective. And do you know something? I felt like killing that boy myself,' my mother said simply. I knew she was referring to Joseph.

'I don't know, Ma. I was just so frightened when he pinned me down like that. Pushing him away was a reflex action. I shudder to think what would have happened if he had fallen over the balcony,' I said.

'He should have stayed away from you when you had made your intentions clear. He had no business to even come and talk to you.' My mother's eyes were slits on her face, she was that angry. I had never seen her like this. It had always been me trying to hide things from my mother. I had never openly discussed boys with her.

After all that I had been through – and as a direct consequence of which what my parents had to go through – my mother had changed so much. This was a new version of her, a version I liked very much.

'What do you want to have for lunch?' she asked.

'Anything. Shall I help you?'

'No, go to your room and read or do something. I shall make something special for you.'

I went to my room and took out *LIFE'S LITTLE NOTES.*

I opened the book and wrote **Note 7.**

No matter how different our parents' outlook towards life is from ours, the one thing we overlook is that they are_always on our side. They try and do what is best for us. When we are very young, they place restrictions on us where it concerns our safety. When they think it endangers us, they tell us not to do certain things. 'Don't play with matches. Don't touch electrical wires. Don't go to the edge of the terrace. Don't cross the road without looking.' They repeat it so many times that it becomes ingrained in us. We never question these rules because the implications of breaking them are obvious.

But sometimes the implications are not so obvious. We doubt them then.

I think it is okay to doubt them. In fact, it is important to question them. That is the only way we grow. That is the only way we become adults – by weighing our opinion heavily against theirs and then taking a decision based on facts that are evident to us. Sometimes we hide these facts from our parents. We know that they will not understand, as their perspective or world-view is different from ours.

All is good as long as we do not get into trouble, and are able to manage things on our own. But nothing's in our control. Things go horribly wrong. We do not know what to do. We turn to our parents then.

Whether we follow the rules or not, they are always there for us. They do the best they can in the given circumstances. They may scold us, reprimand us, shout at us, but mostly, they take care of us.

If you have a set of parents who are in your corner, no matter what, it is a massive strength. Parents can be your wings when yours are broken, and you need a little help to fly.

With care, love and understanding, anything can heal. Anything.

●

When my father got back home, I rushed out.

'What happened, Dad? Did you meet Mrs Asthana?' I asked.

'Yes, I met her,' my father said. I could see that his anger had cooled off considerably.

' And?' I asked.

'Strangely, she said she had no idea about this particular book. She couldn't remember it. She said there were no records of it in the file. It was not indexed at all. She said she would look into it, and try and find out how it got there. So I left it with her,' he said.

'Oh, no! Why did you do that?' I asked. I still wanted that book. Mrs Asthana had clearly said I could have it. It was such a rare book. But my father had other views.

'Look, Ankita. I do not want that book in our house. It has a negative energy. You are not in a state to read such a book right now. You saw what happened when you opened it last time. What if there is another situation like that? I cannot risk it. Your life is too precious, Ankita. Even if there is one percent chance of any negative consequences, I do not want to risk it,' my father said.

'I agree with him. Don't look at anything that can influence your mind. What kind of a book is that anyway? It should be banned,' my mother said.

'I think it is banned in France,' I murmured.

'See? Those people are smart. Everyone should follow suit,' my mother declared.

I was touched by their fierce concern. I might have got annoyed earlier, but now I could see why they were saying it. The way they expressed their love was not through hugs, but through action – like my mother making my favourite dishes and my father rushing off to college to confront the authorities.

There was one more thing that my father did. He dialled Dr Neeraj's office and made an appointment for the next day. It filled me with terrible anxiety. I remembered all the past psychiatrists I had met. Dr Mukta still gave me nightmares. So did Dr Kohli. I remembered how insensitive they were. Then I remembered Dr Madhusudan and how kind he was. I tried to reason with myself. Just like people, there were good psychiatrists and bad ones. But it did not help. I was still terrified; I did not know which category Dr Neeraj would fall into.

Also, I knew my father was right. There was no point resisting just because I was frightened. If I didn't do this now, who knew how things would turn out? Better safe than sorry.

So I braced myself for the visit that was to come. I had to go through with it.

I was so stressed thinking about the doctor's visit that I couldn't sleep that night again. I did not want to lie in bed and keep thinking negative thoughts. The appointment was already made.

Instead of lying there wide awake as I usually did whenever sleep evaded me, I decided to read the *Dream Dictionary*. I wanted to know what it meant when we had terrifying nightmares. I wanted to know what the dream of the grotesque creature meant.

The *Dream Dictionary* explained all the common dreams. It talked about how we dream, and the hidden meanings in our dreams. It talked about the symbolism of dreams and how it varied depending on the culture we were raised in. There were explanations of what it meant if you dreamt you were naked, if you dreamt you had lost a tooth, or dreamt you were falling. There were thousands of dreams explained and sorted in alphabetical order.

But there was nothing close to what I had dreamt of. There was no description of that creature I had seen. I couldn't get it out of my head. I decided to look up the meaning of a dream with dragons in it, even though what I had seen was not a dragon. I was astonished when I read the explanation. It said that a dragon in a dream could represent someone (possibly me) with a fiery personality. It could also mean that a person got carried away by passion and lost control. In eastern religions, it could represent luck and fortune. Then I looked up the meaning of a dream where one is eaten by a monster or a sea creature. The *Dream Dictionary* said that the monster could represent the society or situations that were a threat. It could also indicate disgust over something happening in your life that you needed to address. It could also indicate that the monster was the 'idle gossip' of the people around you; maybe they were talking about you.

All these explanations made sense to me. I was afraid of facing everybody in college. As long as I was at home, protected and comforted by my parents, I was safe. I was in a cocoon, in fine, caring hands.

But college would reopen soon. I would then have to face the Freddys of the world. I would have to face Parul too.

Parul who I trusted as a friend.

Parul who walked away.

Parul who betrayed me.

Then I remembered Mrs Hayden's assignment and I broke into a cold sweat. I wasn't ready to write about the mistakes of my life at all. I wouldn't be able to do this assignment. I wasn't ready to face my college-mates after what happened.

The monster was not just in my nightmares. It was outside now, and I didn't have a clue how to face it. It was gnawing at me from both the inside as well as from the outside. It had stolen my peace of mind, my sleep, and I was scared it would steal my life.

26

Wake Up, Life is Calling

My mother woke me up the next day. I had barely slept a wink. My eyes were burning again. Functioning on too little sleep had become a way of life now. I got out of bed without a fuss. Then I got dressed. My father and mother tried to make conversation throughout breakfast, but I barely replied. I just wanted to get it over with, the visit to the doctor's. I couldn't eat breakfast either. I had helped myself to a single toast and wasn't even able to finish that.

'Eat, Ankita. Don't be so nervous,' my father said.

'Relax. We aren't going to leave you there. We talked this over yesterday, remember? You agreed that it makes sense to meet him once,' my mother reminded me.

I nodded. They were right. But it still didn't make it any easier for me.

Dr Neeraj's clinic was in Santa Cruz and my father drove us there. I sat in the backseat, my stomach in knots. When I had walked out of NMHI, I had been so confident that all of this was behind me. Yet, here I was, once again. My father's words – that this was different, that it wouldn't deteriorate into something which required hospitalisation – all of it flew out of the window. I couldn't remember anything. The chants began in my head again:

Worthless.
Mental patient.
Failure.
You hurt those who love you.

I willed myself to calm down. If I was a bundle of nerves when I was visiting the psychiatrist, it would do me no good. I closed my eyes. My father looked at me through the rear-view mirror.

'Don't worry, we are with you,' his glance seemed to say.

But it did not help.

Dr Neeraj's clinic was on the fourteenth floor of an old commercial building. We got off the elevator and walked down the corridor leading to his clinic. This floor housed other offices – a travel agency, a financial company, an ad agency. As I passed each one, my nervousness grew. Why wasn't I like any of the people working in these offices? Why did all of this have to happen only to me? Why was I so *different?*

The receptionist greeted us and asked, 'Who is the patient?'

I wanted to scream then.

I am not a patient. I am fine. This is just a check-up.

But I said nothing. My father gave her my name.

We waited outside along with others. There were two people ahead of us – one, an older man carrying a file, the other a mother with a child. I idly wondered what the matter was with them and why they were here. They looked completely okay.

Then I realised that from the outside, I looked fine too. Nobody would be able to tell I had a mental health issue. Freddy's words came back then.

She has that unmistakable look of insanity.

I sat with my head bent, looking at my toes. When my mother tried to hold my hand, I angrily withdrew it. I watched the older man go inside and then emerge after a while. I watched the mother and her child go inside and then emerge. At last, it was my turn.

My father and mother both accompanied me in.

I had thought Dr Neeraj would be young. But he was an old, lanky, bearded man. His beard was salt and pepper and the sparse hair on his head matched it. He wore a light blue full-sleeved shirt.

'Hello, Ankita! Hello, Mrs and Mr Sharma! Do have a seat,' he said.

I sat between my father and mother, looking at him in sheer terror, hoping that my expression would not reveal what I felt inside.

'Dr Madhusudan and I were batch-mates. Our friendship goes back a long way,' he said.

I felt somewhat reassured to hear that. If there was one psychiatrist I was comfortable with, it was Dr Madhusudan. I exhaled. I wasn't even aware that I'd been holding my breath.

'So, how do you feel?' he asked. He was soft-spoken and gentle, his voice almost melodious.

'I feel fine,' I said.

'Any anxiety? Any difficulty sleeping?' he asked.

He had my file with him, and he quickly flipped through it.

I looked at my father; I didn't know what to say.

My father told him that certain incidents had happened that were stressful, but my reaction was not unusual or extreme. He said there was no evidence of any mania.

I wished I could disappear. They were talking about me like I was a caged wild animal that could escape any moment. I wanted to get up and run away. It was horrible to be subjected to such scrutiny. I folded my arms across my chest and dug my nails into my elbows. The next moment, I stopped. I didn't want to do anything that might make this man say that I required hospitalisation. I sat very still, without saying a word.

Dr Neeraj listened to my father with care. Then he said that he wanted to speak to me alone. My parents waited outside.

'Ankita, I know this is stressful for you. To come and meet me like this after what you have been through. I understand completely,' he said.

I nodded.

He asked me if I wanted to tell him about the events that had caused me stress. I didn't want to explain all over again. I had just finished narrating all of it to my parents. But if I didn't tell him, how would he know the real situation? So I forced myself to recount everything – how Joseph had turned up, how that had upset me, more importantly *why* it had upset me, and the pending essay, and how I would now have to go back and face everyone in college.

Dr Neeraj made careful notes as I spoke. This note taking made me nervous. I detested it. But I had no option but to continue.

When I finished, he said, 'I can see you have had a rough time. I think you have coped wonderfully.' He then summoned my parents.

He said he did not think that I needed lithium again as there seemed to be no instances of mania. He asked if the dose that had been prescribed after discharge from NMHI was tapered off and stopped. My father replied that we had followed it exactly as prescribed.

'It is very important that we do not suddenly stop the medication. We have to taper it off gradually, in order to give the body time to get used to it,' he said. 'Since you haven't actually taken the other medicines I had prescribed for anxiety, we don't need to be concerned about them.'

'Ankita, do you think you are strong enough to manage without medication?'

I wasn't sure. I was scared. But I wanted to try. I didn't know what to answer.

'Don't worry, just go ahead and openly say whatever is on your mind,' Dr Neeraj encouraged me.

'I think the previous time I took the medication, it numbed my feelings. It made me dull. It took away my thoughts, my imagination – everything. I *hate* medication. I like to be able to *feel*. I write. I write poetry, I am enrolled in a creative writing course. How will I write unless I *feel*?' I asked.

There was a stunned silence in the room.

Dr Neeraj was the first to speak. 'Ankita, that is a very noble profession. You are a true artist. If you feel you can cope, and there has been no instance of mania, then I think it is fine if you do not take medication. However, from what I understand, sleeping at night is a concern. I am going to prescribe some sleeping pills, completely herbal, with no side-effects. It is made from the gingko tree, which is one of the longest-living tree species in the world. It has been in use for thousands of years. You can take it when you feel you really need it. You regulate your sleep yourself,' he said as he wrote out the prescription.

'So no other medication needed?' asked my father.

'You see, Mr Sharma, psychiatry is such a branch of medicine that no two patients are alike. Now in other branches of medicine, if someone has, say, malaria, we know that if we use chloroquine to treat it, it will work the same way for everybody. But when it comes to psychiatry, there is really no telling whether two patients will respond exactly the same way when the same medication is given. Based on what Ankita has told me, I can easily prescribe five drugs that may or may not help her. But whether they are *needed* – that is the question.' He smiled gently.

I heaved a sigh of relief when I heard that. I decided then that Dr Neeraj was a 'good psychiatrist'. He did not randomly prescribe medication. He took the time to hear me out.

'One thing that can help you, Ankita, is psychotherapy. If you keep getting obsessive thoughts, you could consider it. Even after that, if they get too troublesome, I suggest you see me again,' he said.

I nodded.

'Life is calling, Ankita,' said Dr Neeraj, as we stepped out of his room. 'Wake up!' Then he smiled and waved.

'See, that was not so bad, was it?' asked my father as we walked back to the car.

'This psychiatrist turned out to be good. But what if he had prescribed five medicines? Would you have made me take them?' I asked in return.

My father was thoughtful. He had no answers for me.

'You know, what I wonder is how many people are walking around taking medication they *don't* need and how many more people are taking the *wrong* medication, and how many are *not* taking medication when they actually will benefit from it,' my mother said.

'It all depends on the doctor. If you get the right person to treat you, you are fortunate,' Dad said.

I said, 'I think it depends on the patient too. It depends on how badly they want to overcome something and how much they are willing to cooperate with whoever wants to help them.'

I knew how hard it was. I knew how tormented I felt on a daily basis. I did have a mental health issue. I had accepted that. When I was at NMHI, I had simply done whatever they told me to do.

I took whatever medication they gave. I remembered the time I spent trying hard to read the children's books, when I had lost the ability to read. I had tried over and over and over. I had not given up.

I knew I would have to do that again. I would have to will myself and put an end to the negative thoughts. I would have to face my classmates. I would have to write that essay. My parents couldn't do that for me.

It seemed like a mammoth task and the problem was I did not even know where to begin. I had spoken bravely at the psychiatrist's clinic. But now courage deserted me and I was frightened of what lay ahead, and how I would cope.

27

Call Me Maybe

On the way home, my father stopped at a medical store, and bought the medicine that the doctor had prescribed for sleep.

'Ankita, if you need it, you can come and ask me, okay?' My mother slipped the medicine foil into her bag.

'Why? Are you afraid I will take an overdose? I told you, Ma, I will *not* do it. Why don't you believe me?'

'It is not a question of trust, Ankita. It is just that your mother will be less worried if it is with her. We know you will not take it. But if there is a small, minuscule chance of temptation… You know what an overdose can do. Especially since you seem to have studied the book…' My father did not complete the sentence.

'Hide all the plastic covers too. And while you are at it, why not put grills over the balconies?' I snapped.

I was angry that even after I had come clean about *everything* with my parents, they just did not seem to trust me. Dr Neeraj had said that I could regulate the medicines myself. I was also frustrated that there seemed to be no 'solutions' in sight for any of my problems.

My father simply did not respond. Then I felt lousy for snapping.

'I'm sorry. I do appreciate that you are all worried,' I said.

'It's fine, Ankita, leave it,' my mother said.

My father dropped us home and left for work. My mother and I got off at the start of the lane that led to my residential complex and walked the short distance home.

'Ma, do you want cutting chai? I feel like having some,' I suggested as we passed the tea stall. I remembered how Vaibhav had waited here for me once. I missed him so much.

'Why not? I am tired of making tea for myself,' said my mother.

'You know, this doctor is as good as Dr Madhusudan,' I said as we stood there sipping tea with the sun shining down on us.

'I am glad we took his opinion. At least we know we are on the right track,' she said.

We walked on after that and reached the lobby of our building. I stood there gaping, scarcely believing my eyes.

Was that Mrs Hayden in our lobby? What was she doing here? Perhaps she had come to visit someone in our building?

My first instinct was to duck. I didn't want to meet Mrs Hayden. She would probably ask me if I had been working on my essay and I didn't have an answer for her.

'Ma, that is my professor,' I whispered, nudging my mother.

'Where? Who?' she said, looking around.

'Oh god, Ma! Can't you be more subtle? She has seen us!' I hissed.

Mrs Hayden was waving at us.

There was no escape now.

I waved back.

'Hello, Mrs Hayden. This is my mother, Mrs Sharma,' I said, introducing them.

'Hello, ma'am,' my mother said.

'Oh, please, there is absolutely no need to call me ma'am,' Mrs Hayden told my mother.

'So, Mrs Hayden, did you come here to meet someone who lives here?' I asked. I couldn't contain my curiosity.

'You could say that,' Mrs Hayden's eyes twinkled. 'But only if she invites me in.'

It took a few seconds for me to understand what she was saying. Mrs Hayden had come to meet *me*? Why in the world? I was at a loss for words.

'We would be happy to have you over,' my mother responded before I could.

'Do you live close by?' my mother asked as Mrs Hayden got into the elevator with us.

'I live fairly close by. It is a ten-minute drive. I come to this area often as I am associated with the Mount Mary church, which is located here, in Bandra,' she said.

Ma opened the door, and Mrs Hayden followed us.

'Have a seat, please,' said my mother.

Mrs Hayden sat in our living room, and all of it felt so surreal to me. I was only used to seeing her in class, at college. Her being in my house seemed so bizarre.

Ma asked Mrs Hayden what she would have, and Mrs Hayden replied that she was okay and didn't want anything. But my mother insisted on her having tea or coffee or lemonade. In the end, Mrs Hayden settled for lemonade.

I didn't know what conversation to make with her.

Mrs Hayden had walked into our balcony by now and she admired the plants my mother lovingly nurtured.

'You have a lovely balcony garden, Mrs Sharma,' she complimented as my mother walked in with the lemonade.

What was happening here? Did Mrs Hayden come here to admire the plants on our balcony? The contrast between my very beautiful, very Indian, saree-clad, bindi-and-mangalsutra-wearing mother, and the tall, elegant Mrs Hayden in her lilac skirt and heels couldn't have been starker. And yet here they were, discussing plants on the balcony like old friends. This was crazy! I was also dying to know the real reason she was here.

They finally finished the conversation about plants, fertilisers, flowers and nurseries, and came inside.

Then Mrs Hayden said, 'Mrs Sharma, I was hoping to meet both you and your husband together. I was informed that your husband visited the college. I am here to apologise to him and you as well.' Her gaze was down as she said it and her soft voice went softer.

'Apologise? But for what?' asked my mother.

'For the book your husband brought to college. It belongs to me. I am Ruth Hayden,' she said.

There was a moment of silence as this sunk in.

The book belonged to Mrs Hayden. She was Ruth! What did the note mean? Why had someone gifted her the book? I was stunned.

'I want to apologise to your husband and you for the grief it caused you,' she said.

My mother was embarrassed. She said, 'No, no. It's fine. I will convey this to my husband.'

'Please let him know that I had lost the book. I did not intend for it to turn up in the library. It was definitely not my intention for Ankita to have it. When I knew that he had come to college and returned the book, it came as a surprise to me. I was perturbed that I had caused your family distress. It was completely inadvertent. And I take full responsibility for it. It is not a book for students and no student shall ever lay hands on it again. I am terribly sorry,' she said.

'It's fine, it's okay,' my mother said again. I could see she was squirming, and silently cursing my father for putting her in this situation.

Mrs Hayden was very apologetic and my mother was very embarrassed. And if I wasn't this mortified and bewildered at the same time, I would have laughed.

Now there was an awkwardness in the air. I think Mrs Hayden realised it too. We needed to change the topic quickly.

'So, Mrs Hayden, what are the activities you volunteer for at Mount Mary church? I have seen it from the outside. It is a splendid building,' I said.

'Yes, it indeed is. The Corinthian pillars and the semi-gothic architecture are beautiful. It is more than a hundred years old,' Mrs Hayden said. 'I am involved in a lot of activities there. Right now, my focus is on helping them set up a library in the area. There are so many books that have been donated, and my biggest task is to put them in some order. They are piled up at my home at the moment, all higgledy-piggledy,' Mrs Hayden said.

'Oh, that is a lovely task, Mrs Hayden,' I said.

'It indeed is. But it is a *lot* of work, as the books are heavy and the donation pile grows on a daily basis,' she said.

I imagined the pile of books and I imagined going through them. I remembered the date I had with Vaibhav when we had gone through the tunnel of books at Flora Fountain. What a delight it had been. An idea struck me then.

'Mrs Hayden, I would love to volunteer. I can help you sort out the books,' I offered.

'That is very kind of you, Ankita. I was planning on asking around for a volunteer,' Mrs Hayden said. Then she turned to my mother. 'Mrs Sharma, would you be okay with Ankita coming over to my place for an hour or so? It would be a big help.'

'Of course! She isn't doing much at home anyway,' my mother said.

'Come on, Ma! Don't let me down so badly,' I protested.

Mrs Hayden laughed. 'That's what all mothers say. I used to say that too,' she said. There was a faraway look in her eyes. I could have sworn her eyes misted up.

Then she asked me to get a paper and a pen. She carefully wrote down her address, and drew a map to her home as well.

'It is the oldest building in that lane. It is right at the end of the lane. It would be impossible for you to miss it. The place is full of large shady trees. I live on the ground floor,' she said.

I was to start helping her from the day after.

'Ideally, I would have liked you to start tomorrow. But I have a wedding to attend. So it would be great if you started day after, at around 11.00 a.m. Does that suit you?' she said.

I told her I would be there. Once Mrs Hayden told us about the books, the prospect of spending an hour or so with my professor didn't seem bad at all. The pile of books at her home sounded like a treasure chest and I looked forward to helping her.

After she left, the faint fragrance of the perfume she wore still lingered in our drawing room. The air was scented lavender.

'What a lady! She seems like an English queen,' my mother said.

'Yes, Ma! This is exactly what I thought when she walked into the classroom the first day,' I said.

'And I am glad your father didn't meet her at your college when he went there. She is so gentle. I would have hated it had your father shouted at her or picked a fight with her in his anger. She doesn't deserve that,' my mother said.

'She definitely doesn't,' I agreed.

That evening, when my father returned home, my mother narrated all the details of Mrs Hayden's visit. She described Mrs Hayden in great detail. My father was surprised to know that she had taken the trouble to come home to apologise.

'Just shows that she is a classy person and genuinely regrets the book falling into the wrong hands,' my father said.

I went to my room, rifled through my cupboard and found the card that had fallen out of the suicide manual. Then I carefully placed it in my bag.

I decided I would return it to her when I went to her house.

•

The next morning, I learnt that Vaibhav had come back, and had even played badminton with my father. I was stunned when my father casually mentioned this over breakfast.

'Vaibhav played so well today. If not for him, we wouldn't have won so easily,' my father said. My stomach muscles clenched.

'Oh! When did he get back?' I asked, trying not to appear confused. Vaibhav had not even bothered to contact me. I had been so certain that he would get in touch with me when he got back. He had discarded me so easily, and instead met my father. How could he? I hoped my anguish did not show on my face.

'I think he got back the day before yesterday. He said he would meet me on the courts today,' said my father.

My heart almost stopped when I heard that. So he *was* avoiding me. That was the reason he hadn't come upstairs. I was sure of it. But my poor mother didn't know. I hadn't told my parents anything that had transpired on the day before Vaibhav left town.

'Why didn't he come up?' asked my mother, puzzled. I think she looked forward to Vaibhav visiting us as much as I did now.

'He mentioned he had to rush back as his boss was visiting and there's a presentation. Looks like he is immersed in his training requirements,' Dad said.

How easily my father was satisfied. But I wasn't. It bothered me no end that Vaibhav did this.

'When did he call you yesterday, Dad?' I asked.

'It must have been between 6.00 and 6.30 p.m. I was watching the news when I took his call,' my father replied.

I had gone with my mother to the supermarket at that time. She had wanted me to accompany her, and I had gone along. No wonder I wasn't aware of this.

I wanted to know where I stood with Vaibhav. What was this strange game he was playing? I *had* to know. I didn't have his phone number. But I knew I could easily get it; the electronic cordless telephone, which occupied a place of pride in our drawing room, stored the last five incoming numbers.

That night, when my parents went to bed, I took the cordless phone, and looked up the last five incoming numbers. It was easy to identify Vaibhav's number. The other four phone numbers were the same. They were my father's office numbers, and I recognised them instantly. The only number on that list I didn't recognise was Vaibhav's.

My hand trembled slightly as I pressed the buttons to call him. One hand curled around the phone in the dark, listening to it ring on the other side, as I bit the nails of my other hand waiting for him to answer. I didn't know what I would say. All I knew was that I wanted to talk to him. I was desperate to hear his voice. I couldn't take another minute of not knowing where I stood with him. But the phone kept ringing. Nobody answered.

28
Abide with Me

Though I had hardly slept, I woke up early. A quick glance at my bedside clock told me it was only 6.00 a.m. I knew from the stillness of the house that my parents hadn't woken up yet. If they had, I would have heard my mother bustling about in the kitchen, and my father getting ready for his badminton. I lay in silence, absorbing the quietness of the morning. The excited chirping of the birds in the distance, the faint glow of sunlight on the horizon – all of it came floating in through my window, heralding the arrival of dawn. It should have made me happy, but it didn't. The sadness of Vaibhav not contacting me was wedged like a stone in my heart. I felt terrible about it. I couldn't understand how he could come right up to my building, play badminton with my father and then *leave*. Like I didn't exist. I could have never done that to him.

I reached out for my notebook and began to write **Note 8.**

In a relationship, we expect others to behave the same way that we behave towards them. That is the biggest mistake we make. We think that just because we are kind and considerate, others will be the same towards us. We are shocked when they behave differently from how we expect them to. How can they do this to us, we think. We do not deserve this, we think. We would have never done this to them, right?

But perhaps we aren't stepping into their shoes. Maybe their yardstick for a relationship is different from ours. Maybe they have their own definition of love and it doesn't match ours.

The measure of what constitutes love is different for everyone. For some, calling once a week and talking for a while is enough expression of love. For others, calling once a day is adequate. Then there are those who like to make short calls several times a day. When it comes to love, there is no one-size-fits-all. Love is tailor-made for the one who loves.

If love should thrive, communication is a must. If you do not communicate, love dies. Also, being busy is just an excuse when people do not want to keep in touch. If you really want to keep in touch, you will find a way. You will prioritise the other person over everything else. If someone wants to talk to you, they make the time, otherwise they make an excuse.

If someone has not kept in touch and you want to maintain contact with them, you should try to get back in touch once, or at the most twice. After that, no matter how painful it is, you must let go. There is no point chasing after someone who doesn't want to stay in your life.

Let go.

That is the best way, and the only way. It will hurt. But then it will hurt a tiny bit lesser the next day. And a little lesser the day after that.

Eventually it stops hurting. And we heal.

But we will always carry that emptiness where their love used to be.

My mother peeped into my room.

'Up so early and studying, Ankita? So nice to see this,' she trilled.

'Yes, Ma. I have to go to Mrs Hayden's house today,' I said.

'Oh, yes, get ready. But you will have breakfast, right? She asked you to come only by eleven.'

'Of course,' I said.

I kept waiting for the doorbell to ring, kept expecting Vaibhav. When my father was leaving for badminton, I couldn't resist asking, 'Off to play with Vaibhav?'

'Oh, no. He said there was some team outing to Mahabaleshwar. Not in town again.'

How many more excuses would Vaibhav make to avoid meeting me? He should at least have the guts to tell it to my face that it was over. I decided I would never call him again. He had my number, he had access to my house, and he could come any time. I hated feeling helpless. I wanted him to call and explain his silence. But I remembered what I wrote in my note.

No matter how hard it was, I would have to refrain. No matter how much it hurt, I had to learn to let him go.

•

I found Mrs Hayden's home easily. The directions she'd given were perfect. It was exactly as she described. The cab I took went right up to the gate of her compound. I gasped in delight as it came into view. How magnificent! A forest in the middle of Bombay. I paid the driver and got out of the car. I stood for a moment and looked up, staring in awe at the trees. All I could see was a canopy of giant green trees. They seemed to rise upward forever, and through the dense green foliage little snippets of a bright blue sky peeped at me, as though the sun was laughing.

The building itself was very old, probably constructed during the British era, but impeccably maintained. The windows sported ornate decorative grills that curved outward gracefully.

I went up the two stone steps leading to her house. On either side of the steps were giant poinsettias in large pots, and it was like walking right into Christmas! It was almost magical. There was an iron knocker with the head of a lion instead of a doorbell and I knocked twice. Then I waited. This felt like a house in an enchanted forest.

A middle-aged lady opened the door and said that Mrs Hayden would be with me shortly. The living room had a very large comfortable deep brown leather sofa that I could sink into. Antique bookshelves lined up against one side of the wall. The room opened into an open courtyard. It was full of plants of all kinds: chrysanthemums, daisies, roses, jasmine and many others whose names I did not know. In a tiny pond, beautiful pink lilies flowered. A marble bird-bath stood by the side, with birds perching on the edge, having a dip and flying out. All around were green vines and flowers in every colour.

Mrs Hayden greeted me then.

'Hello, Ankita, so lovely to see you on time,' she said.

'Mrs Hayden, you live in a fairy tale!' I exclaimed.

'I am fortunate to have inherited this house, which is an annexe. If you notice, there are no houses above mine. The adjoining main building has ten floors. If I'd got a house there, I would have had an apartment above me. Here I have the open skies,' Mrs Hayden said.

'You have furnished it marvelously. I have never seen anything like this in my life.'

'Ah, Ankita,' said Mrs Hayden. 'We all need to create beauty in our lives in all the ways we can. Life can be so hard,' she said as she looked away.

I gawked around Mrs Hayden's living room. It even had a real fireplace. One of the walls sported a series of abstract paintings, each one framed in a simple black wooden frame. The minimal framing enhanced the vibrant colours leaping from every picture. Everywhere I turned, there was only loveliness.

'These paintings are so unique, Mrs Hayden,' I said.

'Thank you, dear. They are all painted by my son,' she said.

'What does he do, Mrs Hayden? Is he a professional artist?'

She paused. Then she swallowed and said. 'He was. A very good one at that. He is no more.'

'Oh, I am so sorry,' I said.

'No. It's fine, dear. He is in a good place now,' Mrs Hayden said.

She removed her glasses and wiped them. I wished I had not asked her about her son. But she wasn't done talking about him.

'That's his picture there,' she pointed at the mantel.

I walked to the mantel to have a closer look. There were three photographs encased in silver frames. One was a picture of a good-looking smiling young blond with green eyes. The other was a picture of a woman in a white wedding dress and a tall blond man in a suit. The woman was laughing and looking into the eyes of the man as he looked back at her. There was so much love and joy in the picture. It was a perfect wedding photo. The third was the picture of a green-eyed golden-haired baby grinning, looking straight into the camera.

'Mrs Hayden, is that you in this wedding photo? And is this a baby picture of your son? ' I asked.

'Yes, dear, your guesses are correct. That is my husband, Michael. We got married in a church in England. Each time I look at the photo, I can still hear the song they played that day when this photo was clicked,' she said.

'Which one was that, Mrs Hayden?' I asked.

'*Abide with me,* have you heard it?' Mrs Hayden looked serene as she spoke about it and yet there was sadness in her eye.

'No, Mrs Hayden, I don't think so.'

'It is a beautiful hymn. I listen to it all the time. Would you like to hear it?' she asked.

'I'd love to hear it,' I beamed.

Mrs Hayden went to the record player on a rosewood sideboard. Though I knew what a record player was, I never thought people actually used them anymore. She put in a record, and music filled the house.

The music felt sacred and it is difficult to put into words how I felt when I heard it. I was elevated, transported to a different place. The music touched something deep inside me, stirring my very soul. It was divine. I was almost moved to tears by the music.

We sat in silence and listened to the hymn. There was sadness in the notes, and yet it was an orchestral exuberance. When it ended, Mrs Hayden said, 'Do you know that the person who wrote this splendid piece died three weeks after he wrote it? The story goes that he had visited a dying friend many years back. The friend who was dying kept saying, "Abide with me". It stayed in his mind and years later, when he knew he was dying, he wrote the poem.'

'It is beautiful, Mrs Hayden,' I said.

'That's the thing about the words we utter. We have to choose them carefully. They have the power to affect others, and maybe affect the course of things in ways we can never imagine.

Sometimes we remember something someone said years later. It gets imprinted in our memory and refuses to go away.'

I thought of what Freddy had said then.

'Yes, and it is unfortunate if those are words that hurt,' I said.

'If it hurts, you have to learn to let it go, Ankita,' Mrs Hayden said.

She was looking at me carefully now. It seemed like she knew something about me, and was waiting for me to speak about it.

'It is very difficult, Mrs Hayden,' I murmured.

She sighed. 'Yes, it indeed is. I know that too well. But it is not impossible,' she said.

Then she led me inside, where the pile of books lay waiting.

29

Blue Balloon

All the donated books were in the far corner of the dining room, stacked up against the patterned wall.

'Mrs Hayden, the dining room too opens out to the garden!' I exclaimed, as I followed her and drank in the sight.

'Yes, dear. The entire house is planned in such a way that each and every room opens out into the garden.'

'The bedrooms too?' I asked.

'Yes, all the rooms, including the kitchen. You just have to step outside and you are in the garden,' she said.

I fell in love with her home at that moment. It was an unbelievable place. Each room was tastefully furnished. The dining room had an antique rosewood six-seater table with intricately carved legs and matching chairs, upholstered in the same deep brown leather the sofas were made of. At the centre was an ornate candle-holder with three candles. The white curtains had lace panels that hung to the floor.

Mrs Hayden introduced the lady who had opened the door for me as her housekeeper, Grace. She said Grace would join us to sort out the books.

Mrs Hayden had the methodology all figured out. She was like a military sergeant issuing orders, and the details of 'Operation Book-sorting' were meticulously planned. Mrs Hayden told us we could start by discarding the books that were too damaged or torn to be used. After that we were to sort them out alphabetically, which would make it easier for her to organise them in the library. Grace fetched some markers and chart paper. We made 26 cards, with each letter of the alphabet, and lined them up from one end of the room to the other. Each book had to be carefully examined and assigned to the right place, according to the last name of the author. All the non-fiction books were to be clubbed together.

For the next two-and-a-half hours, all three of us worked side by side, going through the pile of books. Each time I found a book I had read, I made a happy sound. Invariably, Mrs Hayden would have read it too, and we would launch into a detailed discussion about the plot, the characters and the setting. It was delightful for me to talk to Mrs Hayden so freely. I enjoyed myself thoroughly and this did not seem like work at all. Discovering an old book you once read is like meeting an old friend after a long time.

I hadn't heard of certain books, and Mrs Hayden told me which ones were a 'must-read' and what they were about. She said I could keep a few aside to borrow, and that I could return them after I was done.

'Oh, thank you so much!' I said.

'My pleasure. It is always a delight to discuss books with another bibliophile,' she said.

She was my professor, but when it came to books, we were chattering away like monkeys. The more time I spent with her sorting out the books, the friendlier we became. Books were binding us together in a strange way, bridging the gap between us.

After we had worked for nearly three hours, Grace excused herself to cook lunch.

'Why don't you join us for lunch, Ankita?' Mrs Hayden invited me.

I knew my mother would be waiting for me, so I thanked her and told her I couldn't.

'Alright, I think we have done enough work for today. Let's stop now. We have earned ourselves some strawberry crush,' declared Mrs Hayden.

'Shall I make it, ma'am, and serve it in the garden?' asked Grace.

'Yes, that would be lovely,' said Mrs Hayden as she led me to the garden.

Grace served us the strawberry crush in tall glasses. It was delicious. Mrs Hayden said she had made the concentrate herself. Each year she got strawberries from Panchgani, when they were in season, and she made the syrup, which could later be diluted and served anytime through the year.

As we sat under the canopy, I looked around the garden.

'Some day, when I have a home of my own, I want to have a garden like this, Mrs Hayden,' I said.

'Do you know that I tried to recreate the garden I had in England? The weather there is different, and many of the plants that thrive there do not do well here. I had to find substitutes. The strange thing is there are many similar-coloured flowers, but their requirements in terms of care are vastly different. There is such a lot that goes into planning a garden,' Mrs Hayden said.

I nodded. I had seen my mother diligently nurturing the plants at home and knew it needed very careful tending to.

As we sat there sipping the strawberry crush, Mrs Hayden said, 'You know, Ankita, each time I sit here, I cannot but help reflect on how a garden is a lot like life. We do make a general plan, we sow the seeds. But afterwards? We do not have much control over what happens. We can only hope.'

'It is so true, Mrs Hayden. Nothing goes according to plan,' I agreed.

It was then that I remembered the note in my bag.

'Oh, Mrs Hayden, I have something that probably belongs to you.'

I excused myself, fetched it from my bag, and handed it over to her.

I noticed the flicker of recognition in her eyes. She then took it and ran her hands over it. She turned it over, handling it gently. She was silent for a few seconds, as though she was carefully considering what to say.

I waited for her to speak.

Then she said, 'Thank you so much, Ankita, for returning this. This means a lot to me. I presumed I had lost it forever. This was the first thing I looked for when Mrs Asthana returned the book to me. I was disappointed when I didn't find it.'

'I held on to it, as I didn't want it to be lost when my father took the book back to Mrs Asthana,' I said.

It was the first time we had made a reference to the book.

'I think I owe you an explanation about this note. But would you like to tell me what upset your father so much about the book?'

My heart began to beat fast then. My anxiety, my thoughts, my fear, all of it came rushing back. I had been fine till then. But now Mrs Hayden had asked about my past. How could I explain to her why my father was so upset, unless I told her my life story? Things were fine between us till that point. But if I narrated to her all that had happened, would she judge me? I didn't know.

It was difficult for me to talk about it even though I had narrated all of it to Vaibhav first, then to Joseph. Both of them had not reacted the way I expected them to. Now here was Mrs Hayden asking me about it. I had no idea how to tell her or to explain to her. So I sat silently, not saying anything. I was furiously trying to think of something clever to say. But nothing came to my mind. I just sat there blinking and swallowing and looking away.

'I can see that it makes you uncomfortable, Ankita. We have to learn to make peace with our past. We have to learn to accept ourselves. Only then can we move forward.'

'Mrs Hayden, that's easy for you to say. You have no idea what I have been through. It is not so easy to let go. People don't let you forget.' I shook my head.

The very next moment, I regretted saying it. I hadn't meant for it to come out with so much anger and bitterness. But then I had been bristling silently at the unfairness of it all, and I felt compelled to speak up when Mrs Hayden made a remark like that so casually. As though letting go was that easy!

'People will say many things, Ankita. But what does your inner voice tell you? You have to listen to only your inner voice.'

My inner voice tells me I'm worthless.

Worthless.

Worthless.

Worthless.

'What if it tells you things you do not want to hear?' I asked. My voice was hoarse.

'You have to learn to silence it. You have to learn to tame your mind, Ankita,' Mrs Hayden said. 'It hasn't been easy for me, but over the years, I have learnt how to.'

I was silent for a few moments as I thought about what she had said.

'Mrs Hayden, what if it cannot be silenced, no matter how much you try? What if your inner voice constantly tells you that you are worthless?' I asked.

I wasn't sure why I was telling her this. Perhaps things were bottled up inside me too long and sought an escape. Perhaps it was the relaxed atmosphere in the garden. Or perhaps it was the way Mrs Hayden looked at me – *into* me – and spoke with such kindness. Or perhaps it was only because I wanted some form of validation from Mrs Hayden that I wasn't just a mental patient but so much more.

'Do you actually believe that you are worthless?' Mrs Hayden asked gently.

'Sometimes,' I whispered.

'Then you need to replace those negative voices with positive ones. It is imperative you do this. If not, you are on a path of self-destruction.'

'How? How do I do that? How can I control it?' I asked.

'Ankita, we have something called visualisation exercises. I used to teach it to my students, and they all said it helped them a great deal.'

'I think I need those, Mrs Hayden. No matter how much I try to forget, certain things keep coming back to me,' I confided.

I felt I could trust Mrs Hayden, and more than that, I felt she could help me. Perhaps it was the magic of the place itself, or it was the hymn that Mrs Hayden had played, or it was the way she was looking into my very soul.

She seemed to understand exactly what I was talking about. There was deep wisdom in her eyes as she looked at me. Though she was my professor, I knew I had found a friend in her.

Something had changed between us.

Mrs Hayden sensed it too.

'I could teach them to you, Ankita. Each time you feel a negative thought coming, you could practice this, and destroy that thought.'

She then told me to close my eyes. I did.

'Now search your mind for whatever negative phrase you hear, whether it is "you are worthless" or anything that plays on a loop. Comb every recess of your mind.'

She paused.

I did as she instructed, and all the phrases that I had been hearing in my head began playing out. It was unbearable. The one that stood out the most was:

You are worthless.

Mrs Hayden's soothing voice cut through my pain. 'Imagine each word of the phrase written in air. They can be as big as you like.'

I imagined the letters in my head.

'Now imagine a balloon larger than those letters,' Mrs Hayden said.

I imagined a massive balloon.

'What colour is the balloon?' she asked.

'Blue, sky blue,' I replied with my eyes closed. Her voice had a hypnotic quality. She spoke slowly and I was in a trance.

'Now take those words, shrink them, and put them inside your sky-blue balloon.'

I did as told.

'Now tie up the balloon tight,' Mrs Hayden instructed.

I sat with my eyes closed and did exactly as she suggested.

'Now do it again a second time,' she said.

I imagined 'you are worthless' written in bold letters. The letters were suspended in the sky, mocking me. I imagined each of those letters entering the balloon, one by one, till none were left. I imagined knotting up the balloon.

Mrs Hayden then told me to take another negative phrase and do the same. This time I took 'you hurt the ones you love'. She made me do it a second time too. Then she told me to take another phrase and do the same. I followed her instructions. I now had six balloons full of negative phrases.

'Now imagine all these balloons floating up... up... and *away*. They are getting smaller... and smaller... and smaller. They are now tiny specks in the sky. They have flown far away. All the negative things you constantly hear are gone. They have vanished... gone forever...' Mrs Hayden continued in her soft voice. I sat there with my eyes closed, mesmerised.

I saw those balloons float high and felt lighter and lighter as they went farther away from me.

'Now you can open your eyes,' Mrs Hayden said.

I blinked slowly and opened them.

'Do you feel better?' she asked.

I had no words to explain how I felt. I nodded.

'This is a *very* powerful exercise, Ankita. Each time you are filled with self-doubt or negativity, be sure to practice this. The beauty of this is that you can practice it anywhere. You do not need any equipment or preparation. Anytime you want, you can shut your eyes and do it. It only takes a few minutes, but the results are long-lasting.'

'But how do I know they won't come back?' I asked. I couldn't believe that a simple visualisation exercise could banish all my negative thoughts.

'The patterns have taken time to consolidate in your head, and they will not vanish overnight. But each time you do this, they become lighter,' Mrs Hayden said. 'I have used this over the years, and it has helped me. A lot more than you would imagine.' She looked at me hesitantly. 'Would you like to hear my story?'

30

Both Sides of the Story

I wanted to.
'It is a long story. Are you certain you want to hear it, dear?'
Mrs Hayden asked again.

Yes, I confirmed, I wanted to hear. I wanted to know how she got to be so calm and wise. If she could do it, perhaps so could I.

She cleared her throat. 'I lived in India till I was eight. Then my father, a British officer posted in India, got recalled back to England. He was one of the few officers who decided to take their Indian wives back with them to England, even though he risked social ostracism. Many of the British men had taken "second wives" in India, while their wives were back home, but my father was different. My mother was the only woman in his life. They couldn't bear to be away from each other and so, though my mother hated to leave India, she did. She swore she would come back the first chance she got. I remember being devastated as I was separated from my beloved *ayah*, who I had known all my life. As a child, it was extremely painful for me to leave India – the only world I had known. Though my father told me about England, I think I internalized my mother's fears, about the cold, the culture and the alien world. We set sail from Bombay to Liverpool in 1938.' She sighed and continued.

'The journey by ship took its toll on my mother's health. The cold in England was unbearable. She had no friends, no family. She was isolated, but for my father. I have never seen my parents fight, but in England, I could sense that things were not how they used to be between them. My poor mother caught pneumonia and died soon after. I was shattered. I was raised by my aunt, a spinster who moved in with us. She didn't approve of my Indian roots and frowned whenever I mentioned India. It was easy for her to pretend I never had any Indian connection, as I had inherited my father's looks. My father kept in touch with my maternal grandfather in India. And I longed to come back to India, to meet my grandparents.'

Mrs Hayden had a faraway look in her eyes as she reminisced about her past. I guessed how vulnerable and helpless she would have felt back then. My heart went out to her.

'So did you manage to visit them?' I asked.

Her eyes lit up as she continued. 'I did manage to visit India once, when I was nineteen. I got a chance to come to India as a part of a student exchange programme during college. I met my Indian relatives. My grandfather was delighted to see me, as was my grandmother. I had never received that much love and unconditional acceptance. They welcomed me with open arms. All the relatives from my mother's side met me and chatted excitedly with me. I felt very inadequate as I knew no language other than English. I pored over my mother's photographs. I loved the stories my grandfather and grandmother narrated.'

I couldn't help but smile at the image this conjured up, to imagine Mrs Hayden as a young girl, in a house full of her Indian relatives whom she barely knew. How strange it must have been for her!

'Little by little,' she was saying, 'I discovered my mother. It was the happiest time of my life. My grandfather said that this house was my mother's inheritance, and it would come to me after her. I was astounded at how they treated me like family even though I hadn't met them for so many years.'

'But then you went back to England?' I prodded when she fell quiet, her mind in the happy past.

'Yes, dear, I did. I had to. My father and my aunt wanted me to complete my education and I too wanted to go back to college. But I left my heart here in India. Nothing in England seemed exciting after my visit to India. That was when I met Michael, my professor at college. He was unlike any man I had met. After his lecture, I began seeking him out on the pretext of asking about the course work, about assignments. I was slowly falling in love with him, and I could tell it was reciprocal. I was 21, he, 26. My aunt and my father were over the moon that I had chosen a well-educated British man. I think they had been worried that I'd marry an Indian man as I was so fascinated by my Indian roots.'

'Did you forget about India then?' I asked.

'No, never. How could I? India is a part of me as I am a part of India. But I never got a chance to come back,' Mrs Hayden said.

I nodded as she went on. 'We got married the following year, the year after I graduated. Within a year I gave birth to my son. Ethan was a charmer from the word go. Everyone loved Ethan. When Ethan was about two, I decided to study further. My aunt helped with childcare. I began earning a stipend too when I pursued my doctorate. Side by side, I also taught at the university. By the time I got my doctorate, Ethan was nine.'

Her eyes grew dreamy. 'We were a happy family. I wanted to bring Ethan to India to meet his great-grandfather and great-grandmother. But then disaster struck. I lost both my father and aunt within the next four years. It hit me badly, and I took a while to recover. By then, Ethan was a teenager, and my visit to India remained a dream. I got news of my grandfather passing away, and then my grandmother too. I wept bitterly, and I was sad that I couldn't even attend the funerals and pay my final respects.'

I nodded, feeling intensely sorry for Mrs Hayden. To lose almost your whole family like that was unimaginable for me.

'Then a bigger tragedy struck. I don't think I will ever recover from it, at least not in this lifetime.' Her voice wobbled.

'Ethan killed himself when he was twenty-four. He was the gentlest, most loving and compassionate soul, forever rescuing mynahs, pigeons, wounded animals. He volunteered at animal shelters. As you can imagine, Michael and I were devastated. It was the end of our world. The details that emerged made me realise how little I knew my Ethan, even though, like all mothers, I presumed I did. The fact is, parents do not know their children at all. Children hide a lot from their parents.'

I could so relate to that. I myself had hidden such a lot from my parents. I could understand how Ethan must have felt.

'Why... why did Ethan...?' I asked.

'Ethan had gone up to Scotland to meet a friend when he fell ill. When we investigated further, we discovered he had been diagnosed with Huntington's disease. It had started about four years back, when he was at art school. Can you imagine that? Four whole years and he did not even know that it was progressing; neither did we. The disease progresses slowly and you have no clue about the deceptive symptoms of this horrible disease.

'What happens with this disease is that it attacks the nerve cells in your brain gradually, eating them away. Ultimately it is fatal. There is no escape. But what is even more terrible is that you lose your thinking and reasoning abilities, you lose memory, you lose coordination, and you lose movement. You are just trapped in your own body, waiting to die. With each passing day, you keep getting worse. There is no hope. Only darkness.'

I sat there in shocked silence listening to Mrs Hayden's story unfold. Her sad words felt like arrows being shot into my own heart.

'Couldn't you... couldn't you have done something?' I asked helplessly, listening to all this.

'I beat myself up for many years asking the same question. But, you see, I couldn't have, even if I wanted to. First, he had hidden it from us. Second, there is no cure for Huntington's. And if that isn't enough, you also succumb to psychiatric disorders. It wreaks havoc with your brain. You get anxiety, paranoia, and you become a victim of obsessive-compulsive thoughts and disorders.'

She looked directly at me now. 'My son had left an entire notebook for us telling us how much he loved us. He mentioned that he didn't want to go through any of that. It was the most heart-breaking thing I ever read.

'Huntington's disease is genetic. Michael's father had died of it. But at that time, he had been confined to an asylum, and we weren't really sure what it was. It can skip a generation, and if the defective gene has been passed on, it can appear in the next generation.'

She closed her eyes. I fought an impulse to lean forward and place my hand on hers, but I did not want to disturb her. She said with eyes still closed, 'Michael and I dealt with our grief in different ways. I did a course in counseling, and started working with young people, to help those in depression. I did this for many years, as I saw my son in the young people I worked with. The young are the same everywhere – across generations, across continents. It was my way of healing from this terrible loss.'

'What about your husband?' I asked softly. I could not even imagine how much pain Mrs Hayden must have been in.

'Michael couldn't bear the loss. He began drinking heavily. He would often come home inebriated and head straight to bed. Michael's close friend Scott, who is also a doctor, said Ethan was brave and had chosen this way out. He told Michael to be strong. He said this was a better way to go than to suffer the vagaries of the disease. But Michael wouldn't listen. He beat himself up over our son's death. He wished and wished the disease could have taken him instead of our son. But you have to be careful what you wish for. Five years back, Michael was diagnosed with the same disease. We were in a state of absolute shock. It was a late onset for him. It is a gene variant that determines whether you have an early or a late onset.'

I gasped. I couldn't imagine a tragedy this enormous. How did Mrs Hayden even face any of this?

Mrs Hayden nodded. 'You can imagine what we went through. First, it was our son. Now Michael. Michael started becoming obsessed with death. There was no hope for him. He would only get worse. He didn't want to live that way. He was still active and functional at that time as it was the early intermediate stage. He began reading up extensively about euthanasia and the choices available medically to those with terminal diseases. He knew some people in the academic circles, and through them he got in touch with members of the Hemlock Society. He started advocating the right to die with dignity.

'I saw what the disease was doing to Michael. It was killing him slowly. Initially, I was against people taking their own lives, for whatever reasons. But when I saw Michael suffering, I changed my mind. Watching a person you love degenerate like this is a fate worse than death. It was becoming increasingly unbearable for me to watch Michael deteriorate. There were months and months that I went without sleep. If I did sleep, it was not more than a few minutes at a stretch. Patients with Huntington's disease need a lot of care. It was affecting my health. My hair turned grey and I became frail. I did not know when the day began and when it ended. Months went by. I was deeply depressed. Michael saw what it was doing to me and he felt angry, guilty and helpless.'

Mrs Hayden's voice had grown faint. I got up and poured her some water from the dining table. She took the glass with a 'thanks' but did not sip it before speaking. 'Michael, Scott and I had many, many discussions around this. Michael begged us to help him. Gradually, I was beginning to see Michael's viewpoint. So was Scott. Then when the book *The Best Way to Go* was published, Michael made Scott buy it. Then he gifted it to me. He wrote that note then. He could barely hold the pen. He struggled a lot. It must have taken him many hours to write that note. He asked me to help him die and he asked me to be strong when I did it. He said it was the only way. He said he had made up his mind, and he couldn't bear it anymore. He was completely dependent on me by then.'

Now she paused to sip from the glass. 'I still wanted him to live, Ankita. But one night, Michael was screaming in extreme frustration and yelling at us. He said he couldn't bear the torture anymore. He told Scott and me that if we didn't help him, he would help himself. He had studied the book, and he said he knew what to do.

'Scott decided then that he would give him a lethal injection. He asked Michael if he was sure. He yelled that he was. Scott asked him if he had any last wishes. Michael told him he wanted to go while listening to the hymn that we played on our wedding day. I sat beside his bed and held his hand as Scott played the hymn. He told me he loved me. He thanked Scott from the bottom of his heart.

'Then Scott injected the drug. Michael was supposed to die within seven minutes, but he started convulsing. Scott and I looked at each other helplessly. He was struggling. I couldn't bear it anymore. I picked up the pillow and held it to his face, and Scott helped me. We held it till Michael stopped struggling and then he was gone.'

Both of us sat in silence; we couldn't talk for some time.

Then she spoke again, 'I couldn't bear to live in the UK after that. I came back to India. Since I had many years of teaching experience, the college offered me a full-time position. But I wanted only a part-time one. The church that I attended in England put me on to the church here that I volunteer with now. I threw myself into all the activities I could. I also did up this house – my Indian inheritance. In the years that I was in England, my grandparents had done all the paperwork, and ensured that I got this house. I can't tell you how grateful I was for this place, my refuge.'

She said, 'As I created this garden, I was healing little by little. As the garden grew, I was growing too – though I didn't know it then. This garden has helped me so much. Each day I see the beauty in it, I am reminded that there is still beauty and hope left in life.

'So you can imagine, Ankita, the amount of guilt I carry and the amount of negative thoughts that try to take over every single day. But I have learnt to control them. I play the song *Abide by me* because it is hard for me to listen to it. At first I would break down each time I heard it. Then I learnt to rein in my sadness, and keep it inside me.'

Mrs Hayden got up and walked towards the garden. I followed her, hanging on to her every word. 'On days when my grief and my guilt get unbearable, I allow myself a good cry, but for just ten minutes in the bathroom. Then my crying for the day is done. After that, I sit here in this garden, and any negative thought I have is given the balloon treatment. They have all almost vanished now.'

She turned to look at me. 'Our mind is our biggest enemy, Ankita. But it can also be our biggest friend. There's so much beauty in life. We only have to look.'

31
Trust in You

Mrs Hayden's story moved me in ways I never expected. When I came home that day, I narrated it in great detail to my parents. I left out the part where Mrs Hayden said she had smothered her husband, and helped him die. I also didn't tell them about Scott's role in the whole thing. I felt my parents wouldn't understand that bit, and who knew, perhaps they would judge Mrs Hayden, which I did not want. When pushed to the extreme, we act in ways we never think possible. I knew it was so for Mrs Hayden. I felt strangely protective of her.

Her story was a whirlpool within me. Mrs Hayden seemed so perfect from the outside. Yet there was such darkness inside her. I had tried to kill myself, twice. It was a burden I had carried for so long. But when I thought about Mrs Hayden's story and the guilt that she carries every single day, I felt it was not that big a burden anymore. For the first time since the day I'd tried to kill myself, I felt *okay*. That it is circumstances that make us act in a certain way. We had to come to terms with it, take responsibility for our actions, and then move on. It was a paradigm shift. I had never looked at it that way.

Both my parents agreed that her story was inspiring. I also told my parents about the visualisation exercise that Mrs Hayden made me do, and my father was happy that it helped.

'Do it every day, Ankita. It has to become a part of your daily routine. See how Mrs Hayden is so brave about the difficulties she faced,' he said.

If only you knew the whole truth you would find her even more inspiring, I thought. But I said nothing.

I sat thinking about Mrs Hayden's life that night. How did she endure it? She had lost almost everyone in her life. She was stoic, no doubt. I kept thinking about her life story, and I could see it in my head like a movie. How much of a loss she had faced and yet how she embraced life!

I took out my notebook, and wrote **Note 9.**

Life is difficult. It might give you a few things. You might even be happy for a while, as you achieve whatever goals you set to achieve: a college degree, a job, a nice house, and maybe even marriage to your dream partner. Life keeps you busy with mundane things, and you chug along, happy to receive that promotion, happy to move into a bigger house, drive a better car, earn more money.

Eventually, life comes to collect. It takes away everything that means the most to you. It takes away your youth, and if you are not careful, your health, and your peace of mind too. In the course of your life, you eventually lose your grandparents, and then your parents. Perhaps you even lose a spouse or a child.

How then do you go on? What meaning can you derive from it all? How do you overcome the debilitating grief of losing all you hold dear?

*Face the grief. Acknowledge it. Accept that it exists. Cry
if you must, but limit it to ten minutes or maybe twenty.*

*After that, do things that heal your soul. Find out
what satisfies you on a deeper level. Perhaps it is growing
a beautiful garden, or practising music or art – or anything
that you forgot in your minutiae.*

*To make life more meaningful, we need to create a
treasure trove of memories that will keep us strong. We need
to find our own little sops that comfort us.*

*More than anything, we need to find beauty even where
there is none. It exists. Always. We need to know where to
look.*

I knew that I had captured in the note all that I had learnt that day
at Mrs Hayden's place. I was also deeply moved that she trusted me
such a lot. She had opened up to me and explained what the note
that I had found in the book was all about and why it mattered so
much to her. She wasn't afraid that I would judge her.

I decided then that I would tell her why my father was that
upset about my having the book and why he decided to come to
college. I felt I owed her an explanation.

•

Sharing and trusting brings people closer in ways they never
thought possible. When I reached Mrs Hayden's home the next
morning, she greeted me at the door with a hug. I was enveloped
in her lavender scent. We were no longer just teacher and student,
we were friends.

She offered me chocolate chip cookies.

'I baked them after you left yesterday. Ethan used to love them,' she said.

The cookies were the best I ate. I told her so.

Her eyes crinkled as she laughed. For a moment she looked young and carefree. She said, 'Exactly what my Ethan used to say.'

We worked for three hours that day, in the same fashion we had done the previous day. By the end of it, the books were rightly categorised.

'Thank you so much, Ankita. I can't tell you what a big help this has been,' she said.

'Does it mean I have earned another strawberry crush?' I asked.

'Of course, my dear.' She smiled. 'Come to the garden.'

We sat in the garden, and Grace served us the strawberry crush again. This time it was my turn to speak. I had narrated my life story to Vaibhav, to Joseph, to Dr Neeraj and now here I was, telling it to Mrs Hayden. It was getting easier with each narration. But with Mrs Hayden, I went a step further. I didn't leave out *anything*. I also told her about my relationship with Vaibhav and how hurt I was that he had stopped coming to my house. I knew she would understand.

Mrs Hayden listened carefully, nodding, just like Dr Neeraj had done. The only difference was that she didn't take notes.

When I finished, she said, 'Now I understand why your father was so upset that he came to the college. Rightfully so. It was a dangerous thing you did, Ankita. It must have terrified your parents.'

'It did, Mrs Hayden. I never meant to frighten them.'

'I know you did not. But you must remember one thing, Ankita. You acted that way because you allowed Joseph's words to *hurt* you. Let me ask you something, if I said you had green hair, would you be hurt?'

'Green hair? Of course not. But I don't have green hair. My hair is black,' I said.

'Precisely. When you are confident about what you are or who you are, it doesn't matter what others say. You must remember that it is *their* perspective. If I say you have green hair, it is because there is something wrong with my eyes. It doesn't mean your hair is green. So it doesn't hurt you.'

It was a moment of revelation for me.

Then I thought about it some more.

'But what if my hair is indeed green?' I asked.

'Then you must reflect on whether the greenness bothers you; if it bothers you, you must think about why it bothers you. Is it because you are trying to fit in? Is it because you are afraid to be different? What does it mean to you?'

How right Mrs Hayden was! Why did I feel hurt? It was because I was afraid what he said was true.

'Ankita, we're all wired differently. It is something we can't help. We are all dealt a different set of cards by life. All we can do is use our judgement and make the best use of those cards. You have fought bipolar disorder, you have spent time in a mental hospital and you have successfully coped with it all. That is your strength, not your weakness. You are creative, you are smart and you have a long way to go. How can you let someone else's words hold you back?'

Her words poured down on me like rain on parched earth. I soaked them all up. Deep down I *knew* she was right. I just had to remind myself over and over till they sank in.

Mrs Hayden wasn't done yet.

'You know, Ankita, we are not responsible for other people's actions. Those are choices *they* make. Can we control how others behave? You cannot control how Joseph or Vaibhav or Abhi behaved towards you. You cannot blame yourself by presuming that it was something *you* did that made them act in a certain way. They are free to make their choices. Just like my Ethan made his choice. I couldn't do anything to stop him or make him change his mind. We do not control others. We only control our minds. We should do everything we can to keep it in check.'

She was so right. Nobody had said this to me before. We did not have any control over other people's choices. Yet we beat ourselves over it.

Then I remembered that I had forgotten to ask Mrs Hayden how the book had got to the library.

'You know I kept thinking about that too. Then it dawned on me. It was Grace. I had borrowed a bunch of books from the college library. I left them on my bedside table for a couple of months, as these were reference books that took me a while to complete. Grace used to complain that she was finding it hard to dust. So I told her to put them in a bag, except for the one I was reading. After I was done, I took the bag to the library, not knowing that she had packed *The Best Way To Go* too. That day, when I reached the library, Mrs Asthana was in a hurry to leave, and she said I could leave them there, that she would sort them and mark them "returned" the following day. I did not think much about it then. But looking back now, it all makes sense. The funny part was I always presumed that the book was in my drawing room along with the other books. I did not even miss it,' Mrs Hayden explained. 'It was when Mrs Asthana called me about it that I even realised it was gone. She immediately knew it was mine, as we address each other by our first names. You have no idea how mortified I was, and at the same time relieved that I got it back.

'The first thing I looked for was the note inside the book that Michael had written. When I didn't find it, I presumed it had fallen out of the book and was lost. Afterwards, I felt I owed your parents an apology. I found out your address from the college records, and the rest you know.'

'I am so, so glad you came over, Mrs Hayden. Else, I would have never discovered this magical garden you have created.'

'And we would have not known each other's stories,' she said softly.

●

Time spent with Mrs Hayden was proving to be invaluable. That evening, when my father got home, I excitedly told him and my mother about my day. I told them what Mrs Hayden said about the green hair. I had never thought of it that way.

'I kept telling you to not bother about what others said. But you said that was not possible,' my mother reminded me.

'Ma, all I was telling you is that it wasn't easy. When you said it that way, it didn't make any sense to me. I knew that they had said those things and those things had hurt me. So how could I *not* bother about it? That was what you were asking me to do.'

'Yes, Mrs Hayden explained *why* one should not bother in a way that made sense to Ankita. She has a wonderful way of explaining,' my father said.

'Whatever it is, I am glad you got the point,' Ma said.

'Ankita, what Mrs Hayden said reminded me of another saying: nobody can hurt you without your permission. Remember that always,' my father said.

'What do you mean by that?' I asked.

'It was Gandhiji who said it during the civil disobedience movement. He was beaten physically. But he said it did not affect him as his morals and beliefs inside him were untouched. He said he did not give anyone permission to enter him, and hence he was untouched. What it means is that if you allow someone's words to enter your heart, you are giving them permission yourself. Be very careful who you give permission to, Ankita. You do not have to allow everyone inside,' my father said.

I decided then to remember these words always. I would from now on choose carefully who I let in, and who to leave outside. I decided I wouldn't give my mind-space to *everyone*.

For the first time I decided that what was important was my well-being. I would fight. I would not let my thoughts take over. If Mrs Hayden could embrace life and go on even after all her losses, I could too.

I would grab life and I would *live* it.

32

Let Love Stand a Chance

The next morning I badly missed going to Mrs Hayden's place. I missed her garden, I missed the strawberry crush, I missed the cookies, and I missed her gentle voice. The last couple of days had been like a balm. The time I had spent there was beyond comforting. She had told me to come and visit her whenever I felt like it. But if I turned up there today itself, I felt it would be too soon.

So I dealt with it in the way I knew best; I took out my notebook, and wrote **Note 10.**

We always have a good time with our friends. But is the friendship good for you? There is an easy way to judge this.

One kind of friendship is where everyone has a good time doing something together. It is the shared interest that sustains the friendship. We might go to a restaurant together, talk about what is going on around us, gossip a bit, laugh a bit and then go home. We might get together, perhaps play a game or two, or indulge in a group activity everyone enjoys, eat, drink and then go home.

Then there is the other kind of friendship where you share what's closest to your heart. You talk about your plans for life. You trust the other person completely and believe that they want the best for you. They do not hesitate to tell you when you are going wrong. They tell you things you do not want to hear, what no one else will tell you.

It is the second kind that makes you grow. While you have fun in the first one, the second one is what keeps you on track, on the path you have chosen. The second kind helps you to see clearly.

You can have the first kind of friendship with just about anybody who shares a few interests with you. But the second kind? That is harder. The challenge is to choose carefully the person for the second kind of friendship. If you choose the wrong person, there is a very real danger they will betray you. Only time will tell who is true.

If you have found someone who is completely trustworthy and is right for the second kind of friendship, then you are fortunate.

You have found a real treasure.

I felt lucky to have found the second kind of friendship in my college professor of all people! The shrill ring of the telephone interrupted my thoughts. My mother picked it up. I strained to hear what she was saying. I could hear only one side of the conversation.

'How have you been? It's been so long.' Then she listened.

'You have to ask her!' and 'No, no, I understand,' and then, 'Of course! Please come over.'

'Who is coming over, Ma?' I shouted from my room.

'Are you studying or listening to what I am saying on the phone?' She smiled.

'Both,' I said. 'You know I can multi-task.'

What she said next made my heart dance and sing.

'Vaibhav is coming over. He wanted to know if he can take you out again. I said he could ask you directly.'

I thought my heart would explode with joy. One part of me was angry with him for not having turned up for so long. But the other part of me was ecstatic that he had turned up at all.

The elated part of me said: Vaibhav is coming. You have heard from him. He wants to see you!

The angry part of me said: Snub him. Don't show your eagerness. How can he decide when to walk out of your life and when to walk back in?

'Oh, okay,' I said and pretended to write. I didn't want my mother to see how conflicted I felt. But I think my mother knew. Mothers always know.

'Go get dressed instead of sitting there in your usual clothes.' My mother gave me a nudge.

'For what? I haven't said that I am going out yet,' I replied and scribbled some more in the last page of my notebook. I was doodling mindlessly.

'Make up your mind,' said my mother with a smile.

I looked at the doodles I had made. They were all pictures of flowers blooming and butterflies flying. I had also drawn a cactus.

That was how I felt inside too. I was happy, yet prickly. It felt like spring after a long harsh winter.

I rushed to the bathroom, and quickly made myself presentable. Earlier, when he used to come over on a daily basis, I had not bothered much about my appearance. But now I wanted to look good. I had just finished applying my eyeliner when the bell rang.

I waited for my mother to open the door.

'Hello! Come in,' I heard her say.

I waited for a few seconds, took a deep breath and walked out.

'Hey, Ankita,' he greeted me as if seeing me for the first time, as if nothing had happened between us.

'Hi,' I greeted him back.

Ma asked him about his training programme and how he had enjoyed it.

'It's such a different experience from working in the city, aunty. I got a proper taste of rural life,' he said. He went on to describe their living quarters, which were rustic, the simple village food and the agricultural life the villagers led. He had to stay in a hut with a family from the village; every year the management trainees did that and it was an extra source of income for the villagers. He described the factory set-up, and the way it functioned. Even as he spoke to my mother, I could see that he kept glancing at me. Our eyes met many times, and each time they did, I felt a flutter in my belly.

My mother asked him to join us for lunch, and he did. I was finding it hard to not blurt out my anger at his disappearance. It was with great difficulty that I controlled myself.

'This is Ankita's favourite, vegetable pulao', my mother said, as she opened the covered dish. The aroma made my mouth water.

'This smells so good!' said Vaibhav as he sniffed appreciatively.

I wanted to finish lunch quickly. I wanted to hear what he had to say. But my mother had put a great deal of effort into this meal, and so we took our time, chatting about inane things. It was mostly my mother and he who were chatting. At last, the lunch was over, and I helped my mother clear the table.

'Ankita, shall we go out for a bit?' Vaibhav asked.

I nodded.

'Aunty, is it fine? I will bring her back in a couple of hours,' Vaibhav said.

'Can I join you?' Ma asked, and then burst out laughing. 'I was just joking. You children go enjoy yourselves.'

Earlier when I used to walk with Vaibhav to the building lobby, we'd chat about my course or about his work.

Now the easy chatter was gone, and we were both formal. The silence between us wasn't a silence of discomfort, though. It was the silence of anticipation.

'There is this café by the beach, shall we go there?' he asked.

'Okay,' I said, my heart in turmoil. Perhaps he was taking me to a café to break up with me? I didn't know. I would soon find out.

'Let's get a cab. I haven't hired a car this time,' he said.

'I am glad you didn't. We know how it went the last time you hired one,' I said.

I hadn't intended it to come out as an accusation. The fact was, I was feeling awkward and a little annoyed. I also didn't know what to say.

'Listen, I am sorry about that. I shall explain,' he said.

He hailed a cab, and we reached the place in under five minutes.

'Oh, if it was this close, why did you call a cab?' I asked.

'I didn't want you to walk,' he said.

The café resembled a log cabin. The emphasis and the focal point of the entire decor were the wood panels that ran horizontally on the walls and continued in long slats on the floors. One side of the café was a wooden deck. We sat there because it had a magnificent view of the ocean. We could hear it roar in the distance.

'What will you have?' asked Vaibhav.

'I really don't want anything. We just ate, right?'

'Me too, but if we don't order anything, I think they will throw us out.'

We ended up ordering a chamomile tea (for me) and a basil tea (for him).

Now that we had settled down, we had no option but to talk about what happened.

'Ankita, listen, I am terribly sorry about the way I behaved last time,' he said simply.

'It's fine,' I said. It was an automatic response, because I didn't know what to say. I wanted to tell him that I had been hurt by his long silence, by the fact that he had completely cut me off. But I didn't say any of it, because I was also happy to be there with him at that moment.

'It is not fine. I acted like a jerk. I was so jealous, Ankita. I should have controlled myself. I thought about it for days afterwards. Mine was a knee-jerk reaction. I realise now how selfish I was. Of all the things you told me, I decided to focus on one thing,' he said

'I too shouldn't have hidden it from you. It was my fault too. There was so much happening in our lives. We were so far apart, and there's only so much you can say in letters. Also, this Abhi thing – I myself was reeling under the suddenness of it. Plus, it was so long back, Vaibhav. I was eighteen. What did I even know?'

'I know... I know. All of this made sense only when I had the time to think it through. You have no idea how stupid I felt afterwards. I had meant to tell you about my training stint on the day we went out. But I went off on a tangent. Then I had to leave for my training. The only way I could call you was from the factory manager's room. The villagers, my hosts, didn't have a phone. You should see their life, Ankita. It's a different world. Then after I got back, I called your father. I could have come upstairs and met you. But I did have to hurry back. I had that module to present. Also, I was feeling sheepish. So I thought I would take you out, and explain the whole thing in detail. Then came the team outing. I wanted to call you. But it wasn't something I could do on the phone. Now

I have two days off from work, and I have come rushing the first chance I got. Please forgive me.'

'I… I thought you had broken up with me,' I said.

The waiter came to place our teacups on the table then. Vaibhav waited till he left.

'How can I *ever* break up with you, Ankita? I can't. Not in this lifetime. No matter what you tell me, I am okay. I love you – that means something, doesn't it? 'he said.

I still hadn't told him about Joseph. I knew then that this was the moment to.

Mrs Hayden's words came back to me.

You are not responsible for the actions of others.

'You know, I had used those words "I love you" when I didn't mean them. I have learnt my lesson now,' I began. I told him all that had happened with Joseph. Even though I was scared about his reaction, I continued. It needed to be said. I didn't want another situation like the one we had gone through earlier. Vaibhav listened in rapt attention. I could make out from his face how worried and shocked he was.

'Good lord,' he said when I finished. 'You needed me and I wasn't there.'

He had stolen the words right out of my head. It was what I had felt but never expressed to him. He *understood*.

It was all that mattered.

Vaibhav wanted to hail a cab to drop me back. But I insisted that we walk, as there was hardly any distance. There was a new understanding between us now. All resistance and resentment from my side was gone. I had let him inside.

'You know, from now on, I will never ever let you attend a party without me as your chaperone, Ms Ankita Sharma. I appoint myself your bodyguard. I shall remain loyal and faithful to you,' Vaibhav said, extending his hand as though taking an oath.

I giggled. 'But I haven't appointed you,' I said.

'Self-appointed. Some things need no confirmation. Especially if it is a voluntary service,' he said.

I smiled and squeezed his hand. He held my hand tightly then. He wouldn't let go. I wasn't sure if I was in love with him. The word 'love' terrified me after Abhi and Joseph. But I felt protected and safe with Vaibhav. I was happy. And for now, that was enough.

'Since we are being honest with each other, there's one more confession I have,' he said.

'What? Please don't tell me you are leaving Bombay!' I said.

'No! Of course not. I wanted to tell you something I hid from you.'

'What? Tell me now!' I demanded. I had no idea what he was going to say and I couldn't bear the suspense.

'You know, it was your parents who told me to come home every day, so that you would slowly start making friends,' Vaibhav said.

'What?' I was puzzled. 'What do you mean by "slowly start making friends"? I don't get it.'

'Remember the first time I came to your house?'

'Yes, of course. You were waiting for me on the sofa when I came back from college. How can I forget?'

'So I hadn't impulsively decided to turn up at your place. It was your parents who had requested me to come as often as I could. They didn't want you to know.'

'You mean my parents conspired with you behind my back?'

He grinned. 'When I spoke to your mother on the phone, I had mentioned I was moving back to Bombay. It was she who suggested that I write to you.'

'Oh my god! So, it wasn't a surprise for them? Your frequent visits were planned!'

'Yes. You have no idea how much they love you, Ankita. You were stepping out into the real world after NMHI. They weren't sure how you would cope. They thought my presence would help. I knew you saw me as a pest. Initially, at least,' he said.

I was flabbergasted. I would never in a million years have imagined my conservative parents plotting with Vaibhav behind my back. All of this was *planned*?

'Oh, wait, so if my parents had not requested you, you wouldn't have come home?' I asked.

Did he love me?

Was he just doing this for my parents' sake?

Did he pity me?

My insecurities started their drum-roll again in my head.

'Come on, Ankita. I *love* you. I'd definitely have met you. But I would have waited for a green signal from you. I am not a stalker or a pile-on,' Vaibhav said. 'Your parents requesting me to come often just made it easier for me. I was only too happy to.'

We had reached the gates of my residential complex by now, and Vaibhav let go of my hand.

'Bye, Ankita. Try not to think too much about the past. Take your pill if you have to and go to sleep. You need your sleep, okay?' he said. There was so much tenderness and care in his voice.

I nodded and on a sudden impulse, planted a kiss on his cheek. Then I ran all the way home. Happiness flowed through my heart, warming me up from the inside. It felt so wonderful to have someone all to yourself.

33

Moving On

When I reached home, my father and mother were both in the living room.

'I was not the only one keeping secrets from you. You both kept such a big secret from me,' I said.

'What secret did we keep?' asked my mother, bewildered.

'You both asked Vaibhav to come on a daily basis! And you never told me. You thought I wouldn't find out, is it?' I said.

My father burst into loud guffaws then.

'See, I told you? I won the bet!' he told my mother.

'What! You bet on it? What is going on?' I asked.

'I had predicted to your mother that Vaibhav would reveal this to you. Your mother bet that he wouldn't. I won! See, I know men,' my father gloated.

Ma laughed too. 'Yes, I admit you do.'

'We were so worried, Ankita. Just before you started college, you did not have a single friend here. You didn't want to meet anyone either. Your mother and I were your only friends. That wasn't healthy at all. We weren't sure how you would adapt to college after NMHI. So it was my idea to ask Vaibhav to start coming over,' my father confessed.

'What else are you hiding from me?' I demanded. But I was smiling.

'You are the detective. Go ahead and find out what else we are hiding,' said my mother. She was smiling too.

'We aren't hiding anything, Ankita. We were just worried and watching out for you. That's all. We are your parents, after all,' Dad said.

'I know and I am lucky,' I said.

I had to blink back my tears when my mother said, 'We are luckier.'

I had given them nothing but trouble and pain so far. It was not that I had done it purposely. But my condition had dragged us all to hell and back. I decided then that I would make them proud one day. I didn't know how I would do it. I didn't have an executable action plan. But I wanted it more than anything else in the world.

'I am sorry, Dad and Ma. I promise you I will never ever attempt to kill myself or do anything that causes you worry. If I need help, I will come to you.'

I meant every word of it.

'What a sweet relief it is to hear that, Ankita. You are a fighter. Your mother and I are both proud of you,' said my father.

●

'Please do not wake me up tomorrow. I don't know when I will fall asleep. If I sleep late, I want to ensure that I wake up only when my body is fully rested. You know even a single day's sleep can affect how we think and what we do,' I said as I was retiring to my room after dinner.

I then brought out the book on sleep patterns and showed it to my father.

'Now this is the kind of book you should be reading.' He nodded approvingly as he opened it and went through the index.

I then took out the essay Mrs Hayden had assigned. It didn't seem so difficult anymore. I saw it from a new perspective now. All I had to write was about any failure. I decided I would write about the time I failed to win the Goenka cup. I would make it humorous. I would play with words, say I couldn't digest certain things from my past and hence it resulted in my throwing up. I'd imply that the 'things' were something I ate or an incident. It would be a cleverly written essay.

The words flowed easily now. I wasn't ashamed of my past anymore. I was who I was because of everything that had happened to me. I fought. I dealt with it. I became stronger.

What was it that Mrs Hayden had said?

We can only control our actions, not others'. It struck me like a thunderbolt.

I wasn't responsible for Abhi's death. That was the choice *he had made.*

I wasn't responsible for Joseph's actions. He *chose* to behave that way.

I wasn't even responsible for Vaibhav coming back. He *wanted* me in his life.

'You always hurt the ones who love you' – the sentence flew at me without warning. But this time I was prepared. I had the secret weapon Mrs Hayden had armed me with. I imagined these words engulfed in balloons and floating away. Then I called upon all the other words that had got me down in the past.

I imagined the words 'mental patient', 'psycho bitch' and everything else my inner voice sometimes screamed at me in big bold letters. I shrank them, put them in the balloons and sent them away.

I felt free.

I felt light.

I felt wonderful.

I felt alive.

Life was calling, and I was awake.

Epilogue

A few months later

I stand on the stage in the auditorium where I had stood a few months ago and been sick. The auditorium is full today too. It is the day of our graduation. I am invited to give a speech because I have topped the batch.

I can see Parul and Janki and all our classmates too. Parul has hardly spoken to me after college reopened. But it does not bother me anymore. I have started putting incidents too in balloons and sending them away. I am consciously letting go of anything that doesn't serve my growth. Mrs Hayden's visualisation exercise has worked wonders. Over the last few months, I have practised it many times.

Mrs Hayden taught me affirmations too. Positive thoughts like 'I am creative', 'I am fortunate to have the talents that I do'. They are on cards I carry with me; each time I feel a negative thought coming, I take out a card and repeat a positive affirmation. I am stronger now, my mind has grown muscles.

I stand there proudly, looking at everyone in the audience. My parents are in the front row where Joseph once sat. Vaibhav is here too.

On the stage are Mrs Hayden, the principal of the college, and a chief guest who is the editor of a national newspaper.

'Ladies and gentlemen, and respected members on the dais,' I begin. My voice rings through the auditorium, loud and clear. 'There was a time when I wanted to drop out of this course,' I say. Everyone sits up and takes notice when I say that. I go on to tell them about the various things we have learnt during the course. I talk about how each one of us bagged an internship at reputed media houses. I talk about the contribution of the teachers. I specifically mention Mrs Hayden and all that she did. I look at her as I speak, and I can see the unmistakable pride on her face. Her eyes are steady on me, as though to assure me that she understands, and she is with me.

I end the speech with: 'I was once asked to write an essay on the mistakes I had made in my life, and what I would do differently. You know what? There is not a single thing I would do differently. Each of our mistakes makes us stronger. They are our life lessons. They make us grow. And I think that is the most important thing in life. To keep making mistakes and learning from them, so that we never stop growing. So here's to mistakes and here's to life itself.'

During the standing ovation I receive, I think it is my parents who clap the loudest.

A note from the author

If you have finished reading this book, you might have noticed the unusual chapter titles. Go back and look at them again. Each of them (except chapter 26) is the title of a song! They are all songs I like. How many artistes can you recognize?

Here's the complete list.

Whenever two artistes have sung the same song, I have mentioned the version I like better.

1. (Just like) starting over (John Lennon)
2. Like a virgin (Madonna)
3. Here's your letter (Blink 182)
4. The visit (Chad Brock)
5. With a little help from my friends (Beatles)
6. This charming man (Smiths)
7. Confident (Demi Lovato)
8. The book (Sheryl Crow)
9. Killing me softly (Fugees)
10. When a man loves a woman (Michael Bolton)
11. A kind of magic (Queen)
12. Total eclipse of the heart (Bonnie Tyler)
13. When you're gone (Avril Lavigne)
14. Wishing, waiting, hoping (Tony Owens)

15. One moment in time (Whitney Houston)
16. The winner takes it all (Abba)
17. I took a pill in Ibiza (Mike Posner)
18. Coming back to life (Pink Floyd)
19. Somebody that I used to know (Gotye)
20. Where's the party (Madonna)
21. Falling off (Aerosmith)
22. Rock bottom (Eminem)
23. Falling apart (Papa Roach)
24. We have no secrets (Carly Simon)
25. Everybody hurts (R.E.M.)
26. Wake up, life is calling
27. Call me maybe (Carly Rae Jepsen)
28. Abide with me (Audrey Assad)
29. Blue balloon (Robby Benson)
30. Both sides of the story (Phil Collins)
31. Trust in you (Lauren Daigle)
32. Let love stand a chance (Charles Bradley)
33. Moving on (Marshmello)

Acknowledgements

To my father, KVJ Kamath, and to my mother, Priya J Kamath, from whom I inherit my strength, sense of humour and resilience.

To Satish, Atul and Purvi, who believe in me and my work.

To my readers, who shower me with so much love, and to my closest friend, my lifeline, who I speak to on a regular basis (you know who you are!).

To my fabulous editor and even more fabulous friend, Shinie Antony, who made the book a lot better. Her inputs were invaluable.

To Arup Bose and JK Bose, and the team at Srishti, for the faith and support.

To Murthy and Pradeep for the author photo.

To Pranav Shah and his team for all the technical support.

To all my friends for the love, understanding and happy memories that they gift me.

To Manjula Venkatswamy, for holding the fort behind the scenes.

To Lostris and Hero, who bring me so much joy.

Other books by Preeti Shenoy

Life is What You Make It
Tea for Two and a Piece of Cake
The Secret Wish List
The One You Cannot Have
It Happens for a Reason
Why We Love the Way We Do
It's All in the Planets
A Hundred Little Flames
Love A Little Stronger
The Rule Breakers